PRAISE FOR ANDREA RANDALL

November Blue

The women in this series are bold, strong and independent. Yet they aren't intimidating or stone cold. Their hearts are vulnerable, they are loyal with a passion, and they love deeply and intensely. ~ **Flirty and Dirty Book Blog**

The heated scenes between Bo and Ember were magic. ~ **Tough Critic Book Reviews**

Andrea Randall has a way with words and I can't wait to see what emotion she stirs up next ~ **Candy Coated Book Blog**

Who ever said that the sequel never lives up to the original never read an Andrea Randall book! ~ **The Book Avenue**

I love that this is no cookie cutter romance and it felt more like poetry...or a song than a book at times. ~ **Michelle Pace, co-author of The Sound Wave Series**

It's hard not to get sucked into the world of Ember and Bo ~ **SMI Book Club**

...an excellent writer with a superb talent at crafting words ... that grab ahold of your heart ... An eloquent, master wordsmith - **All the Raeje Book Blog**

I could gush about this book for days...If you read one book of Andrea Randall's this should be it. There's something in here for EVERYONE to love. ~ **Word Blog**

In the Stillness

They had the kind of love that just makes you shake. Cry. Laugh. Ache right down to your soul. It was an irreplaceable love. The kind that, once taken away leaves a hole that no other person can ever fill. ~**Aestas Book Blog**

Gorgeous writing. Eloquent, but in a raw, realistic way. A delicate subject matter, distressing thoughts, and yet, a wondrous growth that the reader experiences every step of the way, with the characters. ~**Maryse's Book Blog**

This is easily the best book I've read all year, and I will be hard-pressed to find a book that will bring out of me such a strong reaction as this book. In the Stillness is a stimulant of the best and worst kind; it is truly captivating and commensurate with the suffering of so many in society. ~ **Romantic Reading Escapes Book Blog**

Author Andrea Randall has written a gut-wrenching, 5++ star piece of dark perfection. This is a journey of redemption, healing, loving, acceptance, and moving forward. ~ **K and T Book Reviews**

ANDREA RANDALL

Books by Andrea Randall

November Blue

Ten Days of Perfect
Reckless Abandon
Sweet Forty-Two
Marrying Ember
Bo & Ember

In The Stillness
Nocturne (with Charles Sheehan-Miles)
Something's Come Up (with Michelle Pace)

BO
& Ember

If you enjoyed this book, please share it with a friend, write a

review online, or send feedback to the authors!

www.andrearandall.com

ISBN 978-1-63202-074-1
Edited by Lori Sabin
Cover Design by Charles Sheehan-Miles
Cover Photo by Erica Ritchie

Permission for use of song lyrics to "Heaven When We're Home" given by Ruth Moody

DEDICATION

To Pamela,
who never stopped
believing in this series,
or in me.

ACKNOWLEDGEMENTS

I'd like to thank:

Randall's Readers, first and foremost. Your DAILY enthusiasm for my writing and these characters kept me going on some pretty angsty self-pitying days. Your humor, encouragement, and love is something I wish every author could experience.

Randall's Bitchin' Betas. You guys have always been there to call me out, tear me apart, and encourage me. The readers should thank you as much as I do. There are pieces of you throughout this story.

Erica Ritchie, from Erica Ritchie Photography. Your work on the photos for this series has consistently exceeded my expectations. To have a unique cover is one thing. To have a unique and beautiful cover is quite another. Thank you for your vision and talent.

Lori Sabin. Thank you for walking through this series with me. Working with you as my editor has made me a better writer. I learn something new with each project. Moreover, you're a dear friend and I will forever cherish you.

Charles Miles. Sure, you formatted the book, and it's lovely. Truly. Yes, you designed the cover, and it's breathtaking. But, you did the most important job of all in loving me. All of me. The crazy, the irrational, the excited, the reckless. But you loved me most by giving me the support to see this through, in spite of (and maybe because of) your knowledge of how emotionally challenging this career can be. You never let me pull back when I'm scared. You only lead me forward. A partner in every sense of the world.

I want to thank all of my "author friends." What a crap term, huh? You all know that you're more than that. I know you're more than that. Texts, chats, messages, and the rare hug are what bind us together and keep us pressing forward. This industry is hard, kids. Chin up, dig in, and never compromise who you are for what you think you want. "I vow." * wink *

Finally, I want to thank you, the reader. Those of you who fell in love with my very first published novel, "Ten Days of Perfect", have helped me become the writer I am today. Your enthusiasm for these characters is the reason the series became what it did. I will miss these characters as much as you do. But, trust me, there are exciting things on the horizon, and I'm honored to have you all by my side.

CHAPTER *One*

Vineyards and Visions

Ember

B O CAVANAUGH.

6'2", broad-shouldered, thick black hair that was long enough to run your hands through—but short enough for the board room—and a charming smile that led you all the way up to his 20,000 leagues-blue eyes. Guitar. Voice. All of it.

He was absolutely everything all of the female—and some of the male—fans of The Six had grown to love over the last two years. Indie rock star. That last bit had him smiling humbly, and me beaming with pride.

The Six hadn't planned on having a "front man." As our first summer tour neared its end, however, it became clear that Bo was what the fans wanted the most. He seemed to be able to capture the essence my parents and their friends had worked for decades to create, while bringing in a new batch of fans that melted at his smile and admired the risks he took with the guitar.

"They love you just as much," Regan whispered into my ear as I spied on Bo doing his sound check for the night's show.

"Get out of my head already!" I hissed back playfully.

Regan muffled a laugh as he dodged the weak smack I threw his way. "I'm serious. It's like Johnny and June, co-op style."

"You have no idea what you're talking about." I leaned my head on Regan as he wrapped his arm around my shoulders.

No matter how many times I'd seen it, watching Bo alone with his guitar still took my breath away. Each time I happened upon that private moment, it was the same as that May night two years ago when I first saw him play. When everything stopped in the most cliché way possible, and all I could see, hear, and feel was him.

Regan kept his voice quiet as he spoke. "*You* have no idea. No. You must. They go just as crazy when you join him on stage as they do when he walks out there by himself. It's not just because he's *Hottie McGuitar*. You two are blindingly in love and people are, like, watching music porn when you're on stage together."

"Lovely," I mused sarcastically.

"It's true. Not only have you kicked the shit out of your guitar skills, your vocals are above anyone I've heard in a long time. Including anyone in this band." Regan moved so he was holding both of my shoulders.

I smiled as his messy hazel eyes twinkled with sincerity. "Jesus, Regan. Did you ever think we'd end up here?"

Regan dropped his hands, shaking his head as he took in the wide green space in front of the stage. "Not in a million."

Here wasn't just the grape-scented air of Napa. It was *here*. Touring together. Me, Bo, Regan, and The Six. *Here* was spending the last year after our first successful summer tour doing tour weekends across the Pacific Northwest and the warm and dry South West. *Here* was having not been back to the East Coast except for once in two whole years. *Here* was me as Mrs. Cavanaugh. Bo's wife. November Cavanaugh.

We were in Napa for the biggest opportunity any of us had ever dreamed of, which is what had Regan biting his nails with a sour look on his face. No doubt from the rosin that always stuck on his skin. Still, he couldn't keep his fingers out of his mouth.

But, the object of Regan's awe was *Live in the Vineyard*, a three-day event in Napa Valley. The opposite of everything you'd consider a "music festival," *Live in the Vineyard* was an intimate experience of acoustic-only performers, playing for an audience of contest-winners. There was no buying your way in. The music was made up of Top 40 artists, as well as "emerging artists," and hosted top chefs and wine makers for private tastings. Perfect pairings, if you asked me.

There were several things special about this event. First and foremost, a band that's not in the Top 40 has to be high on someone's radar in order to obtain a coveted invite. There wouldn't be a hoard of screaming fans here. Again, it was an intimate opportunity to connect with fans. However, there were very real opportunities for bigger record deals here. I say bigger because my parents own their own label, but it's private. And small. With a much, *much* smaller bank account. An invite not only meant there was strong fan interest, but *someone* had to be paying attention.

While The Six as a whole was slated to play a few numbers, Bo, Regan, and I had been given a second billing, which was nearly unheard of. Someone was *really* listening and, honestly, I wasn't sure how I felt about it. I knew my parents and the rest of their original band had no interest in a record deal. They stated several times they wouldn't do national tours again. Maybe one, but that was it. While I wasn't sure where I stood on the matter, I knew what I wanted for Bo and Regan.

Everything.

While Regan would be a hard sell, since he was generally uncomfortable with loads of attention, Bo wanted it. It was in the smile that grew wider over the course of the last two years. A different smile than the one he gave me first thing every single morning. This was a smile I saw on the face of every artist that got to do exactly what they'd always wanted. It came from deep inside their bones. That's why he had his head down going over chord after chord. He wasn't just practicing for the small crowd tonight. He was preparing for an unspoken audition into something greater.

"Are you going to stare at me all day, or were you planning on joining us for practice?"

I jumped and looked to my left, realizing that somewhere in my swirling thoughts, Regan had left my side and headed out next to Bo, where he stood tuning his violin.

Fiddle, though, was how we were to refer to it tonight, and, probably forever. They were the same damn thing, but *fiddle* was hip and *violin* was stiff, according to current trends.

"I'd prefer to stare all day, if that's all right with the both of you. You two make music worth dropping everything for." I picked up my mom's old guitar from its place against the wall and walked to meet the guys. I had my own guitar, but always played hers given the opportunity. It had history in its wood that made me feel at home.

Before taking my place on the stool set for me, I turned to Bo, setting my guitar down before wrapping my arms around his neck.

"I'm madly in love with you," I whispered just before my lips connected with his.

He gave a satisfied sigh as his mouth opened slightly, and his free arm encircled my waist. His lips were home. We'd spent more than two hundred days on the road in the last year, but here inside the warmth of his kiss, I always found where I was supposed to be.

"Ahem..." Regan cleared his throat in the bored and irritated tone that reminded us to get to work.

"I love you more," Bo whispered back to me before releasing his hold.

I pulled my head back and studied those ocean blues of his. Definitely Atlantic. Cool and stormy set in his now-bronzed skin. A few months on the road on the West Coast will do that to most people.

Regan groaned. "Guys, please. Georgia doesn't get here for a few hours, and normally I put up with this love show, but..."

"Sorry, Reeg." I scooted to his side, planting a chaste kiss on his cheek. "How long is Georgia staying?"

Georgia had become one of my best friends. I knew it was hard for Regan to leave her for long periods of time, but the good news was her bakery was too busy for her to come along.

The tension around his eyes dissolved as he grinned. "She'll be here the whole time we're in Napa, and for a few days after.

Her mom and the new employee she hired this summer are going to run the bakery so she can have a ten-day vacation."

"How's her mom?" Bo piped up, waiting for us to tune.

"She's been great. Georgia said the last several months have been better for her than she can remember." Regan drew his bow across the strings and closed his eyes.

Georgia's mother, Amanda, had catatonic schizophrenia. After a lengthy round of ECT a year and a half ago, paired with new medication and therapy, she'd been doing really well. While I always had my mom with me, whether on tour or at home, Amanda Hall still acted like a mother for the youngsters in the band. She and Georgia sent us care packages filled with baked goods on a weekly basis. Georgia joked she wanted to fatten our men up enough to keep people listening to their music, and stop looking at their bodies. I told her not to worry, but I could tell it was difficult for her.

After tuning for a few moments, I looked to the guys. "Okay, so we've got to nail down our set list for tonight. I'm freaking out a little that we have to go on ourselves before the rest of the band does, but..."

I trailed off as Bo started strumming his fingers over his guitar in the middle of a song—as though he'd been playing it in his head for the past few minutes. Regan joined in at the exact moment the fiddle was supposed to. Tears came unexpectedly, clouding my vision as they played an instrumental interlude of "Heaven When We're Home," the song by The Wailin' Jennys that Bo and I sang together with Monica minutes after I met him for the first time.

I entered the song without discussion, letting the notes swirl around us.

...There's no such thing as perfect, and if there is we'll find it when we're good and dead. Trust me I've been lookin', but tonight I think I'll go and take a bath instead...

I was secretly hoping Bo would join me for the chorus, as he'd done when he first blew me away over two years ago. I knew then. I really did.

And it's a long and rugged road...

I closed my eyes as Bo met my hidden expectations, harmonizing with my voice and leading us through the rest of the song. We hadn't sung that song together since our first night back in Barnstable, and I'd be lying if I said it felt exactly the same. No. It felt a million times better.

More than two years ago, the dark, stormy, and sexy stranger who took over my favorite song with me made me want to kiss him. Rendered me confused and lit me up with unexpected feelings. All of that still held true, but this time, as we finished out my favorite song ever, I was singing it with my husband. With the man to whom I'd promised my eternity, and with the man who promised me his right back.

"You like?" Regan nudged my side playfully with his elbow, lifting his eyebrows as he smiled.

I nodded, smiling until my cheeks hurt. "I'm with you jerks twenty-seven hours a day. How'd you..." I turned to Bo, who looked up hopefully through his unfairly long eyelashes.

"You sleep sometimes. As soon as we got the invite to this gig, I told Regan we had to play it. It's the perfect audience." Bo adjusted his mic and quietly strummed his guitar as we spoke.

"But they're here for you." I turned and pointed to Regan. "And for you."

The guys shook their head in unison. Regan spoke first. "You know damn well that executives don't waste their time with superfluous voices if they're looking for just one. I don't know who's looking for what here," he said, gesturing between the three of us. "But if it *wasn't* one of us, they wouldn't have singled out the three of us."

My eyes moved to Bo, who nodded in agreement.

My long-buried performance anxiety started pushing its way through my gut. "Well," I took a long, deep breath, "guess we better get that setlist straight then, huh?"

"That's why Regan and I brushed up on that Wailin' Jennys song. We want to do that tonight. It highlights everything you do best. We can take it from the top, then hammer out the rest of the list."

I slung the strap of my mother's guitar over my shoulder and settled on the stool, taking another deep breath as I tested my mic.

I bit my lip, wondering how I felt about all of the things I thought might be possible for the three of us. Regan was right, and I don't know why I didn't pay attention to it. They wouldn't have asked me to sing with Regan and Bo if someone didn't want to hear *me* sing. Bo didn't need me for an act. He could play and sing just fine.

"Ready?" Regan asked as he prepared to count us off.

"Ready." Bo cleared his throat. "Ember?"

I cleared my throat and swallowed hard before meeting Bo's eyes. He set his hand on my knee and kissed me once on the lips. He didn't need words. All the butterflies fluttering through my veins grounded their flight and allowed me to take one more deep breath before we got down to business.

§

Regan, Bo, and I were afforded a gorgeous evening under the stars for our performance. We'd join The Six for their performance the next day, but for the next half hour, it was just the three of us. We waited inside something that looked like a small pool house before we were called.

"You guys will do great. What do you have lined up for your set?" Georgia asked as she wrapped her arms around Regan, having arrived in Napa only an hour earlier.

Regan chose to kiss her instead of answer, so, with a smile I picked up the slack. "Some Wailin' Jennys, Civil Wars, you know…" I trailed off, huffing out my nerves in a ragged breath. I'd been thinking all day about the implications of tonight.

Frankly, if it didn't go well, that wouldn't matter as far as The Six was concerned, but it was beginning to matter to me. Bo, Regan, and I had been gelling so well over the last few weeks, I was really starting to view us as a trio, a legitimate group with legs of our own if we chose to walk on them.

My mind was spinning. If someone had told me three years ago that I was going to *want* a career in music after spending *a whole year* working with my parents and their band, I'd have checked them for signs of hysteria. This wasn't in the plan.

My old plan, anyway. Bo Cavanaugh was a bit of a game changer in more ways than one. More ways than either of us had envisioned, I think.

"Hey." Bo lifted my chin with his index finger. "You don't get nervous, so don't start now. You're aces, love." He winked and slid his hand around the back of my neck as he pulled me into a kiss.

"Jesus," Georgia whispered loudly, "is he the most romantic person in the universe?"

Regan twisted his lips and nodded. "'Fraid so."

Between Bo's soft assurance and Georgia and Regan's ever-present banter, I was once again calmed and ready for the show.

Just as Jan Lieberman, an organizer for the event, called us out to the garden, I tugged Bo's wrist. His palms were warm, but not yet sweaty.

"What's up?" he whispered as soft applause sprang from the direction of the soft green grass.

I bit my lip, looking up at him as my cheeks flushed. "What-ever this is...I want it."

Bo squeezed my hand, shooting a sideways glance at Regan, who just smiled. "So let's go get it."

We'd had almost all of our contact for this event with Jan, who smiled as we took our places.

"Good luck, guys." She gave us a thumbs-up as she ducked into the shadows with a glass of wine.

As I looked out into the crowd, I realized my previous de-scription of the venue as a "garden" was a gross understatement. We were outdoors, but that was about the extent to which the comparisons to a poolside garden ended. It was more intimate than the thousands we'd played for at the SoCal Music and Arts

Festival over the summer, but the intimate set up made me feel more on display, somehow. Still, I wanted this. I wanted to do well, no matter what it meant. If it even meant anything.

"Thank you, everyone, for being here this evening." Bo's voice was a low hum as his stage persona took over. Smooth and just the right amount of seductive.

"We love you, Bo! Woo!" Squeals from the back of the crowd started a cascade of applause and dreamy sighs.

"Regan!" Another section of fans waved, and Regan brought his hand to his brow and saluted them. My guys were right in their element.

I adjusted my mic to the right height and leaned in. "Thank you for having us. This is such an honor." I jumped, startled as a stampede of applause shot through my ears. Some people rose to their feet before we'd even sung a note, calling my name.

November Blue.

Looking to my left, I found Bo with his head down, taking a deep breath as he always did before we played. Looking to my right, Regan met my gaze and smiled, mouthing, *told you so*, as fans continued to call to me.

"All right, let's get started..." I nodded our count to Bo and we began our set as cheers continued through the crowd.

We started with "Heaven When We're Home" at my request. I needed something familiar to settle me into the set. I always started singing with my eyes closed; something I'd come to realize my mother did, as well. Regan teased me incessantly about it, promising me that I was missing out on half of the experience of performing for a crowd. So, after I sang the intro solo, I opened my eyes and looked to Regan. He winked and nodded in approval as I turned my eyes to the crowd.

I had to focus twice as hard when Bo entered the song. We met each other's eyes three beats before he joined me, and when he did, the whistles and claps from the crowd almost knocked me off balance. We'd received this kind of reaction many times before, through the past several months of touring with The Six, but in this setting it felt almost oppressively intimate.

My emotional connection with my husband always deepened when we sang or played together. He'd spent two years helping me fine-tune my guitar skills, and I coached him on vocals. Together this was what we were meant to do. As the song reach its end, I knew I didn't want to stop. Not tonight, and not for as long as I had a song in my heart.

Before we knew it, our set was up and we had to leave the stage. The standing ovation we received was overwhelming and had me floating all the way backstage.

"Nailed it!" Georgia raised her arms into the air, and Regan swung his pin-up girlfriend around as he kissed her. She'd finally let her hair grow back to its natural chocolate brown color, and it suited her. She looked even more badass than she had the first night I met her a year ago.

"Was it as good as it felt?" I asked, breathless from adrenaline.

Bo squeezed his arm around my shoulders and I could almost feel his muscles vibrating with excitement. "Better. I'm sure of it. God, that was exciting. I can't wait for tomorrow!"

Just as we were starting to look around, wondering what we were supposed to do with ourselves, Jan rushed up to us with a cabernet-laced smile on her face. "Wonderful job, you three. Truly."

Bo stuck out his hand, never losing his deeply ingrained professionalism. "Mrs. Lieberman—"

"Please," she waved her hand, "just Jan. I dropped the Mrs. when I dropped my ex-husband."

He grinned and I caught Georgia rolling her eyes from beside Regan. Georgia was the only person I knew who rolled her eyes more than I did. She thought everyone was always flirting with Bo and Regan. Mostly because everyone always was, though I didn't think that was the case with Jan.

"Jan," Bo continued, "thank you for this opportunity. You've got a great event here." He gave her hand a firm shake.

She turned her attention to me. "Ms. Har—Cavanaugh— sorry, I must say, you have an incredible stage presence. So relaxed, yet beaming with energy. You remind me a lot of your mom. That's her guitar, isn't it?" She pointed a finger at the instrument in my left hand.

I smiled as a sinking feeling took over. This was an *old* guitar she never played anymore. "It is. Have you listened to The Six for a long time?" I questioned. Hoping.

"I hadn't listened to them much until the tour last summer. But, once I saw all of you on stage, I did my homework. You're a spitting image of both of your parents. A gorgeous young lady." As Jan continued rattling off the things she'd learned during her research of The Six, air returned to my lungs.

Now, I know that more times than not, it's who you know that gets you somewhere in this business. Hell, that's why Bo, Regan and I had the opportunity to play with The Six at all. But, I'd been hoping there hadn't been any favor-calling to get us into this event. I was hoping—and right, it seemed—that our hard work over the last couple of years was garnering the right kind of attention.

"So," Jan continued, "we'll see you tomorrow afternoon with The Six. I'm *so* looking forward to that performance."

With a quick kiss on all of our cheeks, Jan swept herself back to the stage to introduce the next act. A top-40 artist I'd fallen in love with over the last year. I studied her body of work like it was the vocal Bible. Just a girl and her guitar, and I loved that. Though, if I were to be completely honest, performing with one of my best friends and my husband kind of took the cake.

Best friend.

"Where are you?" Bo whispered into my ear as he kissed the still-excitable skin of my neck.

I turned to him, my eyes misting over with a mix of emotions. "I miss Monica. I need to call her. Give me a sec, okay?"

Bo nodded as I slipped away to my guitar case, where I'd left my cell phone. Smiling as I picked it up, I saw that I'd missed five calls. All from Monica. I dialed her back as quickly as I could.

"How could you possibly sound better *every fucking time* you sing? Does your vocal perfection know no bounds?" Monica was rarely one for your standard *hello*.

I laughed, sniffling as I realized how much I missed not just the sound of her voice, but her presence in my daily life. "How did you hear it already?"

"I listened to it on that satellite station. Trust me, I tried to find a live video feed, but they seem to have a mobile lockdown on the event." Monica sounded entitled and annoyed. I loved her.

"Did you hear the whole thing?"

She clicked her tongue as if I were a misbehaving toddler. "Of course I did. I've done nothing else all day. Finnegan's sends their congratulations."

I scrunched my eyebrows. "What?"

"I used my *in* at Finnegan's to have everyone shut the hell up so we could blast your set through the bar. The place went nuts."

"Well, thank Josh for me, huh?" Monica's husband, Josh, was the manager of Finnegan's and had always been a soldier on the front lines of good music.

He was the one who drove all the way to Concord, NH two years ago to scope out a potential act for the Barnstable, MA pub.

That "potential act" snaked his arms around my waist and kissed the top of my head as I conversed with my best friend.

"So," I continued, wrapped in Bo's arms, "when are you coming out here again?"

"Uh-uh, sister. When are *you* coming *here*? You're not West Coast, you know. You're too pale and broody for that shit. Come back and touch down on your roots for a hot minute, would you?" While she brushed a powder of sarcasm over her words, I could tell she was serious.

I'd only been back to Barnstable twice since I moved to San Diego a year and a half earlier. Bo and I had gone to New Hampshire two or three times, where all of our things lay in wait at his family's estate, but that was largely for DROP business and fundraising. Monica was right; I needed some Atlantic air in my lungs.

"After this weekend I'll see what our schedule looks like. I really need a trip back there—"

"You know I'm just giving you shit. If anyone out there was listening and has a brain in their head, they're going to offer you a recoding contract. Wouldn't that be insane? Jesus, then you'd be all *over* the place!"

I laughed nervously, not wanting to put too much pressure on myself. "Tell me something about you. I'm tired of talking about myself."

"I went off the pill two months ago," Monica blurted out nonchalantly.

My eyes grew wide. "Yes!" I shouted. Bo had been holding onto me through most of the conversation, but dropped his arms as I cheered and spun around, addressing him. "They're gonna start trying!"

Bo scrunched his eyebrows and tilted his head.

"They want to have a baby!" I squealed, bouncing on my toes.

A smile rose from his toes to his eyes, and he nodded once in approval.

"Yo, Ember, over here," Monica shouted into the phone.

"Sorry! I'm so excited. Shit, see…I should be there for this…"

She snorted. "No, not for this part you shouldn't."

I laughed harder than I had in days. "Not *that* part, ass. Just…baby stuff! We're supposed to, like, live our lives together. Isn't that what best friends do?" My tone grew somber as I ended my sentence.

"We do get to live our lives together," Monica reassured me. "You get to go be a rock star for a few years, I'll have a few kids, then you'll have some, and we get to experience everything together. It'll be okay. I promise. Okay, I gotta go. It's getting loud in here and it looks like Josh's bartenders are just learning how to tie their shoelaces so I'll have to get behind the bar."

"I love you, Mon."

"Love you, too, Ember. Call me when you get your record deal."

I pressed "End" on my phone and looked around, finding Bo, Regan, and Georgia ready to go. I snapped the guitar in its case and walked to the parking lot, wondering what the next several months of my life would look like. For me and the people I loved so dearly.

CHAPTER *Two*

I gotta feeling

Ember

"YOU GOT QUIET. Are you missing Monica?" Bo reached across the center of the car and grabbed my hand, bringing it to his mouth so he could plant a soft kiss on my knuckles.

I nodded. "I do miss her. I'm hoping to carve out some time soon to go visit her. You did awesome tonight, hon." I leaned over to him, kissing his cheek.

"Likewise, Mrs. Cavanaugh." He grinned like a fool every time he called me that.

Regan cleared his throat from the back of the car. "Sergeant Kane reporting from the back seat. I'd like to add that we fucking rocked that. That's all. Over and out."

The four of us laughed, all clearly relieved the nervousness of the set was over, but still riding on adrenaline. Even though Georgia wasn't in the band, she was as active a member as the rest of us. Excellent in her marketing skills, she knew how to get us noticed wherever we were. And she kept us well fed, which the guys were especially grateful for.

"Hey, where are we going? The exit for the campground was back there." Georgia stuck her head between Bo's and my seats. The Six always parked their RVs at campgrounds during tours, opting for as "natural" an experience as possible.

Regan tugged Georgia into the back seat, hooking his arm around her shoulders. "Despite our close living quarters, we can still have *some* secrets."

I whipped my head around to look at Bo and Regan at the same time. "What secrets?"

Bo's lopsided grin took over the entire car. "Regan and I were able to book a bed and breakfast up here for the weekend. Just us." He looked out of the corner of his eye at me. I may have melted just a little. I knew deep down he would always make me melt.

Georgia and I squealed in unison. While Bo and I were used to trying to sneak private moments while on the road, since "free love" wasn't in the cards when the rest of the band consisted of your parents and their friends, it was different for Georgia and Regan. They didn't get to spend nearly as much time together as Bo and I did, given Georgia was burning the candle at both ends at her bakery, Sweet Forty-Two. When they got together they desperately needed privacy that was at a premium.

Georgia leaned forward again. "Wait...when you say *just us...*"

I furrowed my brow, not knowing what she was getting at.

"Just us," Regan reiterated, an impish grin growing on his face that reminded me he was genetically related to our womanizing percussionist friend, CJ.

"The whole place?" I asked, spelling out my disbelief.

"Hey, we're rock stars," Bo shrugged unapologetically before cracking into laughter. "Seriously, Regan and I have been planning this since we got the vineyard gig."

I nodded, a satisfied smile pulling at the corners of my mouth. "Well played, Cavanaugh."

Twenty minutes later, we were checked into The Cottage, and each couple retreated to their own rooms, which were at opposite ends of the thankfully lengthy hallway. As I closed the door to our room, I noticed a small fire crackling in the fireplace, and an unopened bottle of Prosecco chilling in a bucket at the foot of the bed.

"Is it bad that the Prosecco got my attention first?" I sighed, wandering over to the bed and picking up the cold bottle.

"That was intentional. It's been a hell of a few...months? Years?" Bo slinked over to me, taking the bottle and aiming it away from us as he popped the cork. I held out the glasses and he filled them nearly to the top.

I took a sip, sighing as the bubbles worked their way down my throat. "It's always a hell of a ride with you, Bo. In the best ways. I'm so happy we're doing this together. I can't imagine what it's like for Regan and Georgia."

"You're stunning." Bo stared into my eyes, seeming to ignore my words.

My breath grew shallow as I set my glass on the table at the foot of the bed. I never pulled my eyes from his. "You..."

Bo shook his head as I searched for something measurable to say. "You don't have to say anything. Just let me admire my insane luck. My *wife*." He set his still-full glass next to mine and cupped my face in his hands.

I rose on the tips of my toes as Bo bowed his head. Always working in time with each other, our lips pulled us to meet in the middle. A luxurious kiss that pulled a soft groan from my throat.

"Can I say something now?" I whispered as I pulled away.

Bo only shook his head again. Grinning as he bit his lip, he lifted me by my hips and set me on the bed. I wouldn't have been able to speak in that moment if I'd tried. Bo took a step back as fire seared through his eyes. Though I was fully clothed, I felt exposed under his gaze as he removed his shirt.

I arched my eyebrow and shot him a sly grin.

"See something you like?" Bo teased as he reached for the button on his jeans.

"Keep going. I'll let you know," I teased back. Once he stepped out of his jeans and stood in front of me in his dark grey t-shirt and tight black boxer briefs, I spoke again. "Bingo."

His instant lopsided grin turned my temperature all the way up.

"What?" he asked. "You look so serious all of a sudden." Bo sat next to me on the bed and brushed my hair aside, allowing him to untie the string of my halter top.

"I'm the lucky one," I remarked as his fingertips trailed down my back.

Bo's lips grazed my shoulder. "Hardly."

I'd intended to protest, to tell him what I'd been meaning to say to him all night. But, here's the thing, when Bo

Cavanaugh breathes across the back of your neck, the rest of the world disappears. The only colors are black and blue: the color he looks best in set against the wicked hue of his eyes. The only sounds are the moans escaping with your sigh.

"I love you so much," I whispered as I slid out of the rest of my clothing.

"Damn." He grinned and licked his lips. "I don't know why the hell married people complain about their sex lives so much. I'll never get tired of this."

I crawled over him, pushing him against the pillow with the pressure of my kiss. Bo reached his hands to the bottom hem of his shirt and pulled it over his head in one swift motion that left me staring at his solid chest and abs.

"And I'll never get tired of *this*." I brought my lips to the space between his pecs and kissed a straight line down to his belly button, enjoying the shifting of his hips.

Suddenly, teasing was too much for me to handle, and I had to free him from the rest of his clothes. I softly dragged my nails against his skin as I hooked my fingers around the waistband of his boxer briefs, waiting. Silently, he did as he knew I needed him to, lifting his tight backside off the bed, allowing me to slide the useless fabric down his legs and onto the floor.

Bo's hair was a carefully crafted mess held in place by *very* expensive hair wax. That didn't stop me from ruffling it further, causing him to chuckle and grab my wrists.

"Come here." He pulled me flush on top of him and invaded my mouth with his sweet tongue, causing my hips to move back and forth on their own volition.

"Mmm," I moaned into his mouth as I began to throb between my legs. We hadn't been alone in days and I was ragged with desire.

Bo growled and looked to the ceiling. "You drive me crazy with that noise, Ember."

I shifted my hips down his body and slid slowly and easily onto him, never breaking eye contact. I reveled in his eyes rolling back in his head as his teeth clenched. My poker face only lasted as long as it took for him to fill me completely. When he was as far in as he could go, I threw my head back and groaned.

"Jesus, Bo."

He responded by wrapping his hands around my hips and pushing me down further, causing me to lean back slightly so he could go deeper. I closed my eyes and let myself feel him. All of him. Off the edge of the bed, I heard my cellphone buzz and ring with an incoming call, but answering was *not* an option.

Suddenly, Bo and I were face to face as he sat up. I wrapped my legs around his waist as our lips worked into smiles against each other.

"Roll over," Bo commanded, his eyes piercing into mine with greedy intensity.

As I readily complied with his demand, his phone rang from his jeans pocket on the floor. It cut off after the third ring and immediately rang again.

"Ignore it," I begged, needing him inside me again.

"As you wish." Bo winked and wasted no time pushing into me, resuming his earlier rhythm.

It was short-lived. Bo's phone cut off and mine picked up seconds later. Ringing twice, cutting off, and ringing again.

"What the hell?" Bo looked over his shoulder, pulling out of me as I sat up.

"For fuck's sake," I grumbled, scrambling to the edge of my bed, semi-panicking that an emergency was waiting for me.

"Jesus, you've got to be kidding me!" I was out of breath from my interrupted sexual encounter with my hot-as-hell husband.

"What?" Bo asked, sounding as annoyed as I felt.

"Willow!" I shouted as I answered the phone. "Is someone dead?"

Bo put his hands over his face and fake-cried as he lay face down on his pillow. His frustration made me grin, though hearing the loud thumping of bass and music blasting in my ear wiped all amusement from my face.

"Willow?" I repeated, praying for her sake that this was a butt dial.

"Ember?" she shouted to hear her own voice over the drunken noise, causing me to hold the phone a couple of inches from my ear.

"Willow?" I repeated, growing more annoyed by the second.

"Where are you?"

"Excuse me?" I slid off the edge of the bed and paced around the room. "I'm at a lovely bed and breakfast with my husband, enjoying some *privacy*."

"Shit, I thought you'd be at the campsite with the rest of the group. Well, uh...hate me later if you want, but for now you've got to get your ass to Sand Castle."

I stopped dead in my tracks, turning to Bo with my mouth gaping. He had flipped to his back and was openly gawking at my nudity.

"What?" he whispered.

I shook my head. "Willow, I don't have time for this. We've had a long—"

Ignoring all the information I'd given her about where I was, and who with, Willow continued. "I just got into town for your show with The Six tomorrow. Some friends of mine do some production work for *Live at the Vineyard* and had me meet them here. All the execs who were there tonight, or listening, are here...and they're talking about you guys."

"Us guys..."

"You, Bo, and Regan. Listen, I'm not asking you to come here for some contrived meeting. You need to get your asses down here to be seen. All of you. Rub elbows. Keep yourselves on their radar for tomorrow. This is a big fucking deal, Ember." While she was still shouting, Willow was definitely sober enough for me to take her seriously.

"Shit...I've got...Jesus, Willow, okay. Look, text me directions. I've got to get dressed, then go get Regan."

"Done."

I tossed the phone on the bed and began frantically redressing.

Bo sat forward. "Catch me up?"

"Willow is at Sand Castle. It's some dance club by the sounds of the music."

His eyebrows rose so high they nearly met his hairline. "Are you...what? When did Willow going to a club become cause for an emergency?"

I laughed. My accidental-socialite half sister was never one to pass up a club with good music. She often knew where the best club was in each city we toured. If there wasn't one in the town, she'd find one nearby. Lately she'd been trying her hand in the DJ booths wherever she went, and, frankly, was killing it.

"Execs who watched our show are there. They're talking about us with people who were there and people who listened. She—"

Before I could finish my sentence, Bo was on his feet, pulling on his jeans. He grinned like a fool as he fastened his belt.

"You're not all sexually frustrated, are you?" I stopped and turned my back to Bo, who stood and tied my halter back into place.

Bo laughed and kissed the back of my neck. "Oh I'm frustrated, but I know what a big deal this is. We owe Willow huge." He moved to the mirror and ran a hand through his hair.

"You look perfect. Move so I can touch up my makeup." I stood in front of the mirror and rubbed tinted lip gloss across my smile. "How big of a deal is this?" I knew from the seriousness of Willow's voice, and Bo's excitement, that it had to be pretty big.

Bo looked at me through the mirror. "Networking is always a good move. And, if Willow is there we know the music is good. We want to be seen where people are listening to good music. We need to know what they're listening to. Even if it sounds different than what we're doing, that's okay...preferable actually. We just need to know what kinds of sounds get them going."

"But, what about the executives there?" My neck and cheeks heated as the adrenaline and nerves collided.

Bo shrugged and snagged his wallet off the floor, replacing it in his back pocket. "Technically that's the most important part, but we won't talk to them unless they talk to us. My guess, actually, is there are lots of listeners from tonight at that concert. If we can be *seen* mingling with the fans, then that says more about the kind of people we are than our music does. We know that's solid, and a label will either like our sound, or they won't. There's nothing we can do about that. Having a solid image out of the gate is much more important. Less work for their PR." He winked and hooked his arm around my waist, pulling me in for a hot-lipped kiss.

"Ah, there's my Spencer Cavanaugh, MBA, rearing his head." I turned and kissed him on the cheek, using his given first name. While I'd first seen him on stage, I met him as *Spencer* in my office at The Hope Foundation. He was just as sexy in a suit and tie as he was behind a mic.

Okay, he was a bit hotter behind a mic.

Bo pulled away from our kiss and winced. "Regan and Georgia..."

"Rock, paper, scissors to see who has to go interrupt *them*?" I could hold my own with Regan, but Georgia was libel to cut a bitch over *coitus interruptus*.

"My lovely wife, I promised for better or for worse. We'll knock on that door together." Bo laughed and held our door open for me. "You seemed excited when you got off the phone with Willow."

I bit my lip. Normally, I'd be incredibly pissed to have my private moments with my husband interrupted, especially since they'd been few and far between over the last year. Tonight, though, I was filled with a focus I hadn't had since moving to California.

Bo stopped us in the middle of the short hallway and placed his hands on my hips, turning me toward him. "You really *do* want this."

"Shit," I sighed, "I do. I want to keep us on the radar tonight and knock it out of the park tomorrow. You and Regan deserve it more, though. I mean you guys have been musicians your whole lives."

"You have been, too. You just spent a hell of a lot longer fighting it." Bo winked and kissed my nose before nodding to Regan and Georgia's Door. "Ready."

It was fairly quiet, though I tried really hard not to listen too closely. Bo and I reached our hands forward and knocked loudly and quickly, hoping to just get it over with.

"No, thank you!" Regan shouted, causing Bo and me to cover our mouths in laughter.

Bo cleared his throat and knocked again. "Dude, sorry, it's Bo and Ember."

"Well, go away, then!" Georgia shouted.

"You'll hate us in the morning if you don't open the door right now," I added.

A second later, a sheet-wrapped Regan opened the door. His normally tied-back fiery hair was loose and thoroughly sexed. And, he looked pissed.

"If my violin isn't on fire, you better run." He looked between the two of us with manic intensity.

Bo spoke as clearly and quickly as he could, while I trained my eyes on Regan's face. I was married, not dead. Regan had an impeccable body. A little thinner than I care for, but nothing to disregard. Before Bo finished his pitch, Regan held up his hand.

"Meet you downstairs in five."

§

After an anxious ten-minute drive, the four of us arrived in the parking lot of Sand Castle.

"This place?" Georgia looked around.

The club seemed to be in the middle of nowhere, though in the area we were, nothing was the middle of nowhere. Especially not during a *Live at the Vineyard* weekend. The parking lot was packed and people stood in casual clusters outside, smoking and talking. Also, there was an incredibly long line that wrapped around the building.

I put my hand on the door. "I don't usually get nervous in social situations, but—"

Bo put his hand on my arm. "You're right. You don't. You're fine. Be your beautiful self and let everything else take care of itself." He winked again and grinned.

"You're awfully winky today," I teased.

"It's because I get to look at you almost every second of my life." He leaned across the center of the car and kissed my cheek.

"No," Georgia cut in. "You two didn't cock-block me to make me sit through *Lifetime: Bo and Ember*."

Bo laughed and stuck his tongue out at Georgia. "It's just too easy to get under your skin sometimes, you know?"

"You're an asshole, Cavanaugh." She chuckled as she exited the vehicle.

I'd texted Willow when we'd reached the parking lot, so I wasn't surprised to see her standing next to the bouncer outside the door. Her face lit up in an enthusiastic smile. She waved to us and whispered into the bouncer's ear. He grinned, I rolled my eyes, and he nodded us in when we reached the steps.

"Whatever she promised you, she's lying." I smiled at the beefy—but blushing—bouncer.

Once inside, Willow smacked my shoulder. "Why do you do that all the time?"

"Why do *you* do *that* all the time? He looks like he's still in college, Willow. You're almost thirty."

"Oh, shut up. Guys our age are either married, committed, or gay. Plus, the twenty-year-olds are *excellent* in bed. Stamina wise, anyway."

"Amen to that!" Georgia shouted as she weaved her way in front of us and toward the bar.

Willow gestured toward Georgia. "Go, get a drink and do a lap or two. I'll be up in the DJ booth for the next few songs."

"Are you going to tell us who is who?"

She shook her head. "You'll get all self-conscious. Just do you."

With that, Willow danced her way back to the DJ booth, where the current occupant handed her a set of headphones and seemed to immerse her in conversation.

Bo slid his arm around my shoulders, and Regan walked on the other side of me as we met Georgia at the bar. I ordered a cosmopolitan, needing something to quickly calm my nerves but not render me completely useless. It'd been so long since I'd been in a dance club.

Come to think of it, Bo and I had *never* been to a dance club like this together before. We'd been in bars and done shows together at places kind of like this, but never as patrons. Needing to loosen up and not think about how many—if any—eyes were on us at the moment, I quickly finished my drink and set it on the bar.

Bo and Regan leaned against the bar, casually talking as they sipped beer. I tugged Georgia's arm.

"Come dance with me," I said into her ear.

"I don't dance," she mused.

"You're full of shit. I've seen you at our shows."

Georgia could be counted on, at any show she attended, to get the crowd moving.

She grinned. "This is Sean Paul. You guys have a slightly different flavor."

"Just come!" I laughed and she followed.

I caught Willow's eye as she stepped to the front of the controls and took over the beats for the club. She grinned and started playing a mashup I knew she'd been working on in the studio. Rap and Reggae beats blared from the speakers.

Georgia and I worked our bodies to the beats, and I was jealous of the way her curves moved with each step she made. She exuded sensuality with a simple shift of her hips. Still, I used what I knew I had and let the music move me.

"Don't turn around," Georgia arched her eyebrow and looked over my shoulder, "but somebody's liking the way you move."

Thinking she was teasing me about Bo being behind me, I quickly whipped around. Biting my lip as sexily as possible, of course. I was nearly knocked backward by the shock that awaited me.

"Beckett?" My eyes bulged as I struggled to believe my eyes.

"November Blue." He grinned with the sly confidence he'd embodied since he was far too young to know what to do with it.

In the tick of a second I was tossed back to high school, and my first time.

CHAPTER *Three*

The one with all the double standards

Bo

REGAN AND I watched our girls move out onto the dance floor, each silently thankful we weren't being dragged along with them...yet. To be fair, I'd never been dragged anywhere by Ember, because I would basically follow her anywhere. But we'd never danced together in a club like this, and I wasn't sure how I'd stack up.

"So, whaddaya think, man?" Regan took a swig of his beer and leaned back against the bar. "Do you think we have a shot at something big here?"

I took a deep breath and shrugged, then nodded, which made him smile. "I think we do. It feels like we're, like, *right there*, doesn't it?"

"It does. I know there are lots of moving pieces, but..."

"I know. What does Georgia think about all of this?" As I spoke, my eyes were scanning the room. I was searching for anyone I recognized from the constant industry research I subjected myself to in order to feel like I knew a fraction of what was going on around me.

Regan smiled. "She says I've got to grab this by the balls. She knows how hard I've worked, and she's well aware of the sacrifices even a minor recording contract would require. But, she's supportive. What do you think Ember wants?"

I took another breath and looked over the crowd of dancing sex and found my wife, moving with every fiber of her being. "She's afraid to say it out loud, but I think she wants a big label. I know nothing with any label is guaranteed, but if I put myself in Ember's place, a big label is more financially stable and can generate stronger contracts. Plus, more travel."

Regan nodded. "I don't want to get ahead of ourselves, though. Shouldn't we just enjoy where we're at right now? Keep our eyes on the horizon and push, of course, but we have to be careful that our desires don't get further ahead of us than we're ready for."

He was absolutely right. Everything we'd spent the last several days speculating about—months, really, since that's how long we'd known about the Vineyard—was just that. Speculation. If we got wrapped up in the maybes, we'd miss the right now. And that was something the three of us always tried to focus on.

I nodded and clinked my bottle against his. "Voice of reason. Nice. Wanna go out there before they drag us?" I nodded my head to the dance floor.

Regan squinted in their direction. "Looks like someone beat you to it, bud."

Craning my neck to the side, I saw Ember gazing almost stupefied at a guy that looked about her age. He was probably about six feet, and sandy brown hair that hung well past his ears, though it was swiped away from his face.

"Kinda looks like you, doesn't he?" Regan interrupted my thoughts.

"You're a dick." I playfully punched him in the shoulder.

"Wanna go find out who it is? It looks like she knows him."

I tilted my head toward Regan. "Are you a girl? For real. If he's someone I need to know, she'll introduce me."

Regan set his second beer bottle on the bar and nodded back in her direction. "I'd say it's someone you need to know."

I looked over the crowd once more, and found Ember reach up and hug this unidentified stranger. I turned my back to the crowd and eyed Regan seriously.

"We don't do the jealousy thing."

"I respect that." He nodded. "Neither do we."

"If that was Adrian Turner, on the other hand..." I chuckled as I threw back my third beer, finally feeling the nerves from the day slip away.

Regan eyed the DJ booth. "Willow is kicking ass in there. Who knew she could mix like that?"

As I focused my attention on the conversation with my friend, a few young women appeared behind us.

"Excuse me," one of them said as softly as she could for being in such a loud space.

"Oh, sorry." I moved to the side to allow her access to the bar.

"Oh, no...thank you...but, you're Bo Cavanaugh and Regan Kane, aren't you?"

I fixed my gaze on the group, then on Regan who was fighting a smile.

"I am. You are?" I didn't want to assume they were fans.

"Kelly." The medium-height redhead bit her lip as she stuck out her hand. Lip biting, I'd learned, was always intentional. Not always challenging, but always on purpose.

I shook her hand. "Nice to meet you, Kelly. Have we met before?"

She giggled at a decibel that put her age around twenty-one. "No, but we saw your show tonight. Not just tonight, I mean. Yeah, we saw it tonight, but I've listened—"

Her shorter, blonde friend cut her off by attempting to discreetly smack her in the arm.

"So you were at the show tonight?" Regan seemed to intentionally dial up his latent Irish accent.

Kelly blushed the color of her hair and nodded. "I've played the violin for years. Thank you for making it cool."

That comment took Regan off guard. Where he'd tried to be suave and charming at the beginning of the conversation, he was left speechless, scrunching his eyebrows.

"Trust me," Kelly continued, "you make it cool. All my friends at the conservatory are listening to you. I wrote a paper on you guys last semester."

"You did?" It looked like his head was going to explode. He had no idea how to react.

"About the risks you take. Rock and roll on the violin? It's genius."

Regan put his hands up. "I'm hardly the first person to do that."

"Maybe not," Kelly shrugged, "but you're the first person who's gotten us to notice." She turned to me. "And you and Ember? It's so romantic I can't even stand it. Is she here too?"

Just then, Willow started turning a Rihanna and David Guetta mashup I'd heard her working on in the studio over the last several weeks.

"She is," I smiled and started walking toward the dance floor, needing to move with Ember to the incredible beats, "this way."

The girls followed me, and Regan trailed a few steps behind. When we reached Ember and Georgia, I found Georgia dancing with several people, and Ember moving to the music while still talking with the guy I'd seen her hug a few minutes before.

"Hey," Regan shouted to Georgia, who quickly made her way to him while she shook her hips, "she wrote a paper about me!"

I rolled my eyes, nearly cracking into laughter as the few beers he'd ingested erased any shred of humility. We didn't have much time to spend drinking while on tour, and all of us were suffering from a serious case of *lightweight*.

Georgia quirked her lips. "Fiddle. Violin. Ireland. Must have been a short paper." She arched her eyebrow as she smiled wider and danced in front of Regan.

Regan grabbed her hips and spun her around. "Come on!"

"I'm just teasing." She placed her hands on his shoulders and kept her hips moving in time with the music.

As the two of them got lost in the song, I turned to Ember and tapped her on the shoulder, pointing to Kelly when she turned around. "This is Kelly. She wanted to meet you. She was at the show tonight."

I had to lean into her ear to avoid shouting, given we had a show the next day and I certainly didn't need a hoarse voice.

"Oh, November! You have no idea how psyched I am to meet you. You're gorgeous and talented and smart and..."

"Please," Ember smiled and stuck out her hand, "call me Ember. I'm glad you liked the show."

"Liked?" Kelly shrieked. "I have a total girl crush on you!"

After a few minutes, and a promise from Ember that she would email them back if they contacted her, the friends were sent, seemingly starstruck, back into the mix of hot dancing bodies.

"Since I'm out here," I shrugged, "dance with me." I stuck out my hand, and she took it, while eyeing *the guy*.

"Bo, this is Beckett Roth." Ember seemed to blush a little as she said his name, and I immediately scrolled through all the industry information I had to sift out if I should know him from *somewhere*. I drew a blank.

Beckett stuck out his hand with a genuine smile. "So this is the lucky bastard, huh? Nice to meet you, man."

"Nice to meet you. How do you two know each other?" I wasn't jealous by definition. Not my definition, anyway. But something about the club atmosphere, and all the skin that surrounded us, had my system on high alert.

Clubs were breeding grounds for, well, breeding, and I wanted to know who got my wife to blush in a way she rarely did.

"Oh," Ember giggled, "we went to high school together."

"Our parents knew each other when we were little. That's how Ember's parents ended up in Connecticut. We went to the same private school."

For reasons guided only by testosterone, I leaned in and asked him, "Do you know Willow, too?" I nodded to the DJ booth in case he needed a reference point.

"Oh yeah," he chuckled, "we go way back."

Ember smacked his shoulder as her jaw dropped. "How far back?"

"No worries." He grinned and kissed her cheek before addressing me. "Nice meeting you, Bo. I hope to catch up with you guys after the show tomorrow. I'm really looking forward to it." And, with that, Beckett slid his way back through the crowd and entered the DJ booth.

It wasn't until then that it clicked that he was the DJ when we'd first walked in. I hadn't paid a whole lot of attention, but once he put the headphones back on, I recognized him. He and Willow got back to work, and both seemed very involved with the task at hand.

"How far back? No worries?" I flattened my palm against the small of Ember's back and pulled her toward me.

She put her arms on my shoulders and ran her fingers through the back of my hair. "Jealous?"

I shook my head and kissed the tip of her nose. "Not a bit."

"Good. He was horrific in bed."

I dropped my arms and took a step back. "Excuse me?"

"Oh, get a grip, we were seventeen." Her eyes were focused on me, and I could tell she was already bored—or was trying to look bored—with conversation about Beckett.

I wasn't done.

"Seventeen? Didn't you have sex for the first time when you were seventeen?"

Ember playfully covered my mouth with her hand. "Shout that out, why don't you!" She moved my hands to her hips since I'd lost control over everything except rage.

Now, I'm not normally a rage-filled person. I wasn't going to beat the guy up for having sex with my wife before I even knew she existed. But there are just some things a guy doesn't need. And putting a face with your wife's *first time* is number one on that list of *things*.

"Ember, I could have gone my entire life without ever knowing, let alone meeting, your first time."

Ember pulled me through the crowd and didn't speak until we reached the bar and she'd ordered drinks.

"Ainsley Worthington," she said after a long sip of her Cosmo, challenging me with her stare.

"That's...different," I tried.

"Right," she agreed, "because Ainsley is crazy, and actively tried to get into your pants while we were together."

I sighed and growled at the same time. "A.) She only tried, didn't succeed, and B.) We weren't together when that happened. We were—"

"If you say we were on a break, I'll kick your ass, Cavanaugh." Ember set her drink down and kissed me deep enough that I could tell she'd ordered that Cosmo with raspberry vodka.

"Fair enough. Do we have to see Beckett again?" I curled my lip while grinning.

"He'll be at the show tomorrow, for sure. Relax. I haven't seen him since high school, and we were all pretty close when we were real little. Me, him, and Willow."

"When did he move to Connecticut?" I asked, not wanting to be a total meathead about the situation.

Ember looked up for a moment. "Not long before I did... we were twelve or thirteen. Can we be done talking about this and get back on the dance floor?"

"Let me finish my beer?"

"Okay, I'm going to go request a song from Willow." She made a beeline for the DJ booth.

"And Beckett?" I mumbled under my breath when she was far enough out of earshot.

"I swear to God," Georgia quipped as she reached the bar, Regan in tow. "Ember shows up in California, and all of these brand new hot people come out of the woodwork. Who knew hippies could be so hot? Who the *hell* was that guy?"

"Beckett Roth. Childhood friend of Ember and Willow, high school boyfriend to Ember." There was no way in hell I was going to repeat the information that he was the coveted owner of her virginity. Because a Neanderthal thought like that would guarantee me a swift kick in the balls.

"Oh, I get it." Regan nodded solemnly and sipped his beer.

Georgia took a shot and slid her glass back to the bartender. "Get what? That they screwed?"

"She told you?" I planted myself on a stool.

"Ha. No. It was obvious, though. She was all blush and giggles, and he was all sweaty palmed."

"The good news is, he seems to know Willow pretty well." Regan pointed the neck of his beer bottle toward the DJ booth, where Beckett had his arm around Willow's waist while Ember talked with them.

Georgia smacked my shoulder. "You're not jealous, are you?"

I put my hands up in defense. "No. Not at all. We're married. I wouldn't have married her if I had any reason not to trust her."

"It's just a guy thing," Regan cut in, in my defense. "We just don't want to know. Ever."

Georgia rolled her eyes, causing me to challenge her.

"Are you telling me, G, that you want to know about all the gory details about Regan's sex life?" I sat straighter, confident that I'd found a loophole in her condescending attitude.

"Yep." She shrugged and ordered another shot. "Here's the thing. It's no secret that I don't give a shit what people think, but I still have insecurities. It's not like I want to invite Regan's ex-conquests over for tea, but I need to know where I stand."

"You're standing next to me, aren't you?" Regan held out his hands, sounding annoyed, as though they'd been through this before.

Georgia sighed audibly and perched on the stool next to mine. "That doesn't matter. I want to know, in *my own terms* how I stand up. Irrationally, it has very little to do with you, but in the coven of womenkind, I need to know where you went with them. Emotionally, physically, all of that. I need to know in myself that I can give you above and beyond that, so I don't end up on the list of exes. Don't shoot me down with feminist propaganda. This is self-preservation. You're amazing in bed, and I know I am, too. I just want to make sure I'm pushing all the right buttons. The more I know about your sexual history, the more I can do that."

She crossed her legs, allowing her short skirt to ride further up her legs.

"The problem with you guys," she continued, "is you don't want to admit that that's exactly why you *don't* want to hear about it. We view your sexual histories as a challenge worth accepting. You view ours as a threat."

She had a point. I didn't agree with everything she said, but it served the purpose of making me feel ridiculous about how I felt about Beckett.

"Hey, you're Bo Cavanaugh. Great show tonight." A college-aged guy with black hipster glasses and dirty blonde hair held out his hand, interrupting my battle of the sexes with Georgia.

I shook his hand and talked music with him for several minutes, until a familiar song came through the speakers. I'd often heard Ember sing along to the mind-numbingly overplayed pop song while she got ready in the morning, and, apparently, the rest of the club felt the same way about it as Ember did. A brief cheer rose through the club and I watched Ember bound excitedly through the crowd toward me.

"Dance with me. Now." She grabbed my wrist and I followed her, glancing over my shoulder toward Georgia, who just winked and patiently sat by Regan, who was talking with a fan who'd approached him earlier.

"You're hot, you know that?" I ran my hands down her arms as we settled into our crowded spot on the dance floor.

"Mm-hmm," she exaggerated a grin, "I know. What were you and Georgia talking about while I was in the booth? It looked intense."

"Spying on us?"

Ember's gaze turned serious, but she didn't stop her hips. "I never have my eyes on anyone else, Bo. Even if my back is turned, my eyes are always itching for you."

Suddenly I felt like a child for my reaction earlier. "I didn't mean to get weird about Beckett."

"It's okay. We've each got our own history. But, we get a joint future." She kissed me and resumed dancing with the energy of her usual morning routine.

Damn, she's gorgeous.

"Nervous for tomorrow?" I asked, allowing my hands further down on her hips than I did when her parents were around.

"Terrified." She smiled. "But, right now, it's just us."

That's how it always felt with Ember and me. In the middle of a crowded bar or sitting alone on the beach. It was always just us.

CHAPTER *Four*

Honey What?

Ember

It's time for a goodbye

No time for a hard cry.

I don't mind,

But honey, don't haunt my dreams...

A s I SANG lead with Journey to the fast-paced and bluegrass-flavored Six song, "Ghosts Ahead," I let myself sink into the music.

The night before was a trip. Watching Willow work in the DJ booth with Beckett Roth, of all people, was a nice blast from the past. Beckett's parents often jammed with my parents and the band, right up until they moved. I knew Bo was uncomfortable with the fact that I'd slept with Beckett, but, really, it was nothing. He was my first and he said I was his, but, still, we were seventeen. I'm not sure of any seventeen-year-old that brags about their sex life. It was just sex, then we argued like the children we were, and we broke up.

Our parents took it hard. They'd all met and gotten together when they were in high school, and I think they held out a fantasy that we would do the same. Seeing Beckett again was like the final piece of the puzzle of my past that reminded me of the world I'd be stepping back into if Bo and I kept our music careers going. The last year had certainly been a whirlwind, but one we'd gratefully accepted.

Bo and I often acknowledged with each other that second chances in the entertainment industry were rare, and if we were granted something bigger than what we were doing now, we were going to take it.

As my dad plucked the strings of his banjo with fervor, and sweat from Regan's forehead splashed in the glow from the spotlight, I grabbed the mic from its stand and danced.

They tell us the past is never far behind

That ghosts ahead are what the signs all read

I'll take the road less travelled

The one you paved with regret

For me...

While bluegrass wasn't a style I was usually comfortable with, I loved the contradiction of the fast beats and the heavy lyrics. And, fans over the last several months seemed to favor these kinds of songs over our others.

The whole band was involved in this song, and by the time I worked my way over to Bo's stool, using the stage to spread out my nervous energy, it was time for his entrance. I placed my hand on his shoulder as he looked up at me, and whistles and cheers fluttered through the crowd as we started the chorus again.

> It's time for a goodbye
>
> No time for a hard cry
>
> I don't mind,
>
> But honey, don't haunt my dreams...

The humidity stuck some of my hair to my back and chest as I leaned forward to kiss Bo after we finished the lyrics, and he, Regan, and my dad raced the song to its close. My mom worked her slim hips into sensual curves as she shook the hell out of her tambourine, Mags held a beautiful, high note on her flute, Solstice's shoulders moved gracefully as she struck the keyboard, and Michael worked the bass drum with vivid intensity with his right foot as he strummed his guitar.

By this point, the crowd was on their feet, clapping and dancing. Living the music through their bodies, just the way it should be. Watching the crowd's response filled me with a joy that I knew was branded into my DNA. Aside from my wedding night—and anything involving Bo—there was no more beautiful sight in the world than people *feeling* music that I helped create.

While I didn't tend to focus on specific faces in the crowd, because that could cause me to stumble over my own concentration, I searched for Willow. She was supposed to be there with Beckett, and, sure enough, I spotted them near the pool at the edge of the garden.

Willow was moving her ethereal body along with the rest of us and the audience in a flow that looked so much like her mother's it was nearly distracting. Beckett was watching and nodding along with the beat, talking with two people to his right. I recognized Jan Lieberman from the night before. She and Beckett seemed to know each other pretty well, given the casual and friendly facial expression Beckett wore. I didn't recognize the woman standing next to Jan. She was much younger and incredibly attractive. Beckett thought so too, based on the mere flickers of eye contact he afforded her. He always wanted women to *want* him to look at them.

And he was good at making that happen.

I made my way back to center stage and met Journey at our original spot so we could sing the last note together. After holding the long, high note, and reveling in the praise roaring throughout the crowd, Journey and I smiled at each other and hugged tightly.

She kissed my cheek with the tenderness of a mother, and spoke in my ear. "You were on fire tonight, sweetness."

"Thanks to you," I complimented back.

I was thrilled to be singing with Journey. She had a slightly deeper voice than I did, and harmonizing with her was always a blast.

Mags joined us at the front of the small stage and kissed her partner before the rest of the group joined us for our bow.

Journey and Mags had been a mainstay in my life for as long as the rest of The Six. It was of no surprise to me ten years ago when they found themselves in love. I'd watched them in other relationships in their lives, including Mags's brief marriage to the male lead singer of another band they traveled with frequently. That those two women remained friends all of these years and found love right where they'd been all along was always particularly precious to me.

After we took our final bow, Jan Lieberman slid over to my mic, announcing the two-hour break in the afternoon before the evening performances were slated to start. As a matter of habit, I turned and started helping to pack up our instruments. Before I got very far, Jan tapped me on the shoulder.

"Sorry to interrupt, November," she said with an endearing smile. The kind that lures you in. "There's someone I'd like you to meet."

I was grateful my pulse was already faster than usual from the performance adrenaline rush, or I'd have felt faint from the fresh batch of nerves her request presented.

"Sure." I nodded and kept my stage smile at full wattage.

"Bo? Regan? Can you follow us?" Jan called over my shoulder.

Bo slid a casual arm around my shoulder. "Nice high note at the end." He grinned and bit his lip, which made me want to drag him back to the RV.

"Not so bad yourselves, boys. That was a great set." I eyed Regan who had the same post-performance look on his face I always did. Dazed. Bo was always full-throttle energy. Regan and I usually needed a nap.

Jan briefly looked back over her shoulder. "That was one of the most lively shows I've seen in a long time. Great crowd involvement."

She walked us over to where Willow and Beckett were standing. They were still talking with the younger woman, who I was able to get a clear picture of as we got closer. She was taller than Willow, who was 5'10". A quick look at her feet told me she was probably six-feet tall, since she was wearing sparkly ballet flats. Her hair was blonde and professionally thick. The kind of thickness you'd see on a network news anchor.

She turned toward us and smiled as we approached. "Well, here they are now!"

Her smile got impossibly bigger as her unapologetically rich southern accent took over the airwaves.

"Hello." I stuck out my hand. "I'm N—"

"November Blue Cavanaugh." She took my hand gingerly and arched her right eyebrow. My name sounded entirely different coming from her lips. It felt like I was seated on a porch swing sipping sweet tea.

"Yes." I nodded politely, shooting a quick glance to Willow, who gave me a quick wink.

"I'm Yardley Honeywell." She tilted her head to the side, like she was waiting for her name to sink in.

That was going to take a long time.

I know it seems hypocritical for me to bat a single friggen eyelash at anyone's name, given I was named after words people learn in preschool, but, come on.

Always my saving grace, Bo spoke up. "Ms. Honeywell, it's nice to meet you. Your family does some fantastic work over at GSE." He took her hand and gave her a perfect business smile.

"You're sweet, Mr. Cavanaugh."

Out of the corner of my eye, I saw Regan wipe his right hand on the back of his jeans before offering it up. Rosin could feel a little off-putting in the middle of a handshake if one wasn't prepared for it, and Regan was always covered in the stuff.

Grounded Sound Entertainment.

I couldn't believe the name clicked so fast, given I paid a fraction of the attention Bo did to the goings on in the industry side of the business. I remembered Bo and Regan talking the previous week about a list of possible labels that would be sniffing around *Live at the Vineyard*, and this was one of them. Bo had told me that Luke and Ginger Honeywell were grooming their children to take over, and one of their daughters had a particular interest in raw sound. She preferred musicians who could easily sing live, and—most importantly—could play instruments.

The only reason I picked up on this name and the others they talked about was because of the possibility of working with cool people who appreciated our sound, and what we were trying to do. Which was, largely, go back to basics. Voices. Instruments. That's it.

The young woman who I was face to face with, however, wasn't what I expected. Her face looked more pageant than festival ready, and her clothes were a confusing blend of casual and business. The ballet flats, a quite short black skirt and a white long-sleeved button down shirt with the sleeves rolled to her elbows and the top two buttons unbuttoned.

I decided I should close my mouth and watch her for a while.

"I was just talking with Willow and Beck…" Yardley talked at us about the things she liked about all of the other performances during the day.

I stopped listening when she said *Beck*, and his eyes shot to mine as she said it. *Beck* was a term used by two groups of people: people who'd known him in diapers, and people who'd slept with him. I was a rare member of both camps, but had specifically called him *Beckett* the previous evening to assert my position as far as his pants were concerned.

I wanted so badly to arch my eyebrow at Beckett, but I knew doing so would make him think I cared that he slept with Yardley, and I honestly didn't. I don't know why he'd want me to care, but his playful eyes and challenging smile told me he did.

"I want you three to come play for me tomorrow." Yardley's sure statement tuned me back into the conversation quickly. "I was able to call in a favor and snag some studio time."

"Can we have a minute to talk about it?" Regan's voice was confident and friendly, and Yardley returned a smile and a nod.

Jan hooked her arm through Yardley's. "We'll go over and get some wine while you all talk."

Once they were out of earshot, Willow stepped closer to us. "What do you guys think?"

Bo ran a hand over his head and rested it on the back of his neck as he spoke. "Is she seriously wanting to listen to us or is she just playing with her parents' money? I know a bit about both."

I shot my eyes to Bo, focusing on the second half of his statement. I didn't know what he was talking about and it made me a little uncomfortable. He remained focused on the conversation.

Beckett slid his hands in his pocket. "Good question. She's serious. Grounded Sound is a big name, and while her brother and sister might entertain friends of friends, Yardley has a wicked business sense and doesn't ever waste her time on something she's not considering."

"Beckett's right," Willow offered. "He's the one who told me Yardley was on the prowl and had asked specifically about you guys. That's why I called you to Sand Castle last night."

"She was there?" I scrunched my forehead, trying to remember seeing her, but I couldn't.

"Oh, shit!" Regan sounded like he'd had a revelation. "She was with that group of girls who came up to us, remember, Bo? She didn't say much, or anything, but she was there. *That's* why she looked familiar."

I remembered Regan coming up to Georgia and me the night before, talking about girls who'd written a paper about him in school. I wasn't paying a lot of attention, given I'd just run into Beckett for the first time in ten years.

Beckett nodded. "That was her. I asked her about those girls after and she said she didn't know them, but followed them over to you when they'd finally worked up the courage to approach you. She liked your style. Both of you." He pointed between Bo and Regan.

"Smart." I nodded approvingly at her undercover tactics to get to know both the fans of the music she liked, and the musicians who made it.

Bo scratched his jaw then looked at me. "What do you think?"

"I think we should play for whoever wants to listen, don't you?"

I'd spent the last year working tirelessly on developing my craft. Performing as much as I could, and practicing even more. I was so enveloped in training that I hadn't spent any time at all researching the business side of things. I knew Bo's business sense was enough for the both of us, so I silently let him shoulder that. I realized that was a slight misstep on my part; because I felt like I didn't even have enough to stand on to make such a decision.

"I mean, she isn't wasting our time, really," I continued. "She's here, and we've got that concert in a few days anyway, so *we're* here. I just don't see that it's a loss on any front."

Beckett put his hand on my shoulder. "Last night you spent a lot of time talking about how you didn't know anything about *the business*. Playing for anyone who will listen? That's all you need to know right now. Don't underestimate yourself."

I heard Regan chuckle way under his breath behind me.

Bo, however, spoke first. "Beckett, tell me a little bit about yourself. I know you DJ, but what's your experience with labels?"

I didn't hear any sort of posturing in his voice. Cool and collected, as always. One of these days I knew he was going to snap if he always kept it calm like that.

Beckett answered. "As I'm sure you know, my parents jammed with The Six a lot before we moved back east."

The term "back east" irritated the hell out of me. Before he'd moved there, Beckett hadn't been anywhere east of Wyoming.

"When I was at Colombia, I spent a lot of time in the underground music scene," he continued. "That's where I got my start at mixing music. While I followed local artists, every once in a while one of them would get picked up. I started keeping track of who went where and who had the most success and creative freedom. Soon, friends started seeking my advice as a non-benefitting party."

"Impressive," I cut in.

"Turns out there is some good that can come from hanging out in a bar all week." Beckett winked and I laughed.

"What do you think, Regan?" Bo refocused the conversation.

"Let's play for her. Give her something to write home about. Which reminds me. I'm not getting ahead of myself, or anything, but where is *home* for Yardley and Grounded Sound?"

Willow took the lead. "Her family is based out of Savannah, Georgia, but they've had offices and studios in both New York and L.A. for years. Her parents are ready to take a more behind-the-scenes approach, and are giving Yardley her choice of operations. Looks like she's leaning toward New York, but she's scoping prospects all over."

Willow shot a hesitant gaze my way. I knew what it meant. New York. And, even though we hadn't been offered more than a pair of ears, it occurred to me for the first time that we'd have more to consider than the financial details of a contract.

"Let's do it." I leaned into Bo, who wrapped his arm around my shoulders.

"Did I hear a yes?" Yardley cooed almost out of nowhere.

I looked to Bo and Regan and we all eyed Yardley at the same time.

"We'd love to play for you," Bo answered for us.

Yardley bobbed a little on her heels as though she really wanted to jump. "Excellent. I'll meet you all at Tavern Nine Studios at noon tomorrow."

Yardley glided back across the garden and hooked up with Jan, who was talking with a Top 40 manager I recognized from *Entertainment Weekly*.

"Good move, guys," Beckett said as he stretched his arms overhead.

I freed myself from Bo's embrace and walked back toward where the rest of The Six would be waiting for us. "Thanks. How long are you in town, Beckett?"

He pulled his head back and twisted his eyebrows. "I live here."

"Since when?" I mimicked his incredulous look.

"A year and a half ago. I live like a second from here."

"We did a show here last year. Where the hell were you?" I teased, smiling at the memory that our show last year in Napa was the first large show Bo and I had done as husband and wife. We'd married at the campground in Vallejo a week earlier.

Beckett seemed to struggle for an answer. "I wasn't actually in town that weekend."

He seemed to drop it at that, falling back in step with Regan, discussing doing a rock mix with violin for him to use when he worked at a club. Regan sounded excited enough and they talked about the technical aspects of classical music used in the rock world.

I shook off the slightly awkward exchange and grabbed Bo's hand, excited to tell my parents the opportunity—no matter how small—we'd been afforded.

CHAPTER *Five*

Now or never

Bo

"I'M SO GLAD you guys had the foresight to book this place for two nights." Ember drummed her fingers softly on her knees as she bobbed her head to the music playing through the car.

Georgia chuckled. "Amen to that. Just an FYI, I don't care if the President of the United States calls you and tells you to get somewhere. I'm not leaving that bed till morning."

"Amen to *that*," Ember echoed, reaching her hand behind her for a high five from Georgia.

There was a buzzing energy inside our vehicle. Between the performance tonight, which was the best we'd ever played, and the excitement over our recording session at Tavern Nine tomorrow, I wondered if we'd ever get to sleep. Regan had been quiet since we left the vineyard. Looking in the rearview mirror, I saw his face looked calm, but there was certainly something serious brewing behind his eyes. Just then, he looked forward and caught me staring at him. He grinned and shook his head, mouthing, *can you believe this shit?*

I couldn't. However, I'd promised in prayer to my parents after they died that I'd never question things when they were good. I promised to them, and myself, that I'd enjoy every second of joy and, when it happened, every second of pain.

To feel meant that I was still breathing.

Once we were back at the bed and breakfast and in our own private room, Ember seemed to want to pick up where we'd left off the night before. She tossed her messenger bag on the chair and began undressing. The long white sundress she'd worn on stage was the same one she'd worn when she agreed to be my wife, and then did just that mere minutes later. Only those of us who were there that night knew that *this* was the dress, and it helped create a certain energy sometimes when she wore it.

I knew it was a calming one for her. She tended to wear it when she needed to be centered.

"Are you okay tonight?" I asked, gesturing to the dress as I approached her and set my hands on her hips.

She nodded, looking up at me through her lashes. "I was so worked up this morning about who would be there tonight, and what would happen, that I just needed to wear that dress. To remember what the hell we're doing anyway."

"And what's that?" I exhaled slowly as I brought my lips to her neck, allowing me to inhale again and savor the sweetness of her skin.

"Living our wildest dreams. We're doing it already." She paused to moan as my lips worked to her collarbone. "So, I needed to remind myself not to get too worked up or too disappointed about whatever happened tonight or from here on out."

Ember's hands worked quickly to unhook my belt, leaving it in the loops as she unzipped my shorts and let them fall to the floor.

I stepped out of them and led her to the bed. She was wearing a nude colored bra and matching lace panties that drove me wild. While a nude Ember was certainly something to behold, there was something so inviting and wild about the *almost* that her panties beckoned me with.

"Your parents seemed excited about tomorrow." I took off my shirt and tossed it onto my shorts.

Ember placed her hands behind her and leaned back. "They did. They say they want us to chase this."

"Do you think they mean it?"

I knew Raven and Ashby and the rest of The Six were one hundred percent supportive of all of our musical talent and efforts. If they weren't, they wouldn't have gone out of the way to create space in our concert lineup for just Regan, Ember, and me to play. And, given they'd already had a few rounds of national tours a couple of decades ago, it's not like they'd be missing out on an opportunity. They truly seemed content in traveling California and the Pacific Northwest.

Ember leaned her head from side to side, like she was weighing her response. "I do. I mean, it's not like they'd have a problem getting an audience for a show if we weren't there. Their fans are loyal, and the band is special. They'll be playing together until they leave this earth."

"I know. I tell your dad this at least ten times a week, but it's been a hell of an opportunity learning from them and playing with them this past year. It's been like the dream internship or top apprenticeship." Then, it dawned on me. I leaned over

Ember, laying her on the bed as I kissed her cheeks. "If we get some sort of contract without them, you'll be sad not to be playing with them so much."

She grinned, pinching my chin between her thumb and index finger. "Was that a question or a statement?"

I shrugged, leaning forward to kiss her nose.

"How about," she continued, "we don't worry about any of that unless we have to? You know, one day at a time and all of that." Ember glided her hand down my stomach and slipped past the fabric of my boxer briefs, taking my breath away momentarily.

"November Cavanaugh, have you been reading my self-help books?" I teased.

She shrugged. "I've got to do *something* when we're all trapped in that RV together."

"Well. We're not in an RV now..." I gently pulled the silk of her bra to expose one breast, and started kissing and nibbling her soft skin.

"That's true." Her voice took on the airy breathlessness I found intoxicating. "And, we're not sleeping, either."

"Imagine that." I grinned. "Whatever shall we do with our time?"

Ember had been stroking me slowly during our whole exchange, and finally slid her hand back up to help me out of my boxer briefs.

"Damn, you're fine. I don't know why anyone complains about being over thirty," she teased. "It looks pretty divine from where I'm sitting."

"And eternity looks exceptional from where I'm sitting."

Ember rolled her eyes and smacked my chest. "Oh shut up!"

"What?" I hovered over her, my lips inches from hers.

"I can't say one romantic thing without you pulling out the big guns. Let me have a moment, huh?"

In a second, her playful giggle and lip biting turned serious. Her hands moved to my face and she pulled my lips to hers, moaning as we connected.

"You're so beautiful." I spoke softly as I pulled back, resting on my knees so I could slide her panties down her legs.

Ember never talked much during sex and, sometimes, it made me uncomfortable. I wanted to know what was going on inside her head. The looks she shot me had to have a million words behind them, and I wanted to know what they were. She often did her best speaking with her body, though, and tonight was no different.

She wrapped her hands around the backs of my thighs and dropped her knees a little further to the side to allow me in. I took my time, never wanting to waste a second that I had her in bed. Especially since over the last year we hadn't exactly had the typical newlywed experience. Being in an RV for more than 6 months all totaled posed its own stresses. Stresses that were miles away as I put my head down and reveled in the feel of her. Her back arched as I worked my way deep inside of her. Slowly at first, allowing us to acclimate to the always intense feeling.

"God, I love you, Bo." Ember's head rocked back on the pillow, but when she lowered her chin, she opened her eyes.

Reaching for my face once again, Ember kept her eyes on me as I moved slightly faster. Her lips parted and her breath became shorter, and I couldn't look away. Our eyes were locked on each other as we moved together. No words, no directions, no questions. I wanted to go faster. That was the instinct of my body, but as I watched Ember's face, something changed.

A small tear curled out of the corner of one of her eyes and slid across her cheekbone and onto the pillow. She didn't move her eyes even then. When a second tear fell, I slowed. Not to a stop, but slow enough that I could talk.

"What's wrong?" Shifting my weight to one hand, I took the other and brought it to her face, using my thumb to wipe a third tear that sat on the edge of her eye.

She slowly rocked her head back and forth, pulling her lips into a reassuring smile. "This year has been the best of my life, Bo. We have more than anything I'd dreamed we'd have." Her chin quivered as she released a soft sigh, moving her hands down the length of my arms.

"You look sad..." I was trying to understand the mix of emotions she seemed to be wrestling with.

"I'm scared it'll be taken away."

At that, I stopped and slowly pulled out of her. I rolled over and pulled her to my chest. "What do you mean?"

Ember nuzzled her head into my shoulder and sniffed. "I don't know...it all seems too good to be true sometimes. Like, I find myself wondering when the other shoe will drop."

Kissing the top of her head, I left my lips there as I spoke. "You're my happily ever after, Ember. We've dealt with all kinds of shit, and we're fine."

"I'm afraid I'm going to lose you." With the sound of a thousand hearts breaking, Ember's eyes pleaded with me for reassurance.

I held her tighter. "What makes you think you'll lose me?"

"It always happens, you know. When people get famous."

A sharp laugh from deep within my chest startled her. She leaned up on one elbow, looking rather incensed.

"I'm serious, Bo. If it's not drugs, then it's alcohol. If it's not women, then it's money."

"You're kidding, right? Ember, this isn't *Behind the Music*. I'm not...wait...do you not trust me? Wait...no...this is the most ridiculous conversation we've ever had. I don't have any recording contract, and if I don't get one with you, then I'm not taking it."

She sat up and maintained her quiet faraway tone. "Well, that's kind of drastic, don't you think?"

"No more drastic than you thinking I'll turn into some sort of stereotypical burnout overnight." I kept my voice soft and even because, if I knew Ember at all, this wasn't what she was actually upset about.

Ember ran her fingers through her hair, stopping at the back of her head and tightening them until her knuckles turned white. She bent her knees and rested her forehead on them, taking a deep breath.

"Love?" I placed my hand in the center of her back, brushing it smoothly from side to side. "What's this about?"

"Don't you ever think things are too good to be true?" Her voice started shaking, and it was then that it clicked she was having a panic attack.

To my knowledge up until that point, she'd never had one. I received my PhD in panic after my parents died and, luckily, that training took over. I moved so I was kneeling in front of her, and tugged her hands away from her hair.

"Hey, hey, hey..." With each word, I dropped my volume lower in order to get her to focus on it and not whatever mess was trashing her insides. "Babe, look at me, okay?"

I had to say it one more time, but she finally did. Her hands were shaking like crazy and had a thin sheen of cool sweat covering them. Her eyes darted around the room, no doubt searching for an escape.

"November, look into my eyes. Take a deep breath. In through your nose until you can't take in any more, then puff your cheeks as you force the air out, okay? I'll take one with you." I opened my mouth wider than necessary to get her to focus on the breath we were about to take together.

Her shoulders didn't lower all the way in her exhale, so I encouraged one more deep breath. Then another.

"Don't stop looking at me, okay? Watch my eyes. You're safe."

At those words, it seemed, the last of her breath left her lungs. She leaned back against the headboard, and I let her hands go. They immediately covered her face.

"What the fuck was that?" She panted and sniffed as the remains of the attack littered her senses.

I turned and sat next to her, not wanting to show her how rattled it had me to have watched that from the outside. Then I realized how she must have been feeling. "I think it was a panic attack."

"My tongue went numb, my fingers were tingly and I thought I was going to die..." Ember shook her hands, undoubtedly trying to encourage feeling back into them.

I'd tried it a million times myself, and the only conclusion I drew was you couldn't shake anything *in* to anywhere.

"What do I have to panic about? It came out of nowhere and then I started blathering on about the *True Hollywood Story* of Bo Cavanaugh and I didn't mean a word of it. I was just trying to find out why I was so...afraid."

I stretched my arm out and she leaned forward, tilting her body into mine. She was still shaking a bit, and I expected that would last throughout the night, but for now she seemed mostly tired.

"We've had a really intense few days, Em. Lots of possibilities, even more uncertainties, and...it's just a lot."

"You and Regan aren't freaking out." She sounded smug and irritated.

I shrugged, hoping to pacify her. "Not everyone is wired the same way. Maybe we'll freak out tomorrow in the middle of a song at Tavern Nine. Maybe one of us will lose our ability to speak during an interview. Everyone handles things differently."

"Jesus, that was embarrassing." Just like that, Ember's dry and snarky tone returned as she growled and groaned.

I kissed the top of her head. "It wasn't embarrassing."

"Do you still get them?"

When Ember and I started spending the night regularly with each other when we were dating, she often woke me from dark and loud dreams. I started seeing my therapist again after a week had gone by and Ember looked like she hadn't slept at all. I was keeping her awake with things I should have packed away.

I nodded and twitched my lips. The fact was, I was beginning to think the panic attacks would never go away. I would have to learn how to manage life with them. "Sometimes."

"Like when?" She looked up, concern for me masking her own fear.

"At night."

"When you're sleeping?"

"More when I'm trying to fall asleep. I'll lay there awake sometimes, trying to turn off my brain, and...then it happens."

She scrunched her eyebrows and rubbed my knee. "Why don't you wake me up?"

I grinned, placing my hand on hers. "I'm thankful my tossing and turning *doesn't* wake you up. If there's ever anything I need help with, I'll ask. Okay?"

She twitched her lips skeptically. "Promise?" She arched her eyebrow.

"Promise. So..." Once I saw her face relax, I knew I could play a little bit. "Do you wanna just cuddle, or..."

Ember bit her lip and playfully lunged forward, knocking me onto my back on the bed. "Would it be crude of me to ask that we pick up where we left off?"

I grabbed her hips and leaned up, kissing the tight skin on her stomach. "Hell no."

§

The next day, Regan, Ember, and me found ourselves in the smallest of three studios Tavern Nine had in their offbeat looking building. There was exposed brick on the interior walls of the general areas, and each studio was painted with incredible colors and had wild furniture, like a zebra printed chair and a polka dotted love seat.

Tavern Nine had produced some great musicians over the last two years. Still in their infancy, they were able to snag artists who were up and coming and dissatisfied with the lack of attention some of them were receiving from bigger labels. They were able to offer more studio time, fresh PR ideas, and a more personal experience. They focused mostly on small country-western acts, but the fact that Yardley Honeywell had contacts with such a smooth operation comforted me.

We'd arrived about forty-five minutes before Yardley asked, hoping to get some time to warm up before we were under the spotlight. Thankfully, they weren't booked this morning. Right at noon, when Yardley entered the studio, we felt well oiled and ready to go.

"Thank y'all for coming on such short notice," she started, keeping her professional smile from last night.

Her accent was pleasing to the ear, I had to give her that. It didn't sound forced, and that added another layer of my comfort that Yardley wasn't trying to impress anyone. She wanted to run a business.

Ember stepped forward, extending her hand. "Thank you for having us." Suddenly, Ember focused her attention on the recording room, behind the glass. "Beckett?"

A quick click over the speakers and Beckett's Ivy League-cum-surfer voice filled the studio. "Morning." He grinned and clicked off the mic, offering nothing else.

It was noon.

"It won't be a problem that he's here, will it?" Yardley lifted her chin, keeping her friendly smile despite the somewhat challenging gesture.

"Not at all," Ember asserted. "I wasn't aware you two knew each other."

A flash of pink ran through Yardley's cheeks. "Well, Beck's been helpful in some of the details of my takeover of the New York offices of Grounded Sound. For the last several months he's been rounding up talent for me to listen to on my trips up there."

Half of Ember's mouth formed a sly grin as she focused on the control room. "That's nice of him."

For a moment I felt like a foreigner in the room, incompetent in the ankle-deep subtext between the three of them.

"Okay," Yardley redirected the conversation. "I'd like you guys to play whatever you want. Two or three songs and I won't come back in here until you're done. You can practice more if you'd like, but let me know when you're ready to go."

Ember whipped around, looking ready to say something, but Regan chuckled and pressed his index finger to his lips, pointing skyward with his other hand. Reminding Ember we weren't actually alone despite the closed door. Microphones were everywhere.

She comically cleared her throat. "Ready, guys? Let's start with that bluegrass jig?"

Regan and I nodded, and got situated in front of our microphones. Whatever nerves and uncertainty Ember had grappled with the night before, all of that seemed to have vanished as she slung the strap of her guitar over her shoulder and immediately entered the fast-paced song. I glanced at Regan, who shrugged, grinned, and took off when his entrance came up.

I struck my guitar on cue, and before my vocal entrance, I closed my eyes for a brief moment and breathed in a small prayer that everything would work out as it should.

We ended up playing three songs, choosing to use the maximum opportunity we were given. Two slow, one fast. Sure, sometimes songs with trios involving a violin are more fun to listen to when it's a rapid beat, but there is precision in a slow song's tones and swells. Holding longer notes on an instrument and with your voice shows stamina needed for long shows and for a variety of songs.

Our gut instincts appeared spot on, as I watched Yardley nodding with the pad of her index finger pressed onto her lips. She seemed to be suppressing a smile as she stole a glance to her left, where Beckett stood. Beckett's eyes never moved from Ember. When we finished, he grinned and gave her an overly friendly thumbs-up. Did you know a thumbs-up could be overly friendly? Neither did I, until I watched that one. But, I wasn't about to let some caveman jealousy based on precisely nothing screw up this opportunity.

Yardley leaned for the mic and flipped the switch. "Thanks, guys. I'll give you a few minutes to pack up, and I'll meet you in Conference Room One."

She clicked the mic back off and walked out of the control room, Beckett strolling behind her with his hands in his pockets.

"She's got one hell of a poker face," Regan mused as he put his violin back in its case.

"That's good though, right? I mean we don't need someone who's going to fawn all over everyone or tell them they suck and to get out...right?" Ember shrugged, a smile still on her face from her killer rendition of our new ballad.

I nodded in agreement with her. "Let's get to that conference room and see what she has to say."

With our clunky cases and nerves in hand, we walked a few doors down to the conference room. Yardley was alone, and I was grateful to be free of Beckett for a few moments so I could think clearly, rather than try to interpret his intentions with my wife. Old friends or not, he'd slept with her. I don't care if they were in high school, connecting with a girl like Ember does something to your insides. I saw it on his face and wanted to smack it off. There was no way in hell I wanted to talk to Ember about any of this since it was fleeting, and Beckett and I would eventually get over our silent pissing contest.

Yardley motioned for us to sit around a large round table. I liked that the table was round; there was no positioning of sitting down from her. We were all on an even plane, but even if it was imaginary it made me comfortable.

"As you know," Yardley started without any lead in, "Grounded Sound has several divisions. We're open to all sounds, all artists — except rap. We just don't have a good ear for that." She chuckled, folding her hands in front of her as her southern accent poured out like honey over her words.

"I like your sound," she continued. "You're a few steps ahead of an exciting emerging trend, and we can't ignore it. People are craving musicians. Not just people who can match a pitch to an electronically produced note. You've got talent on all sides. And stage presence, which can't be taught. Look at you, for goodness sake. You're all beautiful." She waved her hand toward us and smiled.

It was hard not to return her smile. Regan blushed, and so did Ember. I lifted my chin, begging my cheeks not to turn. They stayed cool as I spoke.

"We want to thank you again for listening to us this afternoon." I kept my voice pleasant and even. Business was in my blood, and if Yardley had done any homework on us whatsoever, she'd know that about me.

Yardley exhaled quickly through her nose before lifting her chin to match mine. "It was a pleasure, Mr. Cavanaugh. I've been following you three for several months, and it was my good fortune to mention you to Beckett Roth, who was more than helpful in arranging this meeting today."

Instinctively, I clenched my teeth together, feeling my jaw twitch once before I took a breath.

Ember sat forward, placing her hands on the table. "I'm thrilled the timing worked out."

There was an uncomfortable pause in the conversation. I shot a glance to Regan, who looked at me and shrugged slightly. We all seemed to want to ask her what the purpose was for this pow-wow, but there was no way we'd be the first to speak, lest we seem too self-important.

Yardley sighed audibly but with grace, seeming to use the breath to prepare her next words. She took three careful seconds to make eye contact with each of us who sat around the table before she opened her mouth.

"I'm prepared to make you an offer."

CHAPTER *Six*

The offer

Ember

BACK AT THE Six's campsite, where they'd rented a few cabins, eight sets of eyes, Georgia and Willow included, stared back at me, Bo, and Regan. Regan had talked with Georgia beforehand, and a tentative but wistful smile shone on her face.

"So..." Bo clapped his hands once and took a cleansing breath. "That's the deal. Finish the tour with you all, fly to New York to record for a few weeks, and the label is going to put together an *Indie Tour*." Bo put air-quotes around the phrase.

It was a false term, since we'd be signed with a label and would, therefore, not be independent, but Yardley knew the marketing value of those words. She'd been working her ass off over the last year, scouring festivals and open mic nights, collecting the most popular and most talented unsigned artists she could. Putting a tour together with a sound like ours and with newly signed artists was a way to market the artist and the new "Indie" side of Grounded Sound she was hoping to develop.

I watched my parents closely. They'd said over and over again that they would be supportive of whatever offers we received, if we ever received any. The Six remained adamant that they wanted to stick to the West Coast and maybe a few other dates throughout the year, but they'd had "their day" and wanted to give us ours, if it came.

"Of course," Bo continued, "any songs that we worked on with the band or ones we re-wrote would—"

He was cut off by the entire group of middle-aged hippies jumping to their feet with elation in their eyes. Cheers and whistles cut off whatever it was Bo was in the middle of saying, but I could hardly focus on that as we were tackle-hugged by the Essential Oil Brigade.

"We're so proud of you three!" my mom squealed as she tried to hug the three of us at once.

Bo and I looked at each other nervously, causing a quick calm to settle through the room.

"What is it?" Solstice asked, pulling in her eyebrows.

Regan cleared his throat and grabbed Georgia's hand. "I won't be joining them."

The gasp from the group nearly sucked air from my lungs. "What?" they said nearly in unison.

"But you said—" Michael started, but was cut off by Regan.

"The deal Bo described is also the deal I was offered. But Yardley and I spoke at length, and I was able to negotiate a contract with one of her West coast projects. Same style of music, same amount of control. But...I don't want to leave Georgia behind." He put his arm around her shoulders and kissed the top of her head.

"I told you you could go," she whispered, blushing slightly as she seemed to try to hide her face in Regan's shoulder.

"Of course I *can*, babe," he grinned, "but I don't *want* to. The deal I have is just as amazing. Sure, it'll suck to be separated from those two," he playfully pointed at me and Bo, "but I'd rather be with you. We've spent our whole first year and a half together seeing each other for a few days at a time at most. This is good."

I walked to Regan's side and put my arm around his waist while I addressed the anxious group. "While it sucks that after this tour we won't be performing with him anymore, a year ago I'd have made the same decision."

"I would have, too." Bo grinned and winked at me, sending warmth through my chest.

Yes, it would certainly be bittersweet to leave Regan and the San Diego sun, but by the end of the meeting with Yardley, I was grateful that Bo and I were getting signed together as an act. Everything we did from here on out with music would be together.

As it should be.

The group in front of us broke into people congratulating Regan, and asking him questions about his deal, and hovering over me and Bo.

"Well done, son. Well done." My dad shook Bo's hand and gave Regan a hug before turning to me. "You amaze me, Baby Blue. Every day."

Tears stung my eyes as I hugged him tightly. "Thanks, Dad. I never knew this would feel so good."

I truly hadn't. My love affair with performing was slow and unassuming. Sneaking up on me and slowly coming into focus the way rainbows do after a storm. Never all at once. Bo's spot as my soul mate wasn't revealed through chance glances or years of missed chances. It was inside of one song. In the music. It had thrown me full force into a life I'd tried to escape for years prior. I'd needed Bo to love the music, and the music to bring me to Bo.

Once the twittering of kisses, hugs, and congratulations subsided, Mags spoke up on practical matters.

"How's the deal? Not money wise—that can always be negotiated. Creatively. What's your control?"

I grinned. "We agreed to profit sharing. It's a lower advance, but we retain more control and will get more money if certain songs or albums do well. Since we're already somewhat established in our specific audience, there is less legwork they need to do in certain areas. We already have half an album recorded, thanks to Willow's help, so that's some cost savings for the label as well."

Bo nodded in approval of my interpretation of the meeting. He and Yardley had gone back and forth a few times hammering out details and I'd made sure to pay close attention. My business sense had been exercised in the non-profit sector for years before, and the music industry was a far cry from a 501(c)(3) operation. There would be no tax exemptions granted since profit was definitely the name of the game. Thankfully, though, my focus was in grant writing, so I had to learn the language for all kinds of businesses, including multi-million dollar outfits.

While I'd met Bo during his work with his family's non-profit, DROP, he was well groomed in all forms of business. His father had inherited a century-old New Hampshire newspaper when he was barely over the age of twenty. A well-educated man, Spencer Cavanaugh spent years learning the ropes, then carefully sold the company off in pieces, tripling his net-worth. From that point, he dabbled in several non-profit endeavors, which is something one can do when they're worth over twenty million dollars. He used his experiences to guide his children in shrewd business negotiation. Bo formalized his training with an MBA, but, really, he was head and shoulders above most of his classmates long before diplomas were handed out.

"I know we have a show in two days," Solstice silenced the small talk of contracts—which we still needed to have viewed by an attorney—with her sweetly authoritative voice, "but we should take tonight off and celebrate. Willow is DJing at the Iron Lady tonight, and while all of you were hugging and kissing I called and arranged to have a private room. It'll be ready in an hour."

I turned to Bo. "We should go back to the bed and breakfast to freshen up. The Iron Lady is north of there."

It had been a long and emotionally exhausting day. A good shower was in order before celebrating the rapidly approaching next chapter of my life. Our life.

"We'll come with you guys." Georgia looked like she was dying for a little space. It had been an emotionally charged afternoon for her, as well. Until Regan could calm her down enough to show her that he wasn't giving up any opportunity, I'd thought her head was going to explode.

Once we were in the car, the four of us exhaled in near-unison.

"Well," Regan said as he drove us down the road, "that was one hell of a day, huh?"

"Can we squeal yet?" I bit my lip as a dumb grin erupted through my body.

Bo clapped his hands loudly, and then started drumming on the ceiling of the car. "Woo hoo! A record deal, baby!" He leaned over and grabbed the back of my neck, pulling me into a kiss.

It was a rare and beautiful sight to see Bo so animated. He was always honest with his emotions, but he was also very even-keeled. That was necessary, as far as being in a relationship with yours truly was concerned, but this was something I didn't get to see very often. Bo Cavanaugh: Unglued.

I was willing to bet he handed out those smiles like candy in high school. But, by the time I entered his path, life had done a good job of training his guard. Funny, how I thought I was the guarded one. Watching his youthful glee during the discussion of our record deal showed me I still had a great deal to learn about the deep down hidden places in the core of my husband.

"I can't believe I'm married to a rock star," I teased, kissing his nose.

He licked his lips and a flicker of dangerous passion shot through his eyes. "I can't believe I'm married to the hottest rock star the world has yet to meet."

Regan eyed us through the rearview mirror. "Who are you two going to have look over your contracts?"

Ah, reality.

We had a deal. It was well written, emailed to us with the final details an hour after we left our meeting with Yardley. The I's were dotted and the T's were crossed, but it technically wasn't signed. Yardley stated she'd have her lawyer give the deal a once-over and would be in contact with us by Tuesday. That gave us two days to find a lawyer and have them look over the terms in order to give the impression that we had our act together far more than we actually did.

"I've been thinking about it," Bo sat back and put his business mask back on, "I could certainly run it by the board at DROP, though none of them actually specialize in entertainment law, which is a whole different thing."

"They might know someone else?" I suggested.

He shrugged, looking quite serious. "I suppose, but we need this done rather quickly.

My mind flicked through all the lawyers I'd been in contact with over the last several years. Like Bo's dilemma, mine were far removed from the entertainment industry.

Except for one.

I shifted in my seat, hoping Bo wouldn't notice my attempt not to mention him at all.

"No." He shook his head as authoritatively as he spoke.

With an exaggerated eye roll, I began standing up for something I hadn't even brought up. "Why not? You know he's good. Christ, *you hired him* for DROP because you knew he was top-notch. If you remember his resume, which I know you do because you don't forget a damn thing, he specializes in entertainment law."

"Who's the floating pronoun?" Georgia mumbled to Regan.

"I have no..." He looked confused for a moment before his eyes widened. "Ooh. That must be Adrian, Ember's ex-boyfriend from college."

"Not just college," Bo grumbled.

I chuckled. "You've got to be kidding me. This is two-year-old history, you wackjob. Need I remind you that I had to *work* with your ex-girlfriend *while* we were broken up?"

Georgia turned her head to the back seat. "Ainsley Worthing-ton, right?"

Bo looked at me with an amused smirk, then to Georgia. "Yes." He sighed.

Georgia winked at me, blew a kiss to Bo, and turned back around.

"Can we get back to planet Earth?" I urged. "I'll call Adrian, ask if I can send the contract for him to look over this weekend, and that'll be the end of it. If he says no, we'll send it to your board."

Bo cracked a full smile, shaking his head and growling. "I'm sorry. I hate when I have these visceral reactions. Call Adrian. I mean, if anyone is going to feel weird, it'll be him. Right? I got the girl." Bo winked and grabbed my hand, kiss-ing it softly.

"Christ," I joked. "It was never a love triangle. Just a jumbled mess of chaos."

"Um, it was definitely a triangle," Georgia shot to the back seat.

I twisted my lips and playfully slapped the back of her seat. "Traitor. Mind your business."

Once we were back at the bed and breakfast, everyone headed for the door.

"I'll hang out here to make the call." I waved my hand to everyone, and they continued on their way.

"You have his number?" Bo asked.

"Google," I called over my shoulder as I walked to a bench at the edge of the parking area.

It was late in Massachusetts, but that meant nothing as far as Adrian's work hours were concerned. His clients tended to keep later hours due to performance schedules, so his office hours followed suit. If his secretary wasn't in, I'd just leave a message and then call his personal line. You can only delete numbers from your phone. Not your brain. Adrian had had the same cell phone number since we were in college, long before I even owned a cell phone. I'd dialed that number from landline phones over a thousand times.

Still, I thumbed through my phone, Googling his law firm and dialing the listed number. As it rang, I started to feel guilty for calling. Adrian and I hadn't spoke for over two years, and I was going to dial in a favor? I volleyed between asserting that we were adults and could handle a business conversation, and condemning myself for a seemingly selfish act. Before I could change my plan, someone picked up.

"Turner here."

Oh, of course he'd answer.

I wasn't given a second wave of emotional barrier by speaking to his secretary. I could have hung up, but my label of "adult" prevented such actions.

"Adrian," I spewed out with a dash of over-enthusiasm, "it's Ember...November Harr—Cavana—. It's Ember." I rolled my eyes at myself. Ember would have sufficed.

I took his extra-long pause as an opportunity to clear my throat. He cleared his in response.

"Hi. I'm surprised...how are you?" He sounded decidedly older and more mature as he seemed to struggle with exactly what to say.

I took a deep breath and forced myself to smile away the rest of my jitters. Crunching from the gravel driveway as a car pulled into the lot did little to pull me out of my nervousness. "I'm really good. Listen, I'm sorry to call out of...the blue... but I have an entertainment contract I need help looking over. I'm not asking for your official representation or anything—"

"Is this for you?" His voice brightened, and for the flash of an instant, I pictured the twenty-year-old lacrosse star all the other girls at Princeton drooled over.

"Mm-hmm."

I took a few minutes to give Adrian the basics of the contract. Several times through the conversation I thought we should have just sent the paperwork to DROP's legal team. But, mixing Bo's non-profit funds with professional endeavors would undoubtedly cause a major problem for someone.

"So," I wrapped up, "if you're willing, I can email you the file as soon as we get off the phone. Make sure you bill me for however long it takes you."

I could hear the long exhale of Adrian's deep breath before he answered. "I'd be happy to do it, Ember. Congratulations on your marriage. Sorry that's a little late." He chuckled and I echoed.

I didn't ask him how he'd heard. Sometimes it's better to not know something.

"Yeah, well...life, huh?" I bit my lip and looked down. In that moment I wanted to race up to my room, wrap my arms around Bo's neck, and thank him for taking me back.

"Yeah." Adrian's voice went somewhere far enough away that I didn't want to go with him. I was glad the conversation was almost over.

"So," I started.

"Right," he interrupted. "Just send the contract over and I'll have it back to you by the morning. From what you said, it sounds pretty standard. A damn good deal, but uncomplicated. I've heard good things about the way Yardley Honeywell does business."

"You have?" My ears perked up

"She's no-nonsense and has a hell of an eye and ear for talent. Comes from money but doesn't leave her wallet open. From what I've seen from some of Pace's clients, she likes to develop long-term business relationships. Definitely not fly by night."

I grinned, as I always did at the mention of Pace. "I thought he was in real estate."

Adrian huffed. "He'll follow money wherever it'll take him. He's a hell of a lawyer, though. I'll give him that."

It seemed the Pace boys' rivalry wouldn't conclude anytime soon based on the half-praise, half-envious tone Adrian always seemed to carry when discussing his older brother.

"Anyway," Adrian continued, "you'll be in good hands with Grounded Sound. Do you have a manager?"

"Not yet, though we're working on it."

Beckett had approached me at the club the other night, before we'd met Yardley, about representing me if I ever chose to go to, or was offered, the next level. I told him I'd think about it, though I wasn't sure there was much to think about. Bo and I hadn't talked about it, but I knew he didn't care for Beckett. He seemed to tighten his jaw when Beckett smiled at me like someone who'd known me my whole life. Because he had.

Adrian's voice retained its professional cool. "Well, when you get settled back on the East coast, if you still need representation, I can make recommendations to you."

"Thanks, Adrian."

"No problem, Ember. It was good to hear from you." A smile seemed to finally pour over his words.

"You too, bye."

"Bye."

Grateful to be through with what turned out to be a not-so-awkward conversation, I made my way inside and back up to our room. As I approached the door, I heard two different male voices. One was Bo's, but the other definitely wasn't Regan's. If my stomach had a face, it would have grinned in that moment. A dry, sarcastic grin of someone settling in to be entertained by awkwardness.

I opened the door and my ears hadn't, in fact, deceived me. Beckett was standing, leaning against one of the posts of the bed, with his hands casually in his pockets. His freeform sandy brown waves looked significantly more carefree than I felt in that moment, given the look Bo shot me as I crossed the threshold.

"Ah, there she is!" Beckett flashed his best smile, one that accented the sun-kissed creases around his eyes. "I saw you on the phone outside when I pulled up, but it looked like a serious phone call, so I thought I'd come up and wait for you."

I pulled my lips into as big of a smile as they would allow, still unsure about the look on Bo's face. "I was just on the phone with the lawyer who agreed to look over our contract. I've got to email it to him. Give me just a sec."

I walked over to the desk and pulled out my laptop, feeling two sets of steely blue eyes on me. I quickly navigated to my mail and forwarded the contract to Adrian. Once it was sent, I closed the laptop again, and turned around slowly.

"So he'll look it over?" Bo asked, despite having been present for the last several minutes.

I nodded and walked to him, lifting up on my tiptoes and kissing his chin. As I suspected, the muscles were as tight as brick. "Yep. He said it sounded standard so it shouldn't take long."

"That was a pretty kickass contract," Beckett agreed. "I was just talking with Bo about the conversation you and I had the other night. About management."

Oh, for God's sake.

I looked up at Bo, who returned a somewhat accusing gaze. "I hadn't had a chance to bring it up yet," I said to Beckett. "The last couple of days were really crazy."

Beckett shrugged, his eyes looking far more amused than I would have liked, though that could have been my own guilty conscience. Even though I didn't think I had anything to feel guilty about. "It's all right. You've got someone looking over the initial contact. In theory you won't really need a manager, unless you want something more, or when the term of your current contract ends. You've got a year."

Bo put his arm around my shoulders as he spoke. "I think we'll probably get settled first, see how recording the album goes, and the tour...and all of that before we decide what to do next."

"Great," Beckett answered. "Well, I'll be heading back to New York in a few days, but I'll see you when you get to town, I'm sure."

"Of course," I agreed cheerfully, needing this exchange to be over.

Beckett extended his hand toward Bo, who shook it firmly. "It's great to meet you, man."

"You, too," Bo replied cordially.

It was often my only tell that Bo was feeling uncomfortable. When he slipped into Mr. Fortune 500 mode. His poker face was fierce...and frustrating.

Beckett turned to me and pulled me into a warm, sunblock-scented hug. "I can't wait to see you tear up those charts, Em. This is amazing."

"Thanks," I whispered, feeling guilty for wanting a childhood friend to leave as quickly as possible. "We'll see you in New York."

Once Beckett left and I shut and locked the door, I turned to find Bo leaning against the same bedpost Beckett had claimed minutes earlier.

"Sorry for not telling you about that talk I had with Beckett the other night," I started. "There were just a lot of *ifs* in that conversation. I hadn't seen him in years, and it really wasn't something I was bothering to consider." Once I studied Bo's face, irritation began to brew. "But, I gotta say, I don't really like the way you're looking at me."

"I don't like the way *he* looks at you." Bo shrugged as if that was the only answer.

"I can't do anything about how people look at me, Bo. You, of all people, should know that we can't do anything about how people *look* at us." My nostrils flared to accommodate my angry breath.

He scoffed. "What's that supposed to mean?"

"Um...everything." I looked around, a self-protective grin forming on my lips. "For the last year and a half, I've heard girls screaming your name, and watched them fawn all over you anytime they got close enough."

"Yeah, but I don't know them."

"So?" I shrieked, sounding more like a teenager than a levelheaded human being.

Bo growled and ran his hand over his face. "Gah! Okay, you know that little freak-out you had the other night in bed?"

"Hardly a *little* freak-out," I mused. "But, yeah."

He walked toward me and put his hands on my shoulders. "I'm having one now. For every groupie trying to get my number, there will be a hot industry exec waiting in the wings to woo you away from me."

I meant to say something profound and romantic and helpful. Instead, I burst into incredible laughter.

"What?" He exclaimed before throwing his head back in an equally loud laugh.

"Jesus," I tried to slow my breath enough to speak, but the laughter kept coming. "We're a goddamn mess and we've had a record contract for less than twenty-four hours!"

Bo squeezed me against his chest as his breathing finally regulated. "You're right. Sorry for being an ass. I love you." He kissed me on the forehead. "Fuck, let's get some sleep so we can finish out this tour and plan our move back east, okay?"

I bit my lip, looking up at his newly scruffy jawline. "I agree. I'm exhausted. Shave your face in the morning, though. Some of those little girly girls might like it, but it makes you look like you're trying too hard. A face like yours ought to be seen."

With a wink and a kiss, everything was on stable ground once more.

CHAPTER *Seven*

Goodbyes never end

Bo

"I CAN'T BELIEVE THAT went by so fast." Georgia looked at Ember and me, and shoved her hands in her pockets as she stood next to Regan in the middle of the airport. "How did that last month disappear?"

Our summer tour with The Six was over, and it was time to honor our new contracts. Ember and I packed up our beachside bungalow, shipped our belongings to my—our—house in Concord, New Hampshire, and were now saying goodbye to our closest friends on the West Coast.

"I know. It was too fast." Ember's voice was quiet, but strong.

While I knew she was sad about saying goodbye to Regan and Georgia, we had a shared excitement about our new adventure that made this goodbye a little easier.

While the girls talked about the last few weeks together, and organizing when they'd see each other again, I nodded to Regan. "When do you start recording?"

A million-dollar smile cropped up on his face. I knew the answer, but seeing him so happy made me happy, too.

"Tomorrow. Remember the lead singer from Sunset Mission? They played after us at the vineyard?" I nodded and he continued. "Apparently they were only together for that weekend, and Yardley was able to snag him. She signed a guitar player who just graduated from college, too."

His excitement was palpable and I couldn't help but smile. "That's awesome, man. Are you guys going straight bluegrass?"

He shrugged. "It's hard to care, really. I'll play anything as long as it means I get to play."

The thing about Regan was, he meant it. Whether he was asked to play nursery rhymes for the rest of his life, or rock music, he really *would* be happy as long as he was playing. A true servant to art.

After a few minutes, I nudged Ember, letting her know we had to navigate through security and get to our gate. Our flight was scheduled to have us in Boston by early afternoon, and we had to haul it to Concord.

Ember and Georgia hugged. It was a sight that choked me up a bit, given where the two had started in their friendship.

I looked at Regan, took a deep breath, and said, "Good luck, man. Keep in touch and we'll see you soon, okay?"

He nodded and we hugged. Not an awkward side man-hug. The real deal. He was the only person left alive who had loved Rae as much as I did. Saying goodbye to him felt like I was leaving a piece of her in California.

"Get out of the way," Ember snapped playfully. "It's my turn."

She hip-checked me out of the way, and while she was smiling, I knew the quiver in her chin would melt into tears as soon as Regan's arms were around her. I was right. Ember's shoulders shook as she buried her face in the shirt of her best guy-friend.

Georgia walked around the pair and shouldered up next to me. Well, her shoulder to my torso since she was almost a foot shorter than me.

"Would you look at those two?" She rolled her eyes and then nudged my side. "Thanks for everything."

"Me?" I questioned.

She nodded. "Star quarterback, cheerleader, band geek? It's like The Breakfast Club with you guys, and I'm glad I get to be a part of it. I'll miss you. Even if I will have to find a new diet routine since I won't be participating in the barf-fest that is Bo and Ember for a while."

I laughed and wrapped my arm around her shoulders. "No one has ever made me laugh like you do, G. That's for sure. I won't tell Ember you called her a cheerleader, though. She'd kill us both."

"Oh...right," Georgia snickered. "Ainsley."

Ember and I finished our goodbyes with our friends, and two hours later we were taxiing toward the runway, ready for our flight home.

Home.

That had been a flexible term over the last year and a half, but I really felt like going back to Concord was going home.

"What are you thinking about?" Ember asked as the plane hurtled down the runway and began to lift off.

I hesitated, not sure if Ember would share the same sentiments about home as I did.

"What is it?" she asked again, tilting her head in concern.

Tears stung my eyes as I realized both the relief and the fear I felt about the next stage in our journey together.

"You're my home, okay? No matter what the next couple of years bring, it's you. It's me. It's us. You're my home, Ember." I lifted my arm as she nuzzled her way into my chest.

She kissed my jaw and rested her head on my shoulder. "You're mine, too, Bo. I think you always have been. Even before...us."

§

Once the plane had landed, we got our rental car and started the drive to Concord.

"It feels a little weird, doesn't it?" Ember asked as she looked out the window. "Being back here and knowing it'll be for more than just a few days? I mean, we'll have to be in New York for a while, but...what?" Ember looked at me as I bit my lip, trying to stop myself from smiling.

"Nothing."

"You're a horrible liar, so you might as well tell me what has you looking like a cat with a canary in its mouth."

"We're not going to New York."

Ember scrunched her eyebrows. "I beg your fucking pardon? Did something happen with our contract I'm not aware of?"

I chuckled. "Yes, but not in the way you think."

"Jesus, what now?"

I'd been holding this in for the last three weeks. Once we got the okay from Adrian that the contract was good as it stood, I went to Yardley with another proposition.

"Our contract is for just the two of us. There's no band. It's just us."

"Right..." her impatient tone made me grin.

"Grounded Sound's offices and studio might be in New York, but we don't *need* to be there all the time if we can secure approved studio time elsewhere."

Ember rolled her eyes. "Great, where will we—" she cut herself off as her eyes grew wide. "Your house?"

"Our house," I corrected.

"They went for that?" Ember's breathing was faster as she smiled.

I nodded. "Yardley will be out in a few days with some of her sound guys. She said if they like what they see in our studio, then we can do most of the recording there. She's smart. She said it bodes better for our sound if we're happy, and I told her we'd be much happier in our home than splitting our time between there and New York."

"How often will we have to go to New York?"

"Yardley and I discussed recording the entire album at our house, and then going to New York for a week or two during pre-production to iron things out."

Ember let out a massive exhale. "I can't *fucking* believe it!"

"I know, I know. I know it's not the same as staying in California, but you know the pressure has been on at DROP lately, and it will be a huge relief to the board to have me nix my *at large* status."

While DROP's community center had been open for almost two years, I had been absent for most of it. There were trusted and excellent members of the team that handled day-to-day operations, but I missed being a part of it. I'd been turning

BO *&Ember* 105

over ideas for the community center, and wanted to get them off and running.

Ember nodded. "Have you told David yet?"

"Not yet. I wanted to run it by you first. I know that I didn't talk to you about it earlier, but I didn't want to get my own hopes up in case it wouldn't work out. I've gotta be honest, Ember. I've loved the last year and a half traveling around the West coast, but if we're going to go on a national tour next summer, I want to get grounded, you know? Us. Get our home established and have something tangible."

Ember sniffed and reached her hand across the car, grabbing my leg. "You know how much that means to me, too, Bo. The time we spent with my parents was great—don't get me wrong. It was literally just like my middle school life was. Sure, as an adult I had a little more perspective, but I still crave a home base. I know we'll always have that with each other, but I'm excited to have that in Concord."

"Are you?"

Ember and I had been flying uncharacteristically by the seat of our pants for a year and a half. While she'd had all of her things shipped to my house before we made our initial move to San Diego, we never officially discussed making my home *our* home. That's how I referred to it, but I didn't want her to feel pressured.

"What do you mean?" Ember's tone dropped and sounded softly defensive and insecure.

"We've never really...talked about if we'd live in my house together."

"Why wouldn't we? It's your house. It's where you grew up. It's the perfect family home. A family needs to live there. Even if it's just us right now, we're family, right?" Ember choked up at the end of her sentence.

I smiled. "What is it?"

Ember forced a chuckle. "It's nothing."

She pointed out the window as we reached the gate of *our* home. I'd been on autopilot for most of the drive, and was taken by surprise that we'd made it there seemingly so quickly.

I put the car in park and put my hand on the door, ready to get out and punch in the code. Ember stopped me.

"Let me see if I've still got it." She jumped out of the car and jogged to the gate, carefully punching in four numbers. She froze in place for a moment before the gate slowly swung open and then put her hands up in victory.

"Well done," I teased as she got back in the car.

Knowing that this was going to be our official *home* now, save for when we went on tour, I had a mix of feelings pulling down the long driveway. Thankfully, I felt the peace that always filled me when the house came into view. Despite all of the heartache that I'd suffered over the last several years, this home always swaddled me. Memories of laughter and love carved into its walls, the house my parents' love built would soon see a rebirth as Ember and I forged our lives here.

Still, there was some stomach-dropping nervousness. There *had* been so much hurt suffered here. I remembered the hollowness that awaited Rae and me when we returned here after our parents' funeral. It was like walking into a strange house, the way all the life had been sucked away like a vacuum. Rae and I had spent a couple of years repairing the emotional structure of the house and once again, three years ago, the house felt like a home.

My first thought about the house when Rae died had been to burn the place to the ground. I'd thought there was no humanly way I could face walking into that house completely alone.

I put the car into park, pulling myself out of the grey memories. Looking to my right, I smiled at the woman who held me in every sense of the word when I took those first steps into the house after Rae died. Even though Ember and I weren't together then, the warmth that filled me as she crossed the threshold on the worst day of my life gave me the sense that I'd never be alone again. That's all I'd been able to hold onto in those months Ember and I didn't speak. I didn't know how, or when, but I carried the comfort that it would be okay.

"You okay?" Ember asked, almost whispering.

I was.

My eyes drifted to the house, and back to her. "I don't think I've ever been happier than I am at this exact moment."

Her barely-tanned cheeks reddened as she leaned across the car. Her lips connected softly with mine, and we shared a long exhale inside of our kiss.

"I love you, Bo. Let's go home."

We stepped out of the car and were greeted by the sweet comfort of Northern New England air. The mid-fall afternoon in New Hampshire blew any day in San Diego out of the water. Of course, that was easy to say when I was standing on lush green grass, surrounded by the fiery oranges and blinding yellows of the leaves above and around us as the trees displayed their most prized artwork.

Ember walked to my side of the car. A warm breeze with the epilogue of summer and prologue of winter wound its way through her hair, throwing her Autumn-hued hair across her face.

"Our things arrived, right?" she asked as her eyes scanned the property with contented familiarity.

I nodded, pulling her close to me. "I asked David to put them in the garage."

We didn't have much that we went to California with, but what we did have aside from our instruments was warm-weather clothes. I chuckled as I felt goosebumps take over Ember's shoulders. It was sixty degrees, which would have felt like a miracle two years ago.

"We need to get our cold weather blood back," I joked.

"I know we've been back here since we moved, but how are you feeling to be *back* here?" Ember kissed my shoulder and wrapped her arms around her body.

I smiled at her vocalization of my thought process only minutes before.

"I'm back here with you, so that means things have gone well since the last time I lived here full time, I'd say." I kissed the top of her head, leaving my lips there for a moment to take in the always fresh scent of her hair.

"Let's go in." Ember tugged my hand and walked toward the stairs.

Once we were on the porch, I stopped her hand as it reached for the doorknob.

"What?" she questioned, pulling her hand back.

I smiled, letting my eyes float from her gorgeous legs up to her eyes. "I never carried you over the threshold."

She rolled her eyes, but smiled all the way to her core. "We have been rather busy, haven't we?"

I pulled her to me, kissing her softly. "I suppose. Getting married in the woods and being on tour for the last year hasn't left much room for tradition."

Ember's face turned serious as her eyebrows angled inward. She forced a smile and looked at me in earnest. "Carry me into our house."

"As you wish, love." I lifted her, reveling in the airy laughter that came from her throat.

Having Ember to hold onto as we entered the home turned out to serve the dual purpose of tradition and transition. A swift wave of anxiety washed over me, but was gone before I had a chance to think about it.

There was a part of me that would always be seventeen in this house. The part that wanted to crash through the front door, drop my football gear at the bottom of the stairs—which Rae always complained about because it smelled— and wander to the kitchen to rifle through the fridge while my parents made dinner. They always cooked together.

While the seventeen-year-old me would feel that longing for as long as I lived, the me that fought to stay present would thank God every single day that this beautiful woman in my arms agreed to forge a new life with me here.

"I love you," Ember whispered, her lips grazing my ear as she spoke.

"I love you." I set her down, holding onto her hips for a moment as I took a deep breath. "Come upstairs. I have a surprise for you."

Ember pressed her tongue against the inside of her cheek, the way she always did when she felt caught off guard.

"You know," she sighed. "I'd ask how you had time to create a surprise for me, since we've been together nearly every second of the last year and a half, but...this is you. I've got to learn to accept that you're a magician of swoon."

I let out a loud laugh that started cracking the remnants of sorrow in the walls of the house. "Magician of *what?*"

"Swoon." She nodded once. "Don't tell me you've never heard the word. You *are* swoon. It's ridiculous. And, I love it."

She took off ahead of me, racing to the top of the stairs. Sometimes I let her get ahead of me so I could watch. I'm merely an animal, after all.

I caught up to her and grasped her hand, leading her down the long hallway, lit only by the light coming from the widow's watch at the top of the spiral staircase behind us. My heart stayed in my throat as we approached the door at the end of the hallway, bypassing my childhood bedroom, and Rae's. My parents' old room. I'd practiced saying *old* for several months, given they hadn't spent a night there in over five years. Neither had anyone else. That was about to change.

I put my hand on the doorknob and watched Ember stare straight-faced. There was no signal of expectation in her eyes, and I could tell by the way she bit the inside of her cheek that she was fighting some nerves.

Without a word, I took a deep breath and opened the door, letting Ember step in first.

She gasped, and then tried to hide it by clearing her throat. I stood behind her, watching her take in the room.

"Bo," she whispered. "What did you...when did you?" She brought her hand to her mouth and took a deep breath.

I positioned myself next to her and wrapped my arm around her shoulders. "I've been planning this for a few months, and had David send me pictures when it was completed last week."

For the past six months, I'd worked with an old high school friend, who was in interior design, to transform my parents' old bedroom into something new. Something beautiful. The room was rearranged to allow the bed to face the windows, which were on the East side of the room. Being able to watch the sunrise while I held her was one of my favorite things to do, and I wanted to be able to do it every day.

I purchased a new bed, a large white four-poster affair with rails connecting the tops of the posts. Sheer cream-colored curtains were bunched on each of the corners, and could be pulled around us as we slept. The walls were covered with distressed white wood planks, which looked nearly identical to Ember's old bedroom in Barnstable. When we'd first met, she talked about the serenity that room gave her, and I wanted to bring a piece of that with us.

Ember walked gracefully to the bed, allowing her fingertips to skim the curtains before trailing the length of the white comforter. She tilted her head as she seemed to study the tiny pale yellow flowers printed on the blanket.

A bright smile filled her face as she turned toward me. "*You* did this?"

I nodded. "For us."

Ember paced over to the dresser I'd had painted a soft sage color, with lavender drawers. "These colors...this style..."

I chuckled to myself. "I've heard you use the term *shabby chic* a lot. I went on that pin-up website you're always on—"

"Pinterest," she mused.

"Whatever. I went on that site, sent lots of pictures to my interior design friend, and...here we are."

Ember walked back over to the bed and crawled onto it, sitting on her knees. "What interior design friend?"

"Tyler. We graduated together."

Ember's eyes lifted to the ceiling as she seemed to be processing something. "You don't mean Tyler M., do you?"

As her eyes widened, so did mine. "Yes...why? How do you know him?"

"How do I know him?" Ember shrieked as she jumped up and down on her knees. "He helped restore like eight historical houses on Nantucket and Martha's Vineyard a couple of years ago. He's a *freaking* genius! He's the *reason* I fell in love with shabby chic! No wonder this room is so spot on!"

I laughed as Ember's excitement filled the room. "I'll tell him you approve."

She stopped suddenly, looking deadly serious. "No, you won't. I will. You're introducing him to me."

I sat next to her on the bed, facing her. "Well, with any luck, you'll be able to see a lot of him. I know I did this room without you, but I told him I'd talk to you about doing the rest of the house."

"Really?"

"You look concerned."

Her eyes scanned the room. "No...I mean...yes. Wait. Breathe. I think it'd be great, but I want to make sure that you really want to do this. I know this room must have felt like a huge step for you."

I placed my hand on her knee. "This house and this property hold lots of memories for me, Ember. But I also want to make new ones. I want this house to be *us* and our family. I'll always have the memories. They won't go away if we take down that awful wallpaper in the dining room."

A comically low growl came from her throat. "Thank *God* you said that. Truly. It's hideous. It's like everything that was wrong with the eighties, and wallpaper, threw up in that room!"

We lay back on the bed next to each other, staring up at the sheer canopy as we laughed.

"So," Ember sighed, "recording an album and renovating the house? We really can't do anything half-assed, can we?"

"Nah," I reached down and grabbed her hand, bringing it to my lips, "what fun would that be?"

CHAPTER *Eight*

Peeling back the layers

Ember

Y ARDLEY AND BO were able to iron out the changes to the contract that allowed for us to record the album in our home. We would only have to travel to New York once the tracks were complete and ready for production.

Bo and I had spent our first two weeks in New Hampshire unpacking, organizing, and packing up other things. Tyler was scheduled to do a quick walk-through with us in the morning to go over all of the decor concepts before we started officially recording in the afternoon.

We wanted to see how evening recording sessions would work, because it would give us an opportunity to work with DROP during the day, when needed. Grounded Sound was going to send out an audio engineer to run the control room while Bo and I were in the studio. We'd been able to do it ourselves, just kind of playing around, but for a professional album we would need…well…professionals.

Bo had left the house early for a DROP creative meeting, and promised he'd be back in time to record. We'd be recording four days a week, with three days off. This worked best for our vocal cords, and scheduling with Grounded Sound engineers. It wouldn't take long to complete the album, even with that slightly relaxed schedule. We'd already knocked off a few songs while still in California.

A light, but rapid knock on the front door pulled me out of my gaze from the kitchen window. We'd leave the kitchen untouched. Bo and Rae renovated it shortly after their parents' death, and it still looked brand new. It was the most updated thing in the house, besides the master bedroom.

Opening the door, I was greeted by a tall and slender man with short brown hair. He wore grey suit pants and a snug grey button-down vest to match, with a white collared shirt underneath it. And, a tie. He was sharp looking, and it was *definitely* Tyler.

"Ember?" He smiled an almost offensively white smile. He had dimples in *both* cheeks and his eyes sparkled like he was perpetually twelve years old.

"Tyler." I nodded, and flashed my hours-long practiced professional smile. "Come in."

Tyler was everything I thought he'd be. I'd seen pictures of him in magazines, and his manicured presence before me looked nearly identical.

"Should I call you Mrs. Cavanaugh?" He arched his eyebrow and a playful twinkle sparkled in his eyes.

I shook my head. "Only if you want me to call you Mr. M."

"Fuck that," he groaned.

In an out of character move for how I normally interact with strangers, I threw my arms around his neck. He didn't hesitate in squeezing me back.

"It's so great to meet you. I had no idea Bo was friends with you, though we never really sat around discussing interior design."

"Look around you," he said as he pulled away. "It's clear he's never discussed it with anyone."

I laughed, pointing to the dining room. "What the hell is on those walls?"

He shrugged. "Misery. That's all I've got."

"Well, should I show you around?"

Tyler set his bag on the chair in the entryway, pulling a professional-looking camera out. "Let's go. I'll take pictures to see where we are, and then in a few days I'll be able to email you some ideas. I put the pictures on my computer and generate ideas."

"Do you have that cool program that allows you to virtually move walls and stuff?" I led Tyler into the dining room.

"Watch HGTV much?" he teased.

"Do you have a problem with them?" I asked, standing out of the way as he took pictures of the dining room from several angles.

He shrugged. "It lacks inspiration most of the time. It's watered down."

"You better be grateful that I watch it. That's how I found out about you."

Tyler grinned from behind his camera. "Point taken. I like you. So," he stood from his crouched position and ran his hands along the wall, "aside from the wallpaper, what else did you see happening in here?"

For a few minutes, Tyler and I discussed the dining room. It felt awkward discussing changes to the house without Bo present, but he insisted he fully trusted Tyler and me. Tyler agreed with me that nothing needed to be done in the kitchen, save for a few color changes on the walls to brighten it up even more. After we worked our way through the living room and office, I led him upstairs.

"How long have you and Bo been friends?"

Tyler took a deep breath. "Since seventh or eighth grade, I guess? We got a lot closer sophomore year in high school." He looked down, furrowing his brow.

"What happened your sophomore year?" I didn't know a whole lot about Bo's high school years.

When we reached the top of the stairs, Tyler leaned against the post. "We made the varsity football team."

My eyes widened, as it seemed Tyler suspected they would. I didn't want him to know what I was thinking.

"Exactly." He seemed to read my mind. "We made the team, and a month later I came out of the closet. In retrospect, that was poorly timed. Seemed there were a band of assholes coming out of their douchebag closets at the same time."

"Wow," I exhaled, "what happened?"

Tyler swallowed hard, his brown eyes drifting somewhere far away. "Bo fought for me. A lot. Actual fights. He spent as much time in the principal's office for his fists as he spent in class."

"Are you serious?"

He nodded, and continued casually as if he'd told me this story before, despite the fact we'd just met. "One time in the locker room some guys had me backed against the lockers. It wasn't that I couldn't defend myself. I could have kicked their asses in a second. I just didn't want to get in the habit of defending myself that way." He paused, taking a cleansing breath. "In truth, I had no idea what the *fuck* I was thinking coming out on a football team in a small town. Anyway, Bo came in and lost his shit. The reputation of his temper had preceded him, given a fight with other teammates earlier in the week. The guys backed off before Bo had a chance to raise his fist. He quit the team that day."

I swallowed back some tears as I thought of a young Bo defending his friend. "But I've seen pictures of him from senior year homecoming."

"Turns out when the town's golden boy walks away from his birthright, that gets more attention than a gay kid getting beat up." Tyler's venom was clearly directed to every person who hadn't stood up for him. "I told him not to do it. Not to walk away. But, he refused. He said I was more important as a person than some letters sewn onto a shitty jacket."

I chuckled as a tear rolled down my face.

"Anyway," he continued, "the team held an emergency meeting without me or Bo. I don't know what was said, but we were both asked back and neither of us had a problem from that day forward."

I sniffed and wiped the tears off my cheeks. "Did you stay on the team?"

Tyler pushed his back off the post and smiled, wiping a tear off my chin. "Hell yeah! I was fucking amazing and I loved the sport. Plus, I wasn't going to give those blockheads the satisfaction of seeing me walk away. It wasn't all of them, but it was enough."

"And you didn't have any more problems with them?"

"Nope." Tyler shrugged and walked toward the first door on the right. "Ready for more design talk? What's in here?"

I nodded. "Rae's bedroom." I couldn't stop the inappropriate chuckle that came from my throat.

The room was void of all of Rae's *things*, but her presence was still very much in the walls and every nook and cranny. A single, unmade bed and an empty bookshelf were all that inhabited the room now, and I don't think any of us knew how long it was supposed to stay that way.

Thankfully, Tyler appreciated dark humor. "Wow, we can really show each other a good time, huh?"

We pressed on, taking an hour to go through the bedrooms. Once we finished the visual tour of the house, Tyler had to go. He promised he'd send an email in the next few days incorporating what we'd discussed, and then we could plan a time to pick colors, fabrics, hardware, etc. I closed the door in a haze, checking the clock and seeing I had two hours before Bo would be home and Grounded Sound would be at our door.

I wandered to our bedroom and curled up in our bed, my mind continuously going back to a vision of a rage-filled high school Bo. He'd always had a big heart for people, and it didn't surprise me in the least that he'd stand up for a friend the way he did for Tyler. But, it was the savage passion behind his cobalt eyes that connected the dots for me.

There was a dark storm brewing in Bo's soul that he never let see the light of day. The thing about storms is, they rarely go quietly into the good night.

$$\S$$

"Honey, I'm home!" Bo hollered from the entryway in his best sitcom voice.

"Go back to the nineteen fifties!" I shouted back from the kitchen. An ironic place for me to have been standing at that moment, I realized.

Bo sauntered into the sunlit room, setting his bag on the table as he loosened his tie. He'd left while I was in the shower this morning, so I missed that he'd put on my favorite tie of his. Blue—the shocking color of his eyes—with the tiniest yellow pinstripes running diagonally across the silk.

"Look at you." I grinned as I turned from my project on the counter and leaned back. "I get the sexy businessman *and* the sexy rock star? Yes, please."

A low, playful noise started in his chest and vibrated his lips as they pressed into mine.

Breathless, I batted my eyelashes. "How was your day, dear?"

Bo walked to the fridge and pulled out a pitcher of water, pouring a glass as he spoke with his back to me. "It was good. Everyone seems excited to have me back around more. David's done a fabulous job at the helm while I've been gone, but it does something different for morale when we can all work together."

"That's great." I turned back to the counter.

"Whatchya making?" he asked, bumping his hip into mine.

"All kinds of gross hippie stuff," I joked.

Bo laughed. "Seriously I've never eaten better in my life than I have over the last two years."

"Well, I figured we should go down to the studio well fed so we don't get all hangry at each other."

Bo and I both had the misfortune of a crap attitude when we were hungry. He'd blurted out *hangry* one day and I nearly died laughing. He'd said it was a real term and I should read a self-help book once in a while. I flipped him off and we went out to lunch.

"We've still got an hour before Grounded Sound will be here, right?"

"Mm-hmm." I finished slicing the fruit and cheese and set it next to seaweed crackers. "Why?"

He finished the last of his water and put his glass in the sink. "Put the knife down and come with me."

I laughed. "Did you really *have* to say 'put the knife down'?"

"I'd rather not have knives in the bedroom." Bo stuck his tongue out and grabbed my hand, leading me through the dining room and up the stairs.

"You're on a mission." I tightened my hand in his.

"I've wanted my hands on your skin all day." He certainly hadn't left his boardroom attitude at the office. He was still in charge as he led me down the hallway, and that's the way I liked it.

Bo opened the door to our bedroom and his eyes immediately went to the white lights I'd strung around the top of the canopy over our bed.

"You like?" I spun in a circle, holding out my arms.

"I admit," he started, trying to sound serious, "it's hard for me to pay attention to anything other than you when I'm in here. But, these are a nice touch."

The first time we'd made love in our new room, it was weird for both of us. I can only say with certainty that it was weird for me, but Bo seemed hesitant as well. We didn't discuss it, because sometimes you don't need to discuss every detail, but things had slowly improved over the past two weeks.

Now, there was no hesitation as I backed up toward the bed, and Bo followed, shrugging out of his grey suit coat and tossing it on the trunk by the foot of the bed. He pulled his tie over his head. When he threw it in the direction of his coat, I caught it mid-air.

"We'll keep this." My cheeks were on fire at my suggestion.

Bo's eyebrows shot up. "For...what?"

With my voice having ducked for cover, I whispered, "I'm sure we'll think of something."

"Oh," he crooned, unbuttoning his shirt as I unbuttoned mine. "So I get the sexy dominatrix *and* the sexy rock star? Yes please." He repeated my teasing from downstairs, only he was far from teasing.

My fight or flight response clicked on, igniting a rush of adrenaline that sent me up onto the bed, grabbing the waistband of his pants as he followed.

I licked my lips before speaking against his earlobe. "I like it when you say 'please'."

§

"Jesus," Bo panted as he pulled me against his sweat-soaked chest.

I looked up at him and shrugged with a sly grin. "I missed you today."

He laughed a loud hard laugh that told me everything else was far away in his mind. The kind where his jaw was loose and his shoulders shook freely.

"Crap." Bo sat up quickly, resting against the headboard. "I totally forgot Tyler was supposed to come over today. Did he?"

My stomach sank at the mention of his name. I nodded as I sat up.

"Sorry I couldn't be here to introduce you two. Are you okay? Did it not go okay, or something?" Bo leaned back, studying my face.

I smiled. "Oh, God no. He's a goddamn dream! We had a blast talking plans."

"So why that look on your face?"

I shook my head. "It's nothing."

If there was one thing I wanted to avoid, it was bringing up heavy subjects after sex. We ended up in those conversations so often when we were naked between the sheets. Sometimes it was a little bit of emotional overload.

"Ember..."

I shimmied my lower body under the blankets, not wanting to be stark naked for this discussion. Bo followed my lead.

"We just got to talking, and I asked him how long you two had been friends..."

Bo looked thoroughly lost. "And?"

I sucked in as much air as I could while looking at my hands. If Bo hadn't told me this story, there must have been a reason for it.

Finally, I looked up. "He told me about high school. And the football team..."

In an instant the tension returned to Bo's beautiful jaw. His eyes darkened as he looked down at his own hands. I couldn't imagine what thoughts were scrolling through his mind. He was silent, so I spoke again.

"Why didn't you ever tell me about that...or about Tyler, for that matter? The only friend I've heard you mention is David's son."

Bo shook his head, not speaking.

"Bo. Bo, why didn't you—"

"Did he tell you the whole story?" he snapped without raising his voice.

I shrugged. "I...I guess I don't know since you hadn't told me *any* of it." I tried to keep my temper in check, since I didn't know what was fueling this change in demeanor.

Bo brought his hand to his mouth, closing his eyes as he took the same controlled breath he always took when he felt like he was losing emotional control. "It's nothing."

He got out of bed after using my earlier phrase seemingly against me. He strode nude into the bathroom and shut the door. I heard the shower turn on.

Arching my eyebrow to no one but my increasingly angry self, I slid out of bed and knocked on the door.

No answer.

"Bo?" I cleared my throat to make sure I wasn't speaking with an unkind tone.

The situation with Tyler clearly went much deeper than what Tyler had told me. That was concerning, given how emotionally gutted I was by the tale. I wanted to handle Bo with care, but I wasn't about to let him start shutting me out.

I knocked once more while entering, the warm steam and the scent of my eucalyptus oil filling my senses. "Bo?"

I pulled the shower curtain open a fraction, peering in. Bo stood facing the torrent of scorching water, his head pressed against the tiled wall beneath the showerhead. Water pelted his neck and shoulders before cascading down the rest of his body.

Slowly, I reached into the water and touched his shoulder. He didn't flinch. He only straightened and lifted his hand to meet mine, tugging slightly.

"Come on." He nodded his head to the side, asking me into the shower.

As I stepped in, I winced at the scalding heat. Bo must have seen the look because he quickly reached around me and turned the heat down.

"You okay?" I asked, my voice barely louder than the falling water.

He nodded. "I am. Sorry about that." He slid his hands down my sides, resting them on my hips as he pulled me into his body.

I wrapped my arms around his torso. His back was cool from being away from the water, but his chest was warm. As I rested my cheek against his collarbone, I resisted the primal urge I had to ask follow-up questions. We were done talking about Tyler and whatever the hell had happened. For the time being.

Once we were dressed and downstairs, we were able to quickly eat the food I'd prepared earlier before someone buzzed at the gate. The sound was slightly foreign.

"You closed the gate when you came home?" I questioned. We rarely had it shut during the day.

Bo grinned, eating the last of his seaweed cracker. I knew he didn't like them that much, but I appreciated the effort. "I didn't want to be disturbed this afternoon. I missed you, too."

He left the table and walked to the intercom.

I lived in a house with an intercom. And a gated driveway.

"Yes?" Bo spoke in his typical business-casual tone.

A loud voice crackled through the speaker. "Beckett with Grounded Sound."

With a crease between his eyebrows, Bo clicked the buttons to unlock the gate.

"Do you know anyone else named Beckett?" he asked.

"No. Do you?"

"I don't even want to know one Beckett," he grumbled.

I laughed. "Grow up."

"I'm serious." He walked behind me and pinched my butt as I cleared my plate.

A minute later there was a knock on the door. I followed Bo into the entryway and couldn't help but chuckle as he opened it and there, naturally, stood Beckett Roth.

"Hey guys." He always sounded like a pumped up surfer just off the waves.

"Beckett." Bo nodded and pulled the door open, stepping aside to let Beckett in. His eyes shot to me and I felt implored to ask the million-dollar question.

I gave Beckett a quick and friendly hug first. "What are you doing here?"

Beckett stuck his hands in his pockets and smiled broadly. "A week after you guys signed with Grounded Sound, I had an offer from Yardley at the New York office. So, I moved back there. She hired me as a sound engineer and last week asked me if I'd be interested in your album as my first project."

"Wow," I forced myself to sound cheerful and supportive, "congratulations! I'm surprised no one told us...including you."

I caught Bo's lightning-quick grin as I grilled Beckett.

"Well," Beckett answered nonchalantly, "I wanted it to be a surprise." He stood up straight and smiled comically large. "Surprised?"

CHAPTER *Nine*

We were just kids

Bo

SURPRISE, INDEED.

Beckett didn't want to surprise Ember; he wanted to make sure he secured his first job, and he knew that would be risky had I known he was assigned to the project ahead of time.

For the first two days of recording with Beckett, we worked through a lot of sound checks and some of our ready-made songs—ones that Ember and I had sung a million times and wouldn't need a lot of work. It didn't take Beckett long to get used to the control room, which made very good use of our time.

Ember and I didn't have a *discussion* about Beckett, because Beckett wasn't the issue. It was me and my archaic jealousy. I'd told Ember weeks before that I was over any unjust animosity I'd had toward Beckett. That was, in part, because I hadn't seen him in several weeks. Out of sight and out of mind.

I hated that he knew things about her that I never would. I couldn't tell Ember that, either, because then she'd push me on my *deal* with Tyler, as she called it. Since I didn't want to go there, Beckett was off the table.

Beckett clicked on the mic in the control room. "Ready, guys? Take 'Lovin' Me Down' from the chorus. Ember, when you're singing the high notes, don't pull back on the guitar. Match your intensity there, k?"

Ember nodded. "Will do."

Out of the corner of my eye, I caught her flex her hands twice. Even though we'd spent the last year and a half playing all over the West coast, two things were different now. First, Ember was playing a lot more guitar than she had with The Six. Second, we hadn't played much in the past few weeks since the move back home. Her fingertips were raw from three days of nearly nonstop playing as she worked to get her calluses back.

"Ready?" I asked her, avoiding discussion about her certainly burning skin. It would just make the pain worse if I brought her attention to it.

"Yep. One, two, one, two, three, four..."

Ember and I began humming the intro to the chorus. "Lovin' Me Down" was a song we'd worked on over the last six months. It was one of the few we'd written without Regan's vocal or instrumental part, so it didn't require any reworking for recording.

Ember rocked her shoulders and half her mouth curled into a sexy grin as she leaned toward the mic.

I was high, oh so high. The tears brought me to the edge.

But you're lovin' me down, baby, lovin' me down

Off that dark, dark ledge...

It's no surprise that we wrote this song together to try to make some musical sense out of a rocky time in our relationship. We'd split up, made mistakes with other people, Rae died...it wasn't great. The one thing that did get us through all of it was our deeply rooted and intense love for each other.

It was that love that allowed me to ask her to leave after Rae's funeral, that love that let her, even though it hurt. It was the love that gave us time to heal while we were apart. And, that love that brought us back together and made us stronger every day.

Mmm, girl, I begged you to go, I begged you to stay...

When I entered the song, I found myself lost in our relationship. The early ups and downs and the smooth sailing ever since. I was one lucky bastard, and I intended on spending the rest of my life paying that luck forward to Ember. She deserved the best of me every single day.

The song ended, and Ember winked at me from behind her mic. The sight of her with headphones on, holding her guitar, filled me with peace and joy.

Before I could say anything, Beckett infiltrated our private moment. I realize we were in a studio recording our album, but the intimacy between Ember and me was always intensified when we were in the studio.

"Excellent, guys, really. You're making my job far too easy." Beckett clicked off the microphone, removed his headphones, and made his way into the studio.

I reached for Ember's hand, but she whipped around as Beckett opened the door.

"Really, Beck? You're not just saying that?" She lifted the strap of her guitar over her head and set it against its stand.

"November, I don't get paid to *just say* things. Trust me. Just saying anything other than the truth would get me fired. That was fantastic. You guys are way ahead of schedule. I wouldn't be surprised if the label began pushing for a small spring tour, rather than waiting until summer."

That got my attention. "Are you serious?"

Beckett seemed a lot less annoying when he was discussing the advancement of our music career.

He nodded and shoved his hands in his pockets. It's like he could never have a conversation with his hands anywhere else. "Oh, hell yeah. In fact, when Yardley comes up tomorrow, she's going to talk to you guys about plans for the Grounded Sound website. You've seen it, right?"

I nodded quickly, encouraging him to get on with it. Ember watched our interaction with a bit of tension on her face. I hadn't given her reason to think I'd be anything but a pain in the ass about Beckett. That was about to change.

"Well," he continued, "demand for you two has been crazy. Ever since the vineyard show."

"Right," I agreed. "The traffic on The Six's website went crazy the night after we performed."

"Yardley's web design team has your page ready to launch. She wants to check a few details with you, but even the second they announced they'd signed you, *their* traffic has increased almost threefold." Beckett eyed Ember with a proud peacock grin.

Ember stood and stretched. The bottom hem of the long sleeved brown shirt she was wearing rode up, exposing a few inches of skin on her stomach. Beckett's eyes stayed on hers, which made me hate him a little less.

"How the hell have I missed this explosion in popularity?" Ember said, somewhat sarcastically, as she rolled her neck back and forth. Every movement of hers seemed uncomfortably sexy in the presence of other men. I knew that was all in my head, but I didn't want them eyeing her the way I did.

That was the blessing and curse of marrying the most gorgeous woman in the universe, I guess.

Beckett sat on a nearby stool, arching a mischievous eyebrow. "Because you've been up here playing house."

"Shit," Ember sighed, "isn't that bad? Shouldn't we be out, like, connecting?"

"No. It's fucking brilliant." Beckett leaned forward, taking his hands from his pockets and leaning forward to rest his elbows on his knees. "The counterculture lovers signed to a big record label, living all Salinger-like in New Hampshire while recording their debut album in their love nest? Do you not see the romance of it all?

Ember hung her head, shaking it back and forth. "You've got to be kidding me."

"Nope," Beckett asserted. "Brill-i-ant."

"We're not really even the counterculture ones." While Ember had surrendered a bit more to her upbringing over the last year, it was still a hard pill to swallow at times.

Beckett snapped his fingers and pointed an inch from Ember's nose. "Don't. Don't even say that. Ever. Your music, your look, your *name*...it's counterculture. It's going to sell. Big. Look at the Top 40 artists this week. Christ, look at the top *ten*. You'll see it dominated with real singers who can actually play an instrument. Auto-tune is as foreign to them as genetically modified chicken. These are your people. *You* are *their* people."

Jesus. Beckett knew his shit.

Ember turned to get my opinion. "Are you hearing this?"

I grinned. "Quick, let's go upstairs and compost something."

Beckett laughed, but spoke seriously. "That's the right idea."

"I don't want to be dishonest..." Ember wrung her hands, looking at me pleadingly.

"Babe," I stood and walked over to her, "it's not dishonest. We had fruit and seaweed for lunch. You grew up on a commune and went to an Ivy League school as an act of rebellion. It's a gorgeous story how you emotionally reconciled with your parents and fell in love again with the lifestyle you've always known."

Ember twitched her lips and arched her eyebrow suspiciously. "How do we explain you, then?"

I shrugged impishly. "Plot twist?"

As Beckett chuckled, a familiar voice trailed down the stairs and into the studio.

"What? The broody millionaire jock-turned-philanthropist? Ah the possibilities of how to *explain* him." By the end of his sentence, Tyler was smirking in the studio doorway.

"Oh, who the fuck asked you?" I teased.

Ember's face lit up. "Hey, you! I was wondering when I'd hear from you again. I thought you were blowing me off. Oh. Tyler, this is our sound engineer, Beckett. Beckett, this is Tyler."

Beckett turned his back to me to shake Tyler's hand. After the introductions, Beckett headed back to the control room to grab the files he needed. Tyler gave a minute nod in Beckett's direction, raising his eyebrows hopefully.

I shrugged, highlighting my ignorance about Beckett's sexual orientation. All I knew about his sex life was he'd slept with my wife when they were seventeen. Ember seemed to think Beckett had slept with Yardley, but I tried not to think about Beckett sleeping with *anyone*.

Tyler nodded approvingly, then turned his attention to Ember.

"I'd never blow you off. Not my style." He winked, causing me to roll my eyes, then continued. "Anyway, I figured since I hadn't actually *seen* Bo since you've been back, I'd bring some of my plans here and we could go over them together. I thought you were only recording in the evenings, though. Is this a bad time?"

Ember nodded to the control room. "We're actually done for the day. Beckett's got a conference call for work so he's heading back to his hotel. We've actually got friends coming up for dinner tonight, but I *need* you to meet Monica. She'll freak."

Honestly, I'd forgotten about our dinner plans. Time and space seemed to shift imperceptibly when I was in the studio.

We hadn't seen Josh and Monica since we'd been back, and I was really looking forward to seeing them.

Tyler looked slightly unsure as he addressed me. "Are you sure? I don't want to crash your plans."

I moved over to where he and Ember were standing and put my hand on his shoulder. "The more the merrier. What's the point of a house this size if we don't fill it with people from time to time?"

"Well then," he smiled, "let's go upstairs and I can show you what I've come up with."

"You guys go ahead," Ember said. "I'll be up in a sec. Just gotta talk to Beckett about something." She turned on her heels and bounded into the control room as Tyler and I left the studio and headed for the stairs.

Tyler and I sat at the corner of the dining room table, and he pulled out his laptop. "That's an insane studio you've got down there, Bo. Really impressive."

"Thanks. I had it built a couple of years ago. Three, I think? I can't remember anymore."

I used to reference time by things that happened before my parents died, and things after. Once Rae died and Ember and I got married, though, benchmarks got fuzzier and I no longer knew if I should anchor the hourglass in the tragedies or the happy moments. I knew my therapist would tell me it wasn't healthy to dwell on anything negative if I wanted to train my brain to focus on the positive, but that was textbook advice that didn't seem to translate into real life functioning for me. I hadn't connected with her since I'd moved back to Concord, though I realized I should schedule an appointment soon.

"Yeah," Tyler sighed, "guess it's been a long time since I've been here, huh?" He ran his thumb against the corner of his mouth and looked down. I don't know if the movement was conscious, but I consciously chose to *not* respond to it.

By not responding to it, though, Tyler and I were thrust into this short burst of incredible silence that made both of us shift in our seats.

I cleared my throat, not wanting to dwell. "So, want to show me what you've got?"

"Wait!" Ember shouted from the top of the stairs. "Don't start yet!"

Tyler laughed and his signature bright smile returned to his face. "She's awesome, man."

I smiled as all the tension left my shoulders. "Yeah. She is."

Ember stormed into the room and sat next to Tyler so she could better see his laptop. "I leave you two alone for three seconds and you're going to try to design the house without me?"

"What'd you have to talk to Beckett about?" I asked, leaning forward so I could see what Tyler was pulling up.

"Oh, some marketing stuff for us. I've been chatting with Monica and she gave me some ideas I wanted to run by him. Live podcast interviews, sample tracks, live recording feed... he left out the basement door. He'll be back tomorrow."

Her face was pink with excitement. I knew it was going to be a tough transition with all the life changes we had going on at once, so it was a relief to see her smiling like that.

"Excellent ideas. What'd Beckett think?" I was impressed with Ember's initiative on the business side of things. She seemed hesitant when it came to anything outside the studio.

"He thinks they're all great ideas. I told him we'd talk to Yardley tomorrow. I just wanted his impression."

Tyler whistled. "Wanna switch gears here?" He pushed his laptop away from him to give us a clear view of the screen.

"Sorry," Ember whispered with a giggle.

"It's okay, you're safe from detention," Tyler teased back.

Once Ember focused her attention on the screen, she gasped. "Wow."

I squinted my eyes, tilted my head, and looked around the room. "That's...that's this room?"

Tyler nodded, eyeing me cautiously.

"Wow is right!" I smiled at the possibilities that lay before us.

With his interior design program, Tyler had a full mockup of the dining room. When he pushed a button, we got to see a "live" transformation of the room as he saw it. The table we were sitting at disappeared and a wider, more country-looking table took its place. The wallpaper was replaced with a pale yellow that made it look like the sun was shining through the windows. The wall behind us slid out of the way and made way for a sunroom addition. I was floored.

Tyler took a deep breath and spoke in the most professional voice I'd ever heard from him in real life. "I know it's a lot. So just take a minute and look. We're able to consider the small sunroom because when your parents remodeled the kitchen and made it wider, it created this short alcove of unused space outside. If we put a sunroom there, it won't really be a loss of yard because you can use it year round. We'll insulate the hell out of it and put a small wood stove in the corner, here." He tapped the trackpad and a wood stove appeared.

Ember sat back in her seat. "This is beyond anything I could have imagined. I was excited for a new table and fresh paint."

"Well, this is kind of what I do." Tyler smiled almost bashfully as he continued staring at the screen.

"We have a couple of choices for the kitchen," he continued. "We can leave it as is, or we can move some things around so you can have two entry points to the sunroom since they'll share a wall..."

For the next hour, the three of us discussed the bottom floor renovations of my childhood home. The living room would receive cosmetic treatment and some built in shelves carved into the wall. My office would be rearranged to fit two new desks, allowing Ember and I to have a shared professional space. Ember protested, saying she didn't have anything that she needed a desk for, but Tyler told her she'd regret it if she didn't have it. He said at the basic level it would be a place to leave her computer at night, since he wanted to keep all electronics out of the bedroom.

"Shoot," Ember hissed as she checked the time on her cell phone. "I've got to get into the kitchen and start dinner. Monica and Josh will be here any minute. Tyler, can you come back tomorrow or the next day to talk about the upstairs?" Ember stood and put her hand on his shoulder.

"Sure. I've got one or two things I want to talk to Bo about, but I'll come back and we can finalize ideas. I can start pricing things for you."

Ember stopped as she crossed the threshold into the kitchen, turning around slowly and looking a bit embarrassed. "Shit. We haven't really discussed a budget."

Tyler looked to me for direction. I took the lead.

"We'll discuss it later. I've given Tyler figures already. Sorry, it slipped my mind." I stood, and Tyler followed suit.

Ember's eyes settled on me for a few seconds. Her lips pulled into a straight line before she came up with a smile and said, "Okay. Well, thanks for everything, Tyler." She gave him a quick hug and returned to the kitchen, burying her head in the refrigerator as she dug around.

Tyler nodded toward the stairwell. Once at the top of the stairs, he rapped a knuckle against the wall. "I want to leave the widow's watch as is. It's brilliant and the light it lets in here is something I could never recreate. I want to talk to you about stripping the hallway, too. Getting rid of all this dark wood. I never remember it being this dark in here when we were kids. Was it?"

I managed a half grin as I prepared my canned response. "Shit happens, and you kind of see things differently, I guess, huh?" I wandered over to Rae's bedroom door and ran my hand down the doorframe. It *was* a little too dark.

"I...I don't know if you're saying that to me or yourself..." Tyler tucked his laptop under his arm and leaned against the opposite side of Rae's door.

I sighed and set my head against the wood. "I guess I don't either."

"Look, Bo." Tyler spoke quietly, no doubt so Ember wouldn't hear. "If it's going to be too weird for you to have me working here—"

I straightened myself and looked him right in his eyes. "Stop. It's not going to be weird. Sorry that I went rogue there for a second. Look, it's fine. It's all over now, right?"

Tyler's face fell right along with his eyes as they swept to the floor. "Yeah," he swallowed hard, "but you know I never meant to—"

"Hey," I interrupted. "We were all just kids. None of us knew a damn thing. But, yeah...do whatever you want to the hallway, okay? You worked a miracle in that bedroom. She's in love."

Tyler's smile was infectious as he met my eyes. "So are you. And, Christ, it's a beautiful thing."

Just then, there was a knock on the door.

"That must be Josh and Monica." I smiled and slapped Tyler's shoulder. "Come down and meet them before you take off."

"This is Ember's best friend, right?" Tyler trailed me, trying to organize himself socially.

"Yep. They went to Princeton together and worked at the Hope Foundation until Ember and I left for California."

"That's domestic violence, right?"

I stopped at the bottom of the stairs and turned, confused, to Tyler. "Huh?"

"The Hope Foundation. They deal with domestic violence."

"Oh, right. Yes. You know about them?"

Tyler nodded. "Amends, brother. Amends."

I gave him a knowing nod as we reached the front door at the same time Ember did. She completely ignored us, throwing the door open and squealing so loud, Tyler and I winced.

"I can order stronger glass for your new windows," he whispered, laughing at the same time.

In a flurry of hugs and tears and manly nods, Tyler was introduced to Josh and Monica before he left, and the four of us went to the kitchen, where Ember had wine and beer waiting for us.

"Oh!" Monica shrieked before she'd even said hi to me. "You've got to show me the bedroom!"

Ember grabbed her wine glass and the girls raced up the stairs.

When order had returned, Josh and I were standing silently in the kitchen holding our frosted pint glasses.

"So," Josh started with a chuckle, "how ya been?"

CHAPTER *Ten*

Here it comes

Ember

"YOU WEREN'T KIDDING." Monica's eyes were wide as she circled the renovated bedroom. "This is amazing!"

"Right? I know you didn't meet him for long, but Tyler is *amazing*. Not just talented, but *super* nice. Did you get new makeup? You look amazing." I felt like I was talking a million miles a minute. Monica and I texted and talked on the phone several times a day, but it was *so* good to see her face again.

Monica stuck her head in the bathroom as I sat on the bed. "Yeah, the MAC counter is my friend. Are you changing anything in here?"

"I want to. I'd like a corner walk-in shower and his and her sinks, but we'll have to see what the cost is. Oh, get this..." I moved to the other side of the bed and Monica joined me. I set my glass on the bedside table and told her about the slightly weird money discussion Bo and I didn't really have in front of Tyler.

"What's weird?" Monica shrugged.

"I don't know...we didn't talk about it, really."

"Were you planning on paying for the remodel?"

"No. But we haven't really talked about money at all."

Monica took a breath. "I wouldn't stress it until you can talk about it later. He's not exactly cash-poor, and neither are you. With your recording contract to boot, I'd say you've got enough money to sort it all out."'

I twisted my lips and looked sideways at my wine glass. "I guess you're right. Well, let's go back downstairs and rejoin the husbands."

"You're pregnant," Monica blurted out, causing the acid in my stomach to rise.

My eyes widened as I took in her red cheeks. "No, I'm not, *you're* pregnant! That's what's with your face being all...glow-y."

"You haven't touched your wine since we've been up here. This isn't my first time meeting you, you know."

"Look at you," I snapped. "You didn't even bring your wine upstairs!"

"Don't fuck with me, November Blue Harris." Monica tilted her head to the side.

I shrugged. "Don't *you* fuck with *me*."

Suddenly the room was uncomfortably silent. I caught the slight quiver of Monica's chin and my tears followed suit.

"Shit, are you serious?" Monica squeaked.

I leaned my head into my hands as I spoke. "Please tell me you're pregnant and I'm not insane."

"You're insane, but I *am* pregnant. I took the test a couple of weeks ago."

I sat up straight. "A couple of weeks ago?"

"You were busy getting a contract and moving here and we hadn't been to the doctor yet, blah blah. Shut up. *You're pregnant!*"

I put my hand over her mouth. "Shh!"

Monica rolled her eyes. "I'm going to tell Josh—"

"No, you're not. I haven't told Bo. I don't even—"

"Did you take a test?"

I leaned over to my bedside stand and opened the drawer, pulling out two *very* positive pregnancy tests. I'd tried to keep it a secret, even from myself, but I couldn't look Monica in the face and deny it. As I held them out, my hand shook.

"When'd you take these?" Monica asked.

"The day after we signed the contract with Grounded Sound." My voice started to shake, too.

"Shit."

"Mm-hmm."

"Are you okay?" Monica whispered as she scanned my face.

I squeezed my eyes shut, wanting the tests to disappear, but they didn't. Tears rolled down my face as I shook my head.

"This is the worst timing in the history of everything. God," I continued. "I've been a wreck since we've been here. I've been able to pass it off as exhaustion, stress, or unfairly taking advantage of Bo's broody mood, but...I'm running out of options. With how stressed Bo's been lately, I just haven't... found the right time. I don't even know how this happened," I said in futility.

Monica put her hand on my leg. "You guys use condoms, right?" She knew my aversion to the pill was strong.

I nodded but slowed it down to a hesitant movement. "Most of the time. But I keep track of my cycle for times when we don't. I mean, we're not careless, but sometimes…ugh. My cycle probably got all fucked up over the summer on the tour…I don't…Jesus. I'm scared. But, I don't want to talk about it right now, okay? I want to talk about you and your baby!"

"Please. Bo Cavanaugh has "dad" written all over his face. If I were you, I would have spilled this the second his mood seemed sour. And, you *have* to tell him, Em. He'll want to be in on every appointment. You can't wait till you're showing to break the news."

Monica's practical sarcasm calmed me down. She was right. I hadn't been thinking clearly while carrying around this secret, especially when I missed my second period. I'd have to tell him, but tonight in front of Josh and Monica wasn't the right time.

I took a deep breath. "How did we end up pregnant at the same damn time?"

Monica grinned. "Bo's your soul mate, and I'm your best friend soul mate."

"You're not mad? I kind of feel like a schmuck since you guys were actually trying and planning."

"Mad? How could I possibly be mad to go through the scariest thing ever with my best friend? This is *perfect*. Too bad we don't live in the same town, or we could hang out together in breast-milk soaked clothes as we dream about wine. Oh! If I'm a little late and you're a little early, we'll be birthday buddies!"

I laughed for a second before my eyebrows shot up. "Wine. Right. I'm going to dump some of this out. If neither of us appears to be drinking, it will be all kinds of obvious. Let's get back down to the guys."

I slid off the bed and Monica tugged on my hand, pulling me into a hug.

"I love you, Ember. Congratulations." She sniffed and pressed her forehead into my shoulder.

I kissed the top of her head. "I love you too, Mon. This is batshit crazy."

We bounced down the stairs and found the guys standing in the same place we'd left them ten minutes earlier. Perched against the counter. The only signs that time had passed in that room at all were the nearly empty pint glasses in their hands.

"Calm down, guys," Monica spit out her best sarcasm.

"What's with you two?" Bo joked as his eyes shot back and forth between us. I tried to control my grin. And failed.

Josh held out his hand. "You told her."

I looked to Monica who wore a guilty smile. "I didn't."

"She didn't," I confirmed. "I could just...tell." I grabbed Monica's hand and gave it a light squeeze, reminding her to keep the status of my uterus on lockdown.

From her back pocket, Monica produced a soft and shiny ultrasound picture. I couldn't make out anything specific, but there was *definitely* something there. I felt my hand instinctively move to cover my lower stomach, but I stopped it, reaching for her picture instead.

I gently took the picture from her and walked to Bo, leaning my shoulder into his arm. "Look at this," I whispered. The lump in my throat prevented any more words to come out.

"Beautiful," he whispered back, kissing the top of my head.

The way his eyes creased at the edges as he smiled killed me. I knew there was a baby inside me, too, and the glimpse of what his face could look like sent chills down my spine.

Monica was right—I was insane to be nervous about telling him. It was a baby. It was *our* baby.

He leaned away from the counter and hugged Monica. "Congratulations, Mon."

I wiped more tears from my eyes and hugged Josh. "You guys...seriously..." I sniffed away more tears as I relished the beauty of it all.

"How far along are you?" Bo asked, unsurprising in his attention to detail.

"Just eight weeks," Monica answered. "But, we got to hear the heartbeat, and everything looks as good as can be expected." She moved over to Josh and leaned into his side as he put his arm around her shoulders.

"Your parents must be thrilled." I had goosebumps just thinking of how excited my own parents would be.

"Oh, you have no idea," Josh feigned exasperation.

"But," Monica cut in, "this means for your summer tour I'll have a newborn strapped to my body during your shows."

My stomach sank and Monica's eyes shot to mine. Suddenly I was reminded of the perfect storm this little baby would create inside the halls of Grounded Sound Entertainment.

The four of us cracked into laughter. A minute later the oven timer dinged.

Josh put a hand over his stomach. "Good lord, let's eat."

"Sympathy hunger?" I teased.

He grinned. "It's uncanny."

§

A few hours later, Josh, Monica, and incubating Baby Dixon headed out for their drive back to Barnstable. I closed and locked the door behind them, sighing in bliss at their new happiness.

I picked up the last of the dishes from the dining room table, and brought them to the kitchen, where Bo was rinsing plates and putting them in the dishwasher.

"That's exciting, huh?" Bo wore a tired but genuine grin.

I bent down to meet his lips as he stacked plates in the rack. "I know. I can't believe it."

"You should have seen the look on your face." Bo's voice sounded like velvet as his eyes followed my movements around the kitchen.

"What do you mean?"

Bo draped the dishtowel over his shoulder, leaning casually against the granite counter. "Your face exploded in joy. I don't see that look much."

I set the wine bottle in the recycling bin and walked back to Bo, wrapping my arms around his waist. "I'm that happy, though. All the time." I exhaled dreamily and kissed his chin.

"I'm glad. You deserve to be that happy all the time."

"So do you." I pulled back to allow him to kiss my forehead. A feeling that would always give me butterflies.

"I am," he reassured me, his hands sliding to my backside as he pulled me closer.

I surrendered fully to the warmth of his hug. I regretted the topic change I was about to pull, but so much had happened today that we needed to discuss.

"So," I started, backing up and resuming my cleanup of the kitchen. "Did Tyler talk to you about our upstairs plans?"

Bo ran a hand though his frazzled hair. "Yep. He also talked about the hallway. Getting rid of the dark wood, or something."

Bo turned back to the sink and I bagged up vegetables and cheese and put them in the refrigerator.

"We haven't nailed down ideas for all of the rooms upstairs, but I'm happy with what he showed us for down here. Are you?" I cleared my throat, fighting anxiety.

"Yeah. That sunroom idea is great. I guess I didn't realize how dark it can get in here sometimes."

I closed the fridge and left my hand on the handle while I took a deep breath. Apparently, I was quiet for a beat too long. Bo turned off the water and called me out.

"What's wrong?"

"Uh," I cleared my throat again, "about the budget..."

Bo took a deep breath through his nose, exhaling in his always-controlled manner. "Ember, I told you it was fine. I sent him the numbers to work with before you met with him. I needed him to know what he had to work with."

"You didn't talk to me about it."

Bo lifted his chin. "You look mad."

"I'm...frustrated."

"Why?"

"We haven't really discussed how we're handling our money. In California we just split the bills and we didn't have that many to begin with. I'm...I don't know. I guess I'm uncomfortable with you paying for everything for this renovation. Some of the things he's talking about are going to carry a big price tag." My palms began to sweat.

I hated talking about money because everyone got weird about it. Furthermore, I was on socially uneven ground. My parents and their friends never dealt with money the same way the rest of the world did. There were work exchanges, co-ops, etc. So, really, I didn't know what was acceptable. All grant writing taught me was how to discuss money on a corporate level. I was at a loss here.

Bo wiped down the counter, closed the dishwasher, and started it. "Look, Ember, I don't know what to tell you. We have projects we want to do on the house, so we'll get them done.

"Right, but we didn't discuss a *budget*. 'Whatever' isn't a budget. What if I wanted to help pay?"

"This is ridiculous. What's mine is yours, what's yours is mine." Bo began pacing in circles through the kitchen.

"Okay, well, if what's yours is mine, did it occur to you to discuss *how* we'd be spending *our* money? What if we wanted to save for trips, or kids, or college, or—"

Bo stopped pacing and put his hands on his hips. "What aren't you understanding, Ember? I can't take it with me when I go. There will always be plenty. Trust me."

I stuck out my hands. "That's the other thing. I don't even *know* how much you…have. God, I hate this conversation."

Without a word, Bo exited the kitchen through the back hallway. I heard the shuffling of papers in his office, and then he returned holding a thick, bound folder. He tossed it to the table, where it landed with a loud thump.

"There." He gestured to the table.

"What's that?"

"My net worth. Open it. It's yours. I'm not keeping secrets from you."

I sighed heavily. Annoyed. "I never said you were keeping secrets from me."

His eyes bugged out as his voice rose slightly. "Then what's the problem?"

"I just want to be consulted!" I shouted. Not angrily, but we were clearly talking past each other and it was annoying.

"About what?" he shouted back. "It's my house, for God's sake. If I wanted to tear the thing down and rebuild it, I would."

I cocked my head to the side, my tone reaching angry. "I thought you said it was *our* house."

I could literally feel my hormones spinning out of control. I was hot and cold at the same time.

"It is. Unless you're going to be a stubborn ass." He cocked his eyebrow and a small grin twitched at the corner of his mouth.

I began to grin, despite trying to remain serious. "Did you just call me an ass?"

Bo sighed and paced slowly toward me, extending his hands to take mine. "Come...sit with me for a second."

Bo led me by the hand out the back hallway and into the grand living room. I eyed the large fireplace with the stone facade and briefly wished for a cozy winter night and a roaring fire. Bo sat on the oversized leather love seat and I plunked next to him.

"Okay," he took another deep breath before continuing, "I need to explain something. And this is hard for me, but I need you to hear me."

I nodded, tightening my grip on his hand.

He smiled and shook his head. "I'm sorry for behaving so indifferently about the money. This is something I'm still adjusting to. All the money."

"I thought your family always had money." From everything Bo had told me, and my own research early on of DROP and Bo himself, I was led to believe he'd always had a charmed life.

"They did. My *family* did. When I graduated from college, I was granted my share of the trust fund. I used some of it to help with the groundwork of DROP and was going to take the rest of it to build my own business."

I'd never talked to Bo about what his intentions were besides DROP. It was so much a part of him and what he did, that we rarely talked about anything else business wise. And, once the music took over, that's the only business we ever discussed.

"What did you want to do?"

Bo pointed to the floor. "Music. Truly. That's why I had that studio built a couple years ago. I'd been scoping out warehouse space before my parents died. Then, I was able to remodel the basement. DROP took up a lot of my time, sure, but music was something I wanted to do. I knew I wanted to play or produce..." Bo kept his hopeful grin as he looked to the ceiling.

"Were your parents supportive of your music interests?" I relaxed my standoffish position of crossed arms and legs and curled myself into Bo's body.

"They were. My mom was an easier sell, as I suppose most moms are. But, when my dad saw that it wasn't just about performing, that I was focused on all aspects of the industry, he gave me a firm pat on the shoulder and told me that he knew

I'd make him proud no matter what." Bo cleared his throat and rested his chin on the top of my head.

"So—"

Bo cut me off before I could finish my sentence. "My point is, Em, that the reason I have all of this money is because my whole family is gone. That's the only reason I have as much as I do. I want us to be able to have a fresh start. Investing in a property is rarely a bad move—why not just take the money and do it?"

I lifted my chin and looked him in the eyes. He had a peaceful look on his face that was no doubt a struggle for him to maintain, given the gravity of this discussion. "I get it. I'm sorry. I just want us to be really careful and make sure we're making decisions as a team, you know?"

Bo tightened his arms around me. "I know and *I'm* sorry. I thought I was just doing something nice without realizing how you might feel about it."

"A bracelet is nice, Bo. An entire house renovation? That's a bit much, don't you think?" I chuckled when he did.

"You're right. So, we'll talk about the numbers I discussed with Tyler, and then we'll make a plan for how we're going to handle everything from now on. Deal?"

"Deal."

I leaned back and stretched my arms overhead, ready to head back to the kitchen. When I stood, Bo stopped me.

"Hey, Ember?"

"Yeah?" I turned back around and watched him stand with a foolish grin on his face.

"What you said earlier about kids and college, and all of that...is that what you really want?" He rested his hands on my hips, and suddenly I wanted him naked on the couch.

I restrained myself. Smiling, I answered, "It is. I want things with you I never even considered before. A music career, kids... what have you done to me?" I lifted on my toes and kissed his taut jawline.

"Made an honest woman out of you," he teased, bringing back his sitcom actor voice.

I smacked his chest and returned to the kitchen. Bo followed, opening up the fridge and grabbing a beer.

The walls were closing in on Baby O'clock, and I was chickening out. The man was my husband, for God's sake. I don't know exactly what I was afraid of. Still, another subject change seemed in order.

"Oh, by the way," I started slyly. "I have something I've been wanting to ask you for months."

"Great," Bo deadpanned as he opened his beer.

"The night we met Yardley, you made a comment to Willow, when you asked about how she handled her money. You said something about wondering if she was serious or playing with her parents' money, and joked that you knew a little about both." I turned, raising my eyebrows in question, but Bo didn't bite.

"And?" he teased.

I took the dishtowel and smacked his arm. "Come on. What'd you mean you knew about both? You seem so focused about money. Did you ever fool around with it?"

Bo rubbed his arm. "You're awfully abusive tonight, you know."

"Oh, shut up."

Bo took a swig of his beer and got a mischievous look in his eyes. "I was twenty-two. What do you want from me?"

"What'd you do?" I was dying to hear about the irresponsible side of my straight-laced husband.

"Oh, you know," he held out his hands and looked to the sky, "bought stuff. Like...a car, and a jet ski...and a snowmobile. And a cottage up on the lake."

My jaw had never dropped so low in my life as it did in that moment. "Bo! Are you serious?"

"Hey," he said, mock-defensively, "I sold that cottage three years later and almost doubled my investment."

I twisted my eyebrows in horror. "You did that all in one year?"

Bo nearly choked on his beer. "Like six months, but, yeah, close enough."

I shook my head disapprovingly as I walked through the dining room and climbed the stairs to the bedroom. Bo followed. "Your parents must have *shit*."

"Yep. They did. Oh, my dad was *so* pissed. I was called into his office and given a total ass-reaming. How he'd taught me better than that...you know...parent stuff." Once in the bedroom, Bo set the beer bottle down on the dresser as he undressed, taking his time to watch me undress, too.

I tossed my clothes in the hamper and slid into a black slinky number that always drove him crazy. "What'd your mom say?"

Bo shrugged and tenderness overcame his face. "She just rolled her eyes and told me to get my act together."

We crawled into bed and situated ourselves as we did every night. Bo held out his arm so I could lay my head on his chest, and he closed his warm arm around me, pulling me in even closer.

"Well, I'm glad you got all of that out of your system." I yawned and kissed his bare chest.

Bo's fingers skimmed the skin around my shoulders, driving *me* crazy. "I just want to give you a heads up. I'm calling Dr. Bittman in the morning." He reached for the side table light and clicked it off.

My heart skipped a beat as I sat straight up. "Turn it back on."

"What?" He sounded panicked as light filled the room again.

"Is everything okay?" I'd never met Dr. Bittman before, but I'd heard plenty about her after Rae died. David Bryson had told me Bo was in her care again, just as he'd been after his parents died. I knew he'd seen someone when we first got to California, but I'd always associated Dr. Bittman with tragedy.

Bo sat up and took my hand, kissing my knuckles and giving me a reassuring smile. "Everything's fine, love. And, I want to keep it that way. The past two weeks have been harder on me emotionally than I thought they would be. Hell, I didn't give much thought to it." He twisted his lips and leaned his head back almost as if he were disappointed in himself.

"I'm sorry," I whispered. "I knew something was off with you, but I didn't want to get into a huge pow-wow about it because I knew we had a lot going on. Moving, renovating, recording..."

I couldn't tell him. Not yet. I'd planned to, but the weight of what he was already dealing with emotionally was too heavy. My body wouldn't let me hold it in anymore, though. My chin began to quiver, and I tried to hide it by shifting my position.

That worked for about five seconds before my nose began to tingle. Then, the eyes. They filled so high with water that Bo became a blurry blob of color within seconds.

"Ember?" Bo shifted, sitting up and placing his hands on my shoulders.

I shook my head while I tried to force a smile. The tears that spilled down my cheeks and over the corners of my mouth ruined my planned facade, though. "It's fine," I managed through whisper.

"You're freaking me out, Em. What is it?"

I could barely hear my own voice as blood rushed through my ears, leaving me feeling dizzy.

"I'm pregnant."

CHAPTER *Eleven*

Heartbeats

Bo

I'M PREGNANT.

That's what she said. Right?

Before she could take a breath, she collapsed into a sobbing mess against my shoulder.

"What? Ember. What? Wait. What?" I knew she likely couldn't hear me over the volume of her cry, but I had to try to get some straight answers.

"I just...I'm so sorry. The timing is—" she cut off again in a loud wail.

I shifted and pushed gently on her shoulders, forcing her to sit up.

"Ember," a smile cracked through the corners of my mouth, "did you say you're pregnant?"

Her eyes met mine and they were filled with thick tears. Her cheeks were red, and I put together signs I should have paid attention to all along. I knew I'd been difficult over the past few weeks, but she truly did seem overly sensitive—even for her. I chalked it up to the stress of the move, and everything else she'd told me was bothering her.

Apart from that was her restless sleep. Ember usually slept sounder than any person I'd met, but over the last two weeks, she tossed and turned most nights. But, most importantly, there was a true glow coming from her over the past few days. Despite the winter settling around us, her cheeks were permanently rosy and her skin was extra flawless.

Her apparent sadness in front of me was baffling.

"Em?" I brought my hand to her face and ran my thumb across her lips.

She sniffed. "I'm pregnant, Bo."

A chuckle drenched in chest-bursting emotion poured from my mouth as I began to cry. There was no work up to this cry. It was open and flowing before I could consider holding it back. But I didn't want to.

Suddenly, all the stresses and problems and emotional baggage of the last several weeks shot into space. My gorgeous, talented, smart, breathtakingly amazing wife was pregnant. With our child. A baby. Our baby.

I was speechless, smiling as my wife dried her tears and stared at me.

"You're not...mad?" Her voice was small as she looked down.

Lifting her chin with my index finger, I said the truest words I've spoken since *I do*.

"Ember, you just made me the happiest man on planet Earth."

"But the timing—"

"Fuck the timing," I cut her off. "You should have felt what was going on inside me when Josh and Monica were here. I was so happy for them, and I realized that in the pit of my stomach was jealousy."

She allowed a small smile. "Really?"

I laughed through still-falling tears. "Really. Ember, this is amazing. A baby."

"The label…"

I shook my head and placed both hands on the side of her face. "Say something real. You're talking about the things you think you should be worried about. Tell me how *you're* feeling about this."

A sob leaped from her throat as she smiled. "I'm so happy, Bo. I love this baby so much already I don't even know what to do with myself. I'm sorry I kept this from you."

I pulled her into a tight hug. "I'm sorry I made you feel like you had to. Things have been stressful and I haven't been leaning on you like I promised I would. Jesus, Ember, I love you so much right now I don't even know what to *do* with *myself*."

Ember yawned. "Lay down with me?"

I leaned back and kept her close to my chest. Ember reached her arm behind her and grabbed my hand. Interlacing her fingers with mine, she brought our hands to the spot on her stomach just below her bellybutton.

There were no words. Just tears. Happy, beautiful, exhausting tears that ushered us into a deep sleep.

§

"Nervous?" the pleasant-looking nurse asked as she took Ember's blood pressure.

Ember nodded. "Yes. This is all happening kind of fast."

Ember called the doctor the morning after telling me she was pregnant. They scheduled an appointment four-weeks out, but called back in the afternoon to tell us there had been a cancellation. Neither one of us slept the night before coming in.

The nurse smiled as she made some notes on the computer chart. "Well, don't worry. We'll take good care of you. Okay, get comfortable. Since you've missed two periods, you're probably at least eight weeks along. The doctor will try to pick up a picture with the external wand, but if it's having trouble, he'll do the internal. For that we'd have you change into a gown, but don't worry about it for now."

Ember had warned me about the internal ultrasound. She Googled about first doctor's appointments in pregnancy. She was less than thrilled at the prospect, but her face relaxed as the nurse told her that might not be an issue after all.

In the few minutes we had alone before the doctor came in, Ember laid back and turned to face me.

"It's all going to get real in a few minutes." She exhaled and I could tell she was still quite nervous based on her shaky breath.

I took her hand, covering my own nerves with a deep breath. To be honest, I was more excited than nervous.

"When do you want to tell your parents?" I asked after kissing her hand.

Ember threw her hand on her forehead. "Oh God, I don't know. When should we tell Yardley? We have to tell her. This will affect the tour and shit, won't it? I don't even know."

"How about we just wait until this appointment is over before we start making all kinds of plans? One step at a time sound good?"

Ember smiled as she exhaled. "It sounds perfect."

Both of us had been so crazy busy over the last year, the thought of taking something one step at a time really felt like a security blanket.

There was a knock at the door, and a tall, young-looking male doctor entered the room. I shifted in my seat a little. I'd never really considered the gender of doctors much before that moment, and suddenly I was *very* aware of his.

At least it's not Beckett...or Adrian.

"Good morning, I'm Dr. Orson." He smiled gently and sat on a chair next to Ember, taking a few minutes to get a general medical history, and, it seemed, to get to know us a bit.

I liked him after all.

"Let's get started then, shall we? Lift up your shirt a bit, please."

Ember did as instructed, and had to shift her skirt down a bit, too. The doctor squeezed some Vaseline-looking stuff on her stomach, and placed the wand down right over it.

"It's cold," Ember whispered as she fought a giggle.

The doctor smiled and turned his attention to the screen in front of him.

"Okay," he said after a few seconds. "Take a look at the screen in front of you." He flipped a switch and a flat-screen TV mirrored the image on the small screen attached to the ultrasound machine.

Ember gasped and moved her arm behind her head to lift it up bit.

"What?" I asked, feeling completely clueless.

"Look. On the right is the head and, then, the rest of the body." She pointed to the screen like she'd never been more sure of anything.

"That's right," Dr. Orson agreed. He moved a mouse-looking thing around and drew some lines over the picture. "Here is the head, and this is the rest of the body, just like she said. You're measuring about nine weeks. Do you see that little flutter in the center?"

I leaned forward and squinted my eyes. "I see it."

"That's the heartbeat."

Ember's hand left mine and moved to her mouth as she teared up.

"Want to hear it?" the doctor asked.

"Yes!" Ember and I answered at the same time.

Dr. Orson flipped a switch, and suddenly the room was filled with the rapid rhythmic thumping of a tiny heart.

I've been into music for as long as I can remember. I've heard and played almost every kind there is. Suddenly, everything suffered in quality when compared to the sound of the strong heartbeat of our baby.

Ember and I were in a trance for what felt like forever. Soon, the doctor clicked off the screen, turned off the sound, and printed a few pictures for us to take home. We were ushered to the receptionist, where we made an appointment for four weeks out, and received a prescription for prenatal vitamins.

On the drive home, Ember and I had foolish grins on our faces.

"Can we wait to tell people from Grounded Sound?" she asked, sounding hesitant. "I just want to get the album produced first. I know we have a contract, but I'm due in June and that's when the tour starts. It kind of changes things."

I reached across the car and put my hand on her thigh. "Absolutely."

"I'm also not telling my parents yet. I just want to sit and breathe with this for a while." Ember bit her lip as she smiled and looked at her still-flat stomach.

"You know," she said after a moment of silence. "I didn't completely hate being on the road with my parents so much."

I lifted my chin and chuckled. "What are you thinking?"

Ember arched her eyebrow. "I'm thinking I have a little perspective on why my parents made the choices they did. I got to live all over the place, which was bearable because Willow was always there. I'm not saying that I want to do *that* with our baby, but...I don't know, at least before they're in school we can still do lots of traveling."

"I think that's a great idea, love." It warmed my heart to watch Ember transform into a mother right before my eyes.

The baby wasn't here yet, but Ember looked drastically different than she did two days ago. There was a protective calmness on her face.

"What? Could you pay attention to the road?" Ember pointed to the windshield.

"Sorry. I was just thinking how much you look like your mom lately." It rolled off my tongue so easily, I hadn't considered that she might find a problem with it.

Ember was quiet for a moment then rested her head back against her seat. "Thank you," she whispered through a yawn.

Later that evening, Ember and I lounged in our bed and stared at our baby's first picture, falling asleep as we laughed about names and whether it would be a boy or a girl. While I always thought I'd want a son, since women scare the hell out of me, the thought of raising a daughter with Ember that had a fraction of her heart was enough to make me reconsider my preferences.

§

The next day, Ember and I were knee-deep in a stressful recording session. We'd finished our first week without so much as a hiccup. Week two, it turned out, was somewhat of a black hole. Yardley was here with Beckett all week, and Ember seemed off. She said she was just tired, but I wondered if she was internalizing my slow adjustment to a new life in my old house.

"I'd like to hear it one more time from Ember's intro." Yardley adjusted some things on the control panel, and Ember took notice. And offense.

"What are you doing?" Ember nearly snapped. "When people listen to us on the radio or an album it needs to sound nearly identical to what it sounds like when we're live."

Yardley took a deep breath and smiled into the mic. "I was adjusting the volume. Don't worry, I know what sound you guys have, and what we need to record. I'm the one who signed you, remember?" With a wink, Yardley clicked off the mic once more and nodded to us to start.

I placed my hand on Ember's knee, beckoning her attention. Covering the mic, I whispered, "Are you okay?" I knew Ember still wanted to wait a while before revealing the pregnancy, but her temper was making it difficult.

The tops of her cheeks reddened slightly. "Yeah...sorry. I need to get some damn sleep tonight before I screw this up for both of us, huh?" She grinned and situated herself on her stool.

We were playing the guitar together in the song. We strummed once to tune, and then picked up where Yardley asked. Ember pulled it together for the rest of the verse, resulting in an appreciative nod from Yardley and Beckett in the booth.

Working with Beckett, it turned out, wasn't so bad after all. He had an incredible depth of recording knowledge, constantly reminding me of the kind of musical royalty, so to speak, that Ember came from. She was born and raised among some of the most talented and influential indie musicians of the last two decades, and she and her friends were heirs to the musical throne. By agreeing to tour with her family last year, and by signing the contract with Grounded Sound, Ember was surrendering to her birthright. Betrothed to the notes, my wife was stepping into a life she'd fought against for so long.

And damn it if she didn't carry it with the grace of a queen. Of course, the surge in poise I'd seen from her could have been, in part, due to the pregnancy. Every day Ember seemed to be more comfortable in her own skin, as if being a mother was something she'd always been meant to do. She had always been confident and classy, but there was this fierce serenity about her that screamed *woman*, and it was hot.

I strummed the last note, my heart pounding not at the adrenaline of the song, but at the way Ember's lips formed a perfect "O" as she sang the last note. Despite her obvious sexiness, Ember carried a strength that I hadn't ever taken for granted. Until now, it seemed, since I was so floored by it.

"Perfect, guys. My *lord,* you two are gold." Yardley's molasses-thick southern accent put an instant smile on Ember's face.

"Well, aren't you sweet," Ember teased back in her best Yardley interpretation. The two of them had spent all week playfully mocking the differences in their vernacular.

Yardley stepped out of the control room, leaving Beckett to work on a few things. She walked toward us with excited intent in her slightly small eyes.

"I'd like you two to come to the city next week if that's okay." Ember and I looked at each other with wide eyes, and Yardley cut us both off. "I know it's sooner than planned, but I'd like to do a special in-studio session. You know, get a couple of listeners from the contest on our website, throw in a few writers from music columns...it'll get some buzz going. This album is coming together so quickly, we'll have to move up the release date."

My eyebrows shot up. "Move it up? Really?"

Yardley threw her hair back into a perfect ponytail. "Yes. I want to get you guys absolutely everywhere I can before the summer tour. You'll have these songs done by next week, easily, and I'd like to finish the recording in our studio so we can get it into production ASAP."

"Then what happens?" Ember asked as she set her guitar in its stand.

Beckett flipped on his mic from inside the control room. "Then the pimping starts." He stuck out his tongue and got back to work.

Yardley rolled her eyes, looking slightly disgusted. "This is why he's not in PR. What he meant, deep down, is that's when we start *promoting* you. We'll start slow, scheduling in-studio interviews and things like that. If it's all right with you, I'd like to have Beckett shoot some of the sessions for the rest of the week. The fans will *eat up* seeing you recording in your house."

"That's great," I interjected. "Who is slated to be on tour with us this summer?"

We knew Yardley was putting the *Indie Tour* together from scratch, and I wondered how she planned to go about doing that.

"Well," Yardley straightened her shoulders, seeming to look even more excited than usual, "I was planning on telling you all when we were together in New York next week, but I'm including Celtic Summer in the tour."

"What?" I asked, as Ember squealed and jumped up.

"Really?" she squeaked again. Turning to me, she smacked my shoulder. "That's *Regan's* group!"

I fist-bumped the air, which is something I don't typically do while sober. I'd forgotten that Regan's fiery trio had a name. That group had been completely pieced together by Yardley, and I was dying to know how they sounded. They had to write a load of songs from scratch, and had been spending some long-ass days in the studio, so neither Ember nor I had talked much with Regan. But, if Yardley was injecting them into the tour, she clearly had high hopes.

"They'll be in New York? Regan didn't tell me that when we talked yesterday." Ember's tone was bright and bouncy.

While she hadn't had much in the way of morning sickness, the nausea had been nearly around the clock and we were both worried it would give away our precious secret before we were ready.

"We just finalized it with them this morning, which is why I haven't mentioned it before. They'll lay some tracks in the studio as well, so we'd like to make a day of it with the contest winners."

Ember, Yardley, and I talked details about the trip to New York the following week before Beckett and Yardley headed back to their hotel for the evening.

"Today's tone picked up quick, huh?" Ember said with a grin as she shut the door and leaned her back against it.

I took a deep breath through my nose, grinning slyly as I tugged on her hips. "Thank you," I murmured as I kissed her nose.

"For what?" She kissed me back and walked through the dining room—which was finally devoid of wallpaper—and into the kitchen.

I followed behind her, unabashedly enjoying my view. "For...following the music. I know it's not what you wanted—"

Ember whipped around once she reached the sink. Her lips held a cautious smile. "I want you. Us. This. Our life is beautiful, Bo, and I want every piece of it." She draped her arms around my neck and started shifting her hips from side to side, dancing without music.

"Are you still sure you want to wait on telling Grounded Sound about the pregnancy? That will make next week a little tricky..." I didn't want to record the last of our album with Ember feeling lots of pressure either way.

"Yeah, let's wait. The last thing I want is a huge *thing*. Let's dash to New York, finish the album, and hang out with Regan."

I grinned and kissed her cheek. "How very rock star sounding of you."

"Well, you know," she playfully sighed, "it *is* a tough life. But, someone's gotta do it."

CHAPTER *Twelve*

It's complicated

Ember

I WOKE WITH THE sun creeping delicately through the sheer curtains. My head was pounding as I sat up and stretched. Headaches and nausea were a common occurrence these days, and I was hoping it would end sooner than later.

Looking to my left, I saw the bed empty. When I peered at the clock, I saw why. It was well past nine in the morning. I jumped out of bed, which shot pain through the back of my head. Not only would Tyler be arriving shortly, but Bo was gone. He'd told me about an early morning meeting he had, but I was left feeling out of sorts that he hadn't woken me up to say goodbye.

Walking into the bathroom, I took stock of myself in the huge mirror. I was a disaster. My hair was sticking out all over the place and my face looked like it was filling in a little. It wasn't the cute kind of pregnancy-plump yet, I just kind of looked hung over.

I stopped my self-assessment when I saw a post-it note tucked at the corner of the mirror. Reaching for it, I smiled.

Morning, love.
Tried to wake you, but you wouldn't budge.
Call me when you're up.
Bo

I brought the note with me into the bedroom and tucked it into the back pocket of my jeans. I had just enough time to throw my pregnancy-induced hair into a reckless bun before the doorbell rang. Bo and I had agreed it would be easier to give Tyler the gate code since he'd be in and out of the house over the next several months to coordinate the project.

I ran down the stairs and opened the door with a smile. Tyler entered the house with a soy latte in hand for me.

"Morning." He smiled mischievously. "You look...rough. Hung over? Maybe I should have brought full-strength coffee."

I took the half-caffeinated drink from him and rolled my eyes. "Hardly. I wish, though."

We wandered to the dining room and he plunked two huge black binders on the table. Today we would be picking out flooring and furniture.

"What is it?" Tyler asked as he sipped his steaming beverage.

I studied his face for a moment while I considered whether or not I'd tell him about my pregnancy. Tyler seemed genuinely interested in what was plaguing me, but I wasn't sure that I should tell him. I thought of the reticence of both Bo *and* Tyler when they each talked to me about their past. Though, given that Tyler was spearheading the Cavanaugh estate remodel, whatever the hell it was that happened between the two of them was buried enough.

I'd been mulling over something only Tyler could really answer for me, and I decided to ask it. "What was he like after his parents died?"

Tyler coughed a little, trying to mask it by clearing his throat. "Huh?"

"I mean was he always this..." I struggled to find the right words.

"Reclusive?" Tyler offered.

I nodded. "That. I know he had a temper in high school, or whatever, from the story you told. But, what was it like after that?"

Tyler shrugged. "We were in college by the time his parents died. He was at UNH and I was at Pratt..."

"Right, but you two were, like, best friends."

Tyler winced. "Guys don't really operate like that." His tone was far heavier than his words.

"Still..." I sensed the same brick wall as when I tried to talk with Bo about Tyler.

"I don't think he went off the deep end," Tyler said after a few long seconds of silence.

"I changed my mind," I cut off whatever else he was planning to say. "I want to know what the fuck happened to you two."

Tyler turned red, then white. Clearing his throat, he gestured to the binders between us. "We really need to get working on this. That wall is coming down on Monday, and I need to have at least the floor ordered by then, or it won't be here when the addition's done. Also, you'll want to consider if you want the sunroom to have the same flooring as the dining room, the kitchen, or if you want all three rooms to be the same, since we're putting a door in the kitchen." His tone was one hundred percent professional, and absolutely zero percent friendly chum who brought me my soy latte.

"Sorry," I whispered, feeling a lump form in my throat.

My ears burned in embarrassment and leftover emotion from the night before. I flipped through the pages, and had to flip faster as my vision clouded with tears.

"I, uh," I cleared my throat and pointed at a page that held wood flooring, "like these."

Tyler leaned forward. "Wood is an excellent choice, and it's gaining popularity. The good thing about wood is, if you're doing all three rooms, it offers a seamless—shit, are you crying?"

I shook my head as I pursed my lips. It was as sorry a lie as I'd ever told. "Wh—what shade do you recommend?" I tried to continue the conversation despite the several tears that escaped and were now rushing down my cheeks.

"Hey," Tyler moved the binder away from me and put his hand over mine, "stop. Did I upset you? I just…shit. I'm sorry. I know I'm gay, but I'm a dude so I don't have enough estrogen to know what's going on here. "

His desperate tone elicited a chuckle from me, and I threw my head back and wiped under my eyes. "No, Tyler, *I'm sorry.* Apparently all I do is cry now. What the hell?" That part was true. Everything seemed to make me cry lately. Commercials, the news, someone saying "hi" with a nice smile…

"I know something happened between you and Bo," I continued. "But the fact that neither one of you want to tell me about it should be enough for me to drop it, but it only makes me more curious. I'm sorry."

"It's okay, Ember. I just don't want to...it's complicated, okay? I know people get to tell their own story, and all of that, but this story is really both of ours. Mine and Bo's... and I don't want to violate his trust by sharing something he wants to keep to himself."

I pulled my sleeves halfway down my hands and wiped my face with them. Moving my legs so I was sitting cross-legged on the old high-backed dining chair, I offered a shrug. "Betchya didn't know I'd be such a mess, huh?"

Tyler grinned, his well-manicured eyebrows lifting as he laughed. "Life's full of fun little surprises." The way he winked at me at the end of his sentence made me question if he somehow knew my secret.

"Christ," I groaned. "You said that wall is coming down Monday." My change of subject seemed to throw Tyler off.

"Yeah..."

"We're leaving for *fucking* New York City Sunday night."

Tyler nodded, looking to the ceiling in thought. "That should be okay. We'll just make sure the three of us are on the same page about what's going to happen while you guys are out of town. I'll plan on being here more than usual just to make sure someone is kind of watching the place."

I sighed in relief. "You've got your shit together."

"One of us has to," he joked.

"Funny."

"So, the wood floor..."

For the next couple of hours, Tyler and I discussed flooring and furniture, and even made it so far as picking out a light fixture for the dining room ceiling.

By the time Bo returned home, I was offering Tyler some lunch, and the three of us sat in the kitchen together to eat. We caught Bo up on the plans for the renovation while we were in New York, and he seemed happy with the progress.

"This is really moving along nicely, Tyler. Awesome job, man." Bo took a large bite of his turkey sandwich and nodded approvingly.

"Thanks, man." Tyler nodded back.

My eyes volleyed between the friends as I contemplated their enigmatic relationship. Bo was generally really open with me, and I hadn't broached the subject about Tyler since our conversation last night, but I sensed this one might be a hard limit.

"What's up?" Bo nodded to me. "You look lost in thought."

Suddenly, both men had their eyes trained on me. I simply shrugged. "Just trying to prepare myself for one more afternoon with Yardley and Beckett."

It was shitty to throw those two under the bus, but what was I to do? In truth, it was kind of fun having this little secret between Bo and me. Monica knew, but she wasn't in the room. Soon enough the whole damn world would know the status of my uterus. I was grateful for the fleeting privacy.

"Yardley seems like a piece of work," Tyler interjected.

Bo laughed. "Yeah, you could say that. She knows her industry shit, though."

"It sure is in a fancy little package, isn't it?" Tyler arched an eyebrow.

"Hey," I sat forward, "you're supposed to be gay!"

Bo and Tyler laughed in unison, and for a split second I saw two high school seniors laughing in the back of the football bus.

Tyler put his hand on my shoulder. "That I am, my darling, but I sure as hell ain't blind."

"You think Yardley is pretty? She doesn't strike me as your female type," I challenged.

"Of course she's pretty. She's a ripe Georgian peach ready for the picking." Bo shook his head and looked down with a grin as Tyler continued. "But that's not what I mean. She's just so…so stereotypically put together. I've never seen her with a hair or an eyelash out of place. Her lips move perfectly when she speaks and her head is nestled on her neck like a pageant queen herself put it there."

I cocked my head to the side. "That's…observant."

The truth was, I'd noticed all of those things about Yardley myself. It was interesting to get a male perspective though, even if it was a gay one.

Tyler shrugged and stood. "I just kind of want to be around when her perfect little head pops off."

"What are you talking about?" I stood and brought my plate to the sink.

Tyler took a deep breath and his eyes flickered to Bo for a split second, though I could have imagined that. "No one that perfect can keep it up for long. I only know that because there is *no* such thing as perfect. Most of us just crawl along doing the best we can and try to hurt as few people in the process."

He looked down for a moment then seemed to force a smile as he looked back up. "Well, Ember, talk over those floor choices with Bo, and shoot me an email when you can. I'll keep you guys informed next week with texts and pictures, and all that good stuff. Go, be rock stars. I'll maintain the fabulous here in Concord while you bring it to the city."

"Thank you, Tyler." In an unguarded moment as far as Tyler and I were concerned, I gave him a tight hug. I knew I was hugging him for more than I had information on, but I think we both needed that hug.

"No problem. Bo," he mock-saluted Bo, who rose and stuck out his hand to shake Tyler's, "see you at the end of next week."

Tyler left and Bo and I cleaned up lunch and prepared for our final Concord recording session with Beckett and Yardley.

"You know," Bo said as he stuffed the last of the baby carrots in his mouth, "working with Beckett hasn't been so bad."

I snorted. "Are you disappointed that none of your horror stories came true?"

"What stories?"

I looked to Bo out of the corner of my eye. "Oh, I don't know, that he and I would suddenly wake up seventeen and in bed together again?"

Bo bit his bottom lip and playfully smacked my butt. "You're such a smartass, you know that?"

"You've got a board meeting tomorrow, right?" I asked, changing the subject.

Bo leaned against the counter and rubbed his hand over his face as he yawned. "Yes. This is the quarterly one. I won't have to leave as early as I did this morning, but I'll be gone through the middle of the day, easily."

"I think I'm gonna take a drive down to Barnstable and hang out with Monica. I know we'll only be in the city for a week, but I still haven't seen that much of her."

"That sounds good. You know you don't need to, like, ask my permission for that. Even if I was going to be here all day you could have gone." He pushed off the counter and walked to the basement door, holding it open for me as he loosened his tie.

"Are you recording in your suit?" I asked, hopefully.

"I hadn't really thought about what I was wearing." He looked down, seeming surprised that he was still in his business clothes.

"Keep it on. It's hot." I kissed the side of his cheek, right by his ear, and let my lips linger there for a minute."

Bo sighed as I felt his cheeks heat. "Don't start, Mrs. Cavanaugh. It'd be embarrassing to finish while Beckett and Yardley are here."

I giggled and walked through the door. As I descended the stairs, I continued my train of thought. "I know, but we haven't really spent much quality time together outside of the bedroom in the last couple of weeks. I just want to make sure we're checking in with each other. You've been pretty busy with DROP."

"They're happy to have me back on Eastern soil, that's for sure. But, since we'll be on tour this summer...or whatever... there's lots of work that needs to be done for the upcoming spring and summer programs. I like to have my hands on that whenever possible. The last thing I want to be is a director-at-large. It's my organization, and I want to run it." Bo's voice was filled with a mix of passion and determination.

"I know, love. I just want to make sure you're not going to burn yourself out. We've had a *lot* of change in the last month, and—"

Bo stopped me with a hard kiss on the lips. "I'm better than I've ever been," he said when he finally pulled away.

Standing in the middle of the studio, it was hard not to believe him. Everything about him became more vibrant when surrounded by sheets of music and guitar strings. Bo and I took a few moments to tune our voices and instruments before Yardley and Beckett arrived to round out this week's recording session.

§

"He didn't really seem different to me the last time we were there, but he hardly says anything as it is." Monica grabbed two popsicles from the freezer as she brewed ginger tea. Her nausea, it seemed, was far from subsiding.

I plucked the green popsicle from her hand. "I know I probably read too much into it, and projected my own anxieties, and all of that, but I'm glad he seems better now."

"Eh," Monica waved her hand, "it's married life, right? Ups and downs. Drama, good and bad, is like the pulse of life. Without it, how would we distinguish between the two?"

I nodded in agreement as I sucked on the frozen treat.

Monica poured her tea and met me at the table. "Have you gotten to the bottom about Tyler and Bo's *history* yet?"

"No." I sat forward, placing my elbows on the table. "Honestly, I don't know if I even want to. It's kind of tagged as a "let sleeping dogs lie" thing in my brain right now."

"You want some ginger tea?"

"No, I hate ginger." I scrunched my nose and stuck out my tongue.

"The only hippie in the United States that hates ginger..." Monica gestured to me as if we were in a crowd of people.

I stood and walked to her cabinet, pulling down some peppermint rose tea.

Monica's eyes focused on the tiny box. "And where the hell did that come from?"

I laughed. "I brought it here the last time I came. I knew you'd never drink it, so I stuck it in the back."

"Are you offended by my tea?" Monica teased.

I steeped the silk bag and walked back to the table. "So, I'm impatient. When are we going to start looking pregnant?"

She rested her cheek on her closed fist. "I feel like I'm a thousand pounds. It's like having three periods worth of bloat at once. Seriously. I don't know, though. I hope soon so I can just move into leggings. Jeans are my enemy at the moment."

"When do you get to find out what you're having?"

The tight sarcasm in Monica's lips shifted into the softest smile I'd ever seen on her. "January sometime."

My eyes filled with tears again. "We're in February, I think. God, I'm so happy for you guys."

Monica shed a rare tear as she sipped her tea. "I'm happy for us. How ridiculous is this? Oh! You had an appointment yesterday, right?"

"Yes!" I jumped to my feet and retrieved the pictures from my bag. "They look just like yours, but...you know."

"Did you hear the heartbeat?" Monica asked as she smiled at my pictures.

I nodded, feeling that comforting warmth circle through my bones. I took a long sip of my tea and smiled.

"Motherhood looks good on you, Ember. I gotta say, you're like a whole new person since you got knocked up."

I snorted, causing me to sputter on my delicious—and expensive—tea. "You're ridiculous."

"It's true." Her eyes bugged out. "You're all extra calm and graceful. You know what? You're all Raven-like these days."

I tilted my head and smiled. "Bo said the same thing."

"Do they know yet?" Monica asked of my parents.

I shook my head. "Soon."

She knew of our plans with Grounded Sound and when we wanted to tell everyone.

"Just make sure you tell them before they hear it on the news."

"No shit. All right, I gotta go." I stood and brought my teacup to the sink and tossed my popsicle stick in the trash.

"Rock New York, super star." Monica saluted me with her empty popsicle stick.

I laughed and rolled my eyes. "You're sick."

"I probably will be in a few minutes," she joked as I shut the door.

CHAPTER *Thirteen*

Reunions

Ember

"T HAT DRIVE WAS easy," Bo remarked as we made our way to Grounded Sound's studio in the heart of New York City.

"I'm glad *you* drove. I hate city driving." We ascended the stone steps that led into the well-maintained brownstone.

It was a gorgeous building. From what Bo and I could surmise from our Internet snooping, the Honeywell family had invested in Yankee real estate since the Civil War when they moved money there to protect their assets. Further digging showed before and after pictures of the Honeywell plantation after it was burned to the ground and they rebuilt in Savannah, where the family home still stands.

After the rebuild, it seems, the family had their hands in everything—arts, entertainment, business...a broad investment plan designed, no doubt, to continue protecting their assets.

Over the past thirty years, they'd found a way to combine the three, and Grounded Sound Entertainment was born.

I had a new respect for Yardley, and the kind of stock she came from, but it didn't do anything to quell the curiosity of what might lie beneath her facade.

We were buzzed in and greeted by a friendly receptionist who looked like she was cut from the same cloth as Yardley. Brunette, but with a perfectly polished bob and a set of white pearls to match her pageant-like teeth.

"You can head right down to Studio A on your right." The young woman with an ID badge that read "Brielle" handed us our own visitor passes that doubled as card access for the studios. Ours didn't say *visitor*, though. I grinned as I read the word "Talent" in bold letters.

"Thank you," Bo and I said in unison.

Brielle smiled at both of us, but her eyes twinkled just a bit more when she nodded to Bo.

From GS's website, we knew this was a four-story building with two studios in the basement, one on the main floor, offices on the second floor, and what we could only guess was an apartment on the top floor for when Yardley or her family came into town. This was as professional an operation as I'd ever seen, and it intrigued me that it all took place behind the facade of a row of brownstones.

"Have you talked to Regan?" Bo asked as we moved down the short, narrow hallway.

I held my ID badge over the swipe pad next to Studio A's door. "No. I called him the other day when we found out about this trip, but he didn't—"

The door clicked as it unlocked, and my sentence was cut short as I opened the door and found Regan talking with two people I didn't know as they stood casually around a set of microphones.

"Regan!" I squealed as I rushed over to him and gave him a hug. It had only been a few weeks since we'd seen each other, but with all the time we'd spent together the past year, it felt like an eternity.

Regan's arms tightened around me and he lifted me a few inches off the ground. "Hey you!"

Once he set me down, he and Bo engaged that manly handshake-hug thing they always did.

Regan took a step back and gestured to who I assumed were the other members of the band. "Bo and Ember, I'd like you to meet the other two massively talented members of Celtic Summer. This is Chris. He's lead vocals and occasional percussion."

A roughly five-foot-eleven, broad-shouldered Chris shook my hand. His brown hair was shorn into a tight buzz cut, and below the hem of his grey short sleeves, I saw the makings of an insanely intricate tattoo. His eyes were clear blue and he had a small gap between his front two teeth.

"Nice to meet you." He spoke with a tinny rasp that I knew had to drive the women crazy.

"And," Regan continued, "this is Shaughn. She's vocals and guitar."

Shaughn was a very petite five-foot-two, or so, with a fire-red pixie cut. She didn't look frail in any way, though, and her strong handshake cast away any lingering doubts.

She spoke in a syrupy-thick Irish accent. "Nice to meet you both. Regan talks a lot about you."

"Great accent!" I cheered excitedly. I was riding high on adrenaline and happiness.

"Thanks," she said in a purely American accent as she sighed heavily.

"Wait," Bo cut in. "What happened to the accent? Which is the accent?"

Shaughn smiled. "Both. I was born in Athlone and lived there till I was in high school. My parents divorced and I moved with my mom to Chicago. I went back to Athlone every summer, though, and still go every chance I get. So my accent is usually muted, but, for Celtic Summer, it's dialed way back to my middle school days."

"Was that your choice or the labels?" I questioned.

"It was Yardley's idea. She heard me talking when I was drunk one night and told me to keep talking like that." Shaughn grinned mischievously, and suddenly I had the urge to drag her to a pub and hear every story that sat behind her dark green eyes.

Several minutes later, Yardley entered the studio, followed by what looked to be her parents, from pictures we'd seen on the Internet. They were the most fascinating pair of socialites I'd ever seen. Their crisp dark clothing was a nod to their Manhattan interests, but Mrs. Ginger Honeywell's expertly pinned French twist and flawless pearls gave away her southern address.

Studio A at Grounded Sound was special in that it had the standard recording room and control room, but there was another room as a part of the floor plan that housed a viewing/ listening area. A soundproof glass window allowed the musi-

cians and the audience to see one another, but kept unneces-
sary noise out of the recording room. The listening room was
equipped with one-way speakers, and looked like it could seat
ten to fifteen people comfortably.

For the morning, Bo and I, and Celtic Summer, were to
take turns recording, while the other group had the opportunity to sit in the listening room. It was important, Yardley
reminded us, to get familiar with each other's styles. Since
we'd be on tour together and giving interviews and talking
with fans, it was imperative that we could be supportive of
one another by talking up one another's strengths, and to
be able to discuss similarities and differences in our sounds.
Yardley had discussed that at least three groups would be on
tour this coming summer, but neither Celtic Summer, nor Bo
and I had any idea what her plans were there.

While Celtic Summer worked through their first song, Bo
and I watched from the leather chairs of the listening room.

"It's weird to be *watching* Regan, isn't it?" I whispered,
despite the knowledge of the soundproof glass.

Bo shot me a sardonic grin. "You forget, I've seen both of
you on stage together before...back when you hated me."

I gasped and slapped his shoulder. "I have never *hated* you!"

"Use your words," Bo teased as he took the hand that
slapped him and offered a soft kiss.

While Bo and I didn't hold any resentment over our time
apart, it was rarely something we discussed or even joked
about. I was glad to see Bo slip into some sarcasm and wit.
He was always so serious, and had been especially over the
past few weeks.

"They are damn good, though," Bo continued. "That guitar looks big enough to swallow Shaughn whole, but she *owns* it."

I nodded in agreement. "And Chris is crazy good. Who knew you could bring a sultry sound into this kind of music?"

"Yardley did," Bo replied. "She's good. Real good. I think we're luckier than we realize to have a contract here."

"Guess that means you've got to be a lot nicer to Beckett, huh?" I teased as I elbowed him.

Bo feigned pain as he held his arm. "God, you're abusive today."

For the next hour, we had the pleasure of watching a seemingly perfectly melded Celtic Summer work through several songs. Even when they had to stop to work on something, it was a quick fix and they were back up and running. While it was definitely disappointing to not be playing with Regan anymore, it was good to see that he'd bonded so well with the others in his group.

As their session ended and Bo and I warmed up, I was getting a little nervous about the summer tour, and our little secret that was going to require a *big* change of plans. Still, Bo and I reminded ourselves a thousand times on the drive down to stick to our guns until the album was done. And, Yardley didn't have a third band lined up for the tour yet, so the dates weren't set in stone.

Bo and I warmed up with a song we'd written near the end of our tour with The Six. We'd titled it "Crimson Minute." It was a soulful ballad that carried enough energy to keep it from drowning. Regan had heard us rehearsing it, but never had the chance to hear the final product before we moved back to New Hampshire. When we finished the piece, Regan lurched toward the glass that separated us and knocked wildly, flashing the thumbs up and mouthing "hell yes!"

After we played two more songs, Yardley left the control room, where she'd been the whole morning, and entered the recording room. She had a professional, but satisfied smile on her face.

"Y'all make my job *so* easy," she cooed as Celtic Summer entered the recording room and situated around us.

Bo smiled his friendly boardroom smile. "You're the one that had the ear for us, Ms. Honeywell."

"Please." She blushed and smiled. Blushed. She did. "I insist that you call me Yardley. I know that we all have a professional relationship here, but I need to know you're comfortable enough in these rooms to call me by my name."

"Well, Yardley," I entered, "thank you for this opportunity. The studio here is great. I'm looking forward to recording more."

Yardley took a quick breath as if she'd just remembered what she'd intended to say all along. "Bo and Ember, you two only have two more songs left to record to complete the album."

"Nice!" Regan exclaimed as he put his hands on our shoulders.

"What I'd like to do is break early for lunch, and give some listeners an opportunity to watch you record them live this afternoon. We won't be releasing any of the sound bites or videos until closer to the album release date, which will be mid-April." Yardley pulled out her phone and scrolled through the calendar.

"Why not until then?" I questioned.

Yardley smiled with drive in her eyes. "We want to keep you relevant, but don't want to do the push until the album release and close to the tour date so the fans don't tire of you before they've heard your body of work. It'll go fast, I promise. You can head up to the second floor. There's a conference room there with lunch waiting for all of you." She winked and walked briskly from the room, leaving the door open behind her.

"When's your album out?" I asked Regan as we all packed away our instruments.

He looked up to the ceiling for a moment. "A week or two after yours, I think."

"How's it sounding?"

Regan's broad smile gave it away. "Awesome. We have some instrumental-only songs in there that are to *die* for. We have four more to record before it's sent to production. We'll be here until we finish, which should only take a couple of days."

Bo was chatting up Chris and Shaughn as we all made our way upstairs to the conference room. Regan and I continued catching up. I asked about Georgia, and his face lit up. While it was hard to be away, he said, they'd recognized their stints apart wouldn't end any time soon and they'd better get used to it. Georgia was working on training and hiring a slew of people just for the summer so she would be able to take longer stints away from the bakery and meet up with him on tour.

"I miss her," I said through a mouthful of vegan spring rolls. "It sucks that we won't see each other until the summer, but with everything going on at the house and with the album, I don't see an opportunity to get out there any time soon."

"Oh, right, the house! Bo told me about some of the stuff you're doing. It sounds great." He paused and looked down at his hands for a moment before continuing. "Are you going to do all the bedrooms, too?"

I knew what he was *really* asking. Would *Rae's* room be remodeled.

I nodded slightly. "We're taking our time with those, though. Bo had our room done, and we need to do the master bath, then we'll slowly work our way down the hallway. We're not actively using the rooms right now, so it's not as urgent as the rest of the house."

As I spoke, my voice trailed off. Of course we'd need to use one of the bedrooms as a nursery. Bo and I hadn't discussed how we wanted to handle that yet, though we'd have to with Tyler eventually.

"You okay?" Regan asked. "You got all weird and quiet for a second there."

I plastered on my *everything's fine* smile and waved my hand. "You're the weird one. Just tired, I think."

Regan shrugged and chewed his food while he talked with Bo.

During the rest of the meal, I had an opportunity to talk with Chris from Celtic Summer. He was a Minnesota native who looked nothing like the Midwest stereotypes. His upbringing, though, was exactly that. Two parents—who were happily married—a sister, and a dog. He was on the debate team in high school, and in the glee club. Things got saucy when he left for school as a political science major, and came home having dropped out and started his own band.

"How'd your parents take that?" I asked, almost nervously.

Chris moved his head from side to side. "They've...taken things better before."

The whole table broke into laughter.

"Man," I cut in, "my parents probably would have killed for me to drop out and sing."

With the little bit of space I'd had from my parents, and being in the company of people with different upbringings, I could appreciate the passion for life my parents held.

Really, all they wanted was for me to be happy, which is why they didn't throw a fit when I'd insisted on attending college or moving halfway across the country. That they let me grow into my own person said more about them than it would have had they forced me one way or the other.

Yardley came into the room as we were finishing our lunches.

"Okay," she smiled, "we've got ten listeners from a flash giveaway on our website from over the weekend. They're ready in the listening room now. Bo and Ember, since you played last, do you want to go first, as you're most warmed up?"

Bo and I shrugged as I answered, "Sure."

"Great. Regan, Chris, and Shaughn, you three can get your instruments and head down to Studio B, where you can warm up some, or just relax." Yardley turned on her heels as she got a phone call, and exited the room.

"Well, good luck." Chris winked and smiled as he shook both my hand and Bo's.

"Knock 'em dead," Regan encouraged as we all made our way for the stairs.

Bo and I were in the lead as we casually descended the steps. My pace, and voice, picked up as I reached the bottom third and saw Willow standing at the reception desk, talking with Brielle.

"Willow! What the hell!" I ran over to her and pulled her into the tightest hug I'd given her since we were in high school.

"What the hell me? What the hell you!" she squealed as she hugged me back.

While we never really settled into sisterly roles while I was on the road over the past year, seeing her in Grounded Sound made me want to make that a priority.

"I've missed you." My eyes watered slightly as I pulled back and studied her.

She'd taken out her braids and trimmed her hair. It sat a few inches below her shoulders and was a soft bed of wild curls.

Willow pointed to her head. "Crazy hair, right? I needed a break from the braids."

"No, I think it's fabulous. Total boho-chic." We laughed harder than people around us may have considered necessary for that remark.

In eight grade, Willow and I were wandering through a shopping center when the manager of a clothing store chased us down and complimented us for our "trendy" boho-chic look. We thanked him, not knowing what the hell he was talking about, since we were both wearing clothes we'd had for years.

We then looked around and realized that girls who looked like they were definitely cheerleaders and the most popular girls at their schools were dressed just like us. To us, it was just how we were. I appreciate that story more now than I did then, because it was the realization of how different I was from the rest of society that spearheaded my desire to move across the country and attend a normal high school.

"Did I miss your session? And, why are you teary? It's just me." Willow flicked her eyes up, then back to mine, instructing me to look to the ceiling as she quickly ran her pinky under my eyes. I felt like she knew. She looked at me like she knew, but I wasn't about to spill it all over the studio.

"You didn't miss it. We recorded some earlier, but we're headed back in now. We have an audience. I'm just really happy to see you." I shrugged and put my arm around her as we walked toward Studio A.

"You didn't tell me you were coming!" I continued.

"Well, of course not. I wanted it to be a surprise. I've been learning some sound engineer stuff, and Yardley has let me practice a bit with Celtic Summer. They're patient." She arched her eyebrow and smiled. It was rare to see Willow admit she was struggling at something. That was certainly a trait we shared.

"Regan didn't tell me either!" I whipped around and caught a glimpse of his face just as he turned for the stairs to Studio B. He smiled and winked as he disappeared.

"Brat," I mumbled under my breath.

"Uh, hi?" Bo called from behind. I'd completely forgotten that he was there, as I'd gotten wrapped up in Willow.

We giggled like the little girls we'd always been to each other.

"Sorry, hon." I cleared my throat.

"Willow," he nodded with a sparkling smile, "good to see you." They hugged briefly and I got goosebumps at how different things were from just over a year ago when I would have taken her out for looking at—let alone touching—Bo.

Bo and I entered the studio, and I noticed Beckett was in the control room again, which filled me with ease. Bo seemed relieved to have him back behind the controls as well as he nodded and waved to him through the glass. While each sound engineer technically had the same job, they each have a different ear and a specific relationship with each client. It was important for Grounded Sound that all of their engineers could work collaboratively on projects, maintaining the consistency of sound.

Willow gave me a quick peck on the cheek before she slipped into the control room and took her seat next to Beckett.

I took a look in the listening room and saw ten people aged eighteen to thirty. A well-crafted listening demographic, which highlighted the tactical marketing on Grounded Sound's website. There were a mix of genders and races, but one thing was common: they were all excited to see us. Smiles and waves and claps put a smile on my face as Bo and I settled onto our stools and placed our headphones over our heads.

Yardley entered the recording room and motioned for Beckett to turn on the mic she pointed to.

"Thank you all for coming," she spoke to the hipster and hippie group that was assembled. "You'll get to hear Bo and Ember perform one of the songs—of their choice—already recorded for the album, and one that they'll record live. At the end of the session, there will be a ten-minute break while Celtic Summer sets up, and then you'll listen to them. Anyone caught using their cell phones will be asked to leave. Let's all have a great afternoon of listening to hot, fresh music."

Yardley waved again to Beckett, who clicked her mic off for her. Then, she addressed us.

"Tom is our media guy. You might see him milling between the listening room and the recording room. There are cameras hardwired into the studios to cut down on bulk, but he'll just be checking the sound, and such, as you warm up. Take a few minutes to do that, and then start with that ballad you played earlier, "Crimson Minute." "

When she left, I turned to Bo and nodded to the listening room. We heard the click of our mics being turned on and I smiled into mine.

"Thank you all for being here. We're excited to share with you what we've been working on. "Crimson Minute" is a piece Bo and I worked on over the summer." I looked at Bo, encouraging him to speak.

"Thanks, love," he started. While we couldn't hear what was happening in the listening room, I could see the love-struck smiles on the faces of the women in the room. "It's been a pleasure recording this album with my wife, and we're ready to share some of it with you. It's kind of a peek into our relationship."

With that, the girls all nearly melted. Bo tried to hide his grin, but it was impossible. We counted together and took off with our love story, as told through music.

CHAPTER *Fourteen*

I didn't even think to pray...

Bo

EMBER AND I had the next day off. Regan, and the rest of his group were scheduled to work pretty late into the day in order to lay a few more tracks before we had another listening session. We spent the day touring around New York, and Ember made sure to purchase at least one "super cute" baby item for Josh and Monica at each store we entered. I cut her off at Dior. I don't know who he is, but babies don't need a $175 onesie.

Do they?

She refused to buy things for our baby, saying she didn't want to have to explain away a whole hoard of things, should anyone happen to come to our room and see everything. She acknowledged it was far-fetched, but she wasn't taking any chances on this secret.

We picked up some sushi at a trendy "must go to" place, and brought it back to the hotel. I never understood how vegetarians like Ember enjoyed sushi places—since she was the kind of vegetarian who didn't eat fish—but she said her

California rolls worked out since pregnant women weren't supposed to have sushi anyway.

"Today was so much fun!" Ember announced as she plunked onto the bed with her sushi and chopsticks. "Yesterday, too. It's great recording at the house—don't get me wrong. But, there was a hell of an energy at the studio, don't you think?"

I nodded as I sat next to her. "There was. It really felt like we were the real thing, didn't it?"

Ember agreed with a mouth full of California roll. "It was like...we're...*doing it.*"

While we'd recorded and performed with The Six, I knew what she meant. We were on our own, so to speak, and part of something that was growing fast.

"I hope Regan's band knocks out a bunch of songs today so we can all spend some time together tonight. I've missed him and Willow like crazy." Ember expertly manipulated her chopsticks as we devoured the high-priced—but worth it—sushi.

She was sexy even when she ate. Her mouth was at the center of my desire for her most of the time. The way she kissed, the way she sang, talked, and even ate. Her lips were perfectly pouty enough to make me want to kiss them, without overpowering her face.

The power in her face came from those eyes. She was tired, as evidenced by the greying circles beneath them. It had been a long few days...or weeks. But their color never dulled. I'd seen her angry, sad, happy, and loving, and the fierceness in the jade color was always enough to stop me in my tracks.

"What are you looking at? Bo? Hello?" Ember waved a soy-soaked chopstick in front of my face.

"Just you. You're incredible, you know that?" I bit my lip and returned to my avocado roll. My time with the counter-culture clan had broadened my palette considerably.

Ember sighed and stared at me for a few seconds. I always felt naked when she did that, like her eyes were giving her more information about me than any of her other senses combined could do. You have to be careful about women with great eyes. They always see more than you bargained for.

"Oh," she snapped out of her hypnotic trance on my face, "after the session today I noticed about three hundred emails from Tyler."

She jumped out of bed and dug her phone from her bag. Though I hadn't ever told her, I thoroughly appreciated that she never had her phone glued to her side. For as serious as she could sometimes be, at least she was always present.

"Sweet," I murmured through my last piece of sushi. "What's going on there?"

Ember's eyes widened as she handed me the phone. "The wall's down." Her tone was excited but guarded.

"I knew the wall was coming down, Em. You don't need to tiptoe around it. I'm just glad they did it before the snow fell."

"That's exactly what Tyler said. He said they wanted to get it down and closed in before the first snow. I wouldn't have ever considered that."

I shrugged. "Some things you've got to leave to the men."

Ember's face turned gravely serious as she snatched her phone back. "Did you just fucking say that?"

I burst into laughter. "Did you just really believe me?"

"You're such a shit!" Ember tossed her phone on the table next to the bed and tackled me backward until I was underneath her. "Not much of a quarterback, are you?"

"That's a sack!" I laughed as I rolled her underneath me. "Not fair! Where are my linemen?"

"Oh good," she giggled, "I was right. The quarterback *shouldn't* be tackled."

I shook my head and playfully bit her lip. "You better study up on football. You're going to parent a legacy one of these days."

"Who says he's going to play football?" Ember sat up on her elbows. "What if he wants to, I don't know, play the banjo and work for Greenpeace? And, what if *he* is a *she?*"

I kissed her on the tip of her nose. "He can do both. Wouldn't you say I'm a bit of a hybrid myself?" I ignored the thought of potentially fathering a girl. Girls terrified me.

"Only as much as I am," she challenged.

Suddenly she took a deep breath and her face paled as she drew her eyebrows in.

"What's wrong?" I backed up, sitting on my heels in front of her as she shifted to a seated position.

"Shit." She threw her hand over her mouth and sped to the bathroom where, a few seconds later, it was clear what was wrong.

I walked to the threshold of the bathroom as Ember crouched on her knees in front of the toilet. "You okay?"

"Get out!" she shrieked. "I'm not a pretty puker."

I rolled my eyes. "Ember, no one is a pr—"

"Out!" She pointed her finger toward the door as she heaved.

Walking from the room, I closed the door behind me and poured her a glass of bottled water. I sat on the edge of the bed and waited for the toilet to flush, signaling her return to the room. When she came out, her hair was tied back in a low ponytail, and her mascara was smudged across the apples of her cheeks.

"Here." I patted the space next to me on the bed. "Think you can stomach some water?"

Ember took a few deep breaths as she sat down and took the glass from me. "And here I thought I'd escaped the morning sickness."

"Ugh. I'm sorry, love." I walked to the bathroom and wet a washcloth, handing it to her as I sat back down.

"It's like as soon as I finished eating it, it came back up. Though trying to wrestle with you right after eating probably wasn't the best idea I've ever had..." Ember cautiously sipped the water and wiped under her eyes with the cool washcloth.

Within a few minutes, her color seemed to be returning. I leaned to the side and kissed her temple. "You're looking better."

"I think I'm done. That was a *lot* of sexy throw up," she grumbled as she lay back on the bed.

"How does your throat feel?"

"Fine, thank God. I'd hate to burn the hell out of it before our recording session tomorrow. Way to be business minded, love." She grinned as she draped her forearm over her face.

"No, no. That's not what I meant." I prepared to defend myself, when she cut in.

"I was being serious. Hey, if I happen to throw up again, like, in the studio or something, let's go with food poisoning, okay? I can't believe you saw me throw up. It's so gross!

Now I'm exhausted." Ember turned so she was facing me, and nuzzled her head into my shoulder.

I kissed the top of her head, suddenly feeling tired myself. "You're gorgeous. Always. Like our vows. In sickness and in heath, you're stunning."

"Mmm." I could hear the smile on her lips. "I like it when you use the word stunning. It's so vintage."

"Let's bring it back," I whispered as we fell asleep fully clothed and on top of the blankets. Our feet dangled off the side of the bed as we slept wrapped in each other's arms.

§

The next morning, Ember seemed better. She was a little slow getting dressed, but once she had some water in her, she was good to go.

We had a long day ahead at the studio and were scheduled to return to New Hampshire this evening. As I shaved in the bathroom mirror, I was half-wishing we'd taken the train to the city, so neither one of us had to drive home at the end of what was sure to be an exhausting day.

Grounded Sound was up and buzzing when we arrived at their offices at nine in the morning.

"Good morning," Brielle said through a painfully wide smile. "There is coffee and breakfast up in the conference room waiting for you."

"Thanks, Brielle." Ember took her badge. "I'm *starving*."

Ember jogged up the stairs and entered the conference room a few seconds ahead of me. By the time I crossed into the room, she was sitting down with a bagel and cream cheese, and a plate full of fruit.

"What?" Regan snarked as I walked in. "You don't feed her?"

I shook my head as I poured some coffee.

"Food poisoning," Ember said between bites of her bagel. "Then we both passed out wicked early."

"Ew, really?" Shaughn looked up from her lox. "From where?"

"Sushi," I said as my nose crinkled, remembering the barf-fest in our hotel yesterday.

Chris chuckled as he set his cup down. "That explains it, then. Sushi would make me puke, too."

Regan grimaced behind his cup of coffee. "That explains why neither of you answered when I called after our session."

We all sat around eating our breakfast and drinking coffee as we caught up on the day before. Celtic Summer made good progress, and did record two songs yesterday, clearing the way to record the last two in front of the listeners today.

As Ember inhaled her breakfast, she updated Regan on what was going on with our house, and he seemed to be genuinely interested. I was, too. But, frankly, I just wanted the whole project to be done. Dr. Bittman, my old therapist, would have cracked the whip at that statement, which is why I hadn't said anything to her. I knew she would tell me to "trust the process" as she always had.

Everything, including life, is a process we must surrender to in order to grow. If we were just thrust out on the other side of something, we'd know no more than when we went in. When the next challenge came along, we'd be less prepared than we were before.

Trust, breathe, trust, repeat. That was the mantra Dr. Bittman and I produced when I was grieving my parents' death. Grieving is the most sinister process to surrender to. There are stages, and each one takes the exact amount of time it takes to get through. You can't rush them any more than you can rush the sunrise. Such was the process of renovating the house. I wasn't stupid. I knew that this project was more than just about the structure of a house. So, I had to go through it. One nail at a time.

Regan's voice pulled me from the mental confines of my therapist's office. "After we get our album set, I want to come to Concord to visit you all. With Georgia, too, if that's okay."

I smiled. "What's the sense in that giant house if we don't fill it with family and friends? You're always my brother, got it?"

Regan's eyes locked onto mine, and I caught the shift of his Adam's apple as he swallowed. "Got it."

Beckett sauntered into the room with Willow just as the atmosphere started to suffocate me.

"All right, you magicians of sound," he grinned at his own joke, "today's going to be busier but more fun than yesterday. We're going to work the same viewer schedule as we did yesterday. You've each got two tracks to lay, and you'll be able to do it in front of a new group of listeners."

"Love it." Shaughn sipped her coffee and I couldn't tell if she was sarcastic or not.

Willow spoke up next. "Also, you'll be videotaped during the recording, but when you're done and the fans have gone home, we want all five of you in the studio together. We want you to jam together. Sing, play, talk, whatever. That will be filmed, too. The idea is to create a montage that presents you all as a family. You each have a different sound, which is evident, but when it comes time for the albums to drop and the tour tickets to go on sale, we want to sell the idea of a friendship experience. Drama is tired. Fans want to know they're watching a genuine experience."

"Well, that's what they'll get," Ember encouraged as she stood and kissed Regan on the top of the head.

"Great," Beckett said as he clapped his hands.

I had no idea why Willow and Beckett were doubling as PR, but I guessed that in this case it had to do with their close relationship with the members of both groups. Artists can be a cranky bunch of self-entitled whiners, so it's best to present new ideas in the easiest way possible.

"Hey," Ember whispered as she pulled me aside before we went into the studio.

"What?"

She looked to her left and right, seeming to make sure we were somewhat alone. "The videos from yesterday and today..."

"Yeah..."

"When we see them in a few months everyone will know I'm pregnant, but in those videos we'll be the only people who know there's kind of one extra person in the room." Embers eyes sparkled as she spoke.

I wrapped my arms around her and kissed her like my life depended on it. "I love you so much. Let's go finish this album, huh?"

Once we were settled in the studio, my hunch was proven correct. We were quickly introduced to the GS marketing team, and Yardley seemed relieved when we told her we were looking forward to the jam session this afternoon.

While Yardley had a sharp industry sense, and a hell of an ear, it was clear she was still shaky on reading people. Asking the five of us to spend an afternoon together goofing off in a studio was far from an imposition. We lived and loved music. We weren't attitudes manufactured to look and act like singers. We were musicians thrilled to be doing what we loved.

Ember and I worked easily through our set. Despite her sickness episode from the night before, she was clearly well rested. She glowed behind that mic, and we nailed both tracks, one of them without having to stop at all.

"You say you have to work at it," I whispered to her, even though I knew the mics were on, "but every day it becomes more clear just how natural you are. I love you."

"I love you, too. Congratulations on finishing the album." She winked and leaned in to kiss me.

"Congratulations to you, too." Before pulling all the way back, I kissed her cheek. I couldn't resist the blush she'd developed through the set, and her skin felt warm beneath my lips.

Ember looked more beautiful to me in that moment than all the other moments I'd had with her put together. I almost felt something inside of me break and float away. Something dead and useless I'd been carrying around for far too long. Hurt, pain, whatever. It was all gone as I focused on my wife and the baby inside of her.

"What's wrong? Your eyes are watering." Ember tilted her head and I watched a flash of fear whip through her eyes.

"Nothing bad. I promise. I just...I feel..." I couldn't finish my sentence. I stood, sliding my guitar to my back, and grabbed her hand, exiting the studio to where Regan and his band waited for their turn to record.

We smiled and waved at them, wishing them luck, before they closed the door behind them.

"Bo," Ember said in a whisper once we were alone. "What are you doing? You're freaking me out."

"I just wanted to be away from the microphones for a minute. I was feeling really overwhelmed in there. In a good way. I'm so proud of you. I'm so proud of *us*. I just...Jesus, I feel like I want to marry you again, right this second."

From down the hall, Willow's voice cut through my romantic mania. "I think one impulsive wedding is enough for all of us, don't you?"

"You're just jealous," Ember quipped.

"Maybe so," Willow replied as she wrapped her arm around Ember's waist. "But, seriously. No more weddings. You're just high from finishing your first project."

Willow turned to Ember, addressing her as if I wasn't there. "Jesus, Ember. Most guys accomplish something and they go out and get piss-faced drunk or buy a car. Not your husband. He wants to *marry you* again. It's just too much sometimes," she teased.

"It's just enough," Ember said quietly as she stepped away from Willow and walked into my arms. "Bo, I'd marry you every day."

It looked like she was going to say more, but her face contorted in an uncomfortable looking fashion.

"What is it?" I asked, holding her hips.

Ember covered her mouth. "I think I overdid it on my post-sushi-puke breakfast."

She turned and raced down the hallway to the bathroom, and Willow followed her.

A few minutes later, the sisters emerged with serious expressions.

"Everything okay?" I scanned both their faces.

Ember twisted her lips. "Well, Willow knows."

Willow flashed a sympathetic smile and spoke in a hushed tone. "Yes, and I support the waiting to tell everyone, but I'm glad you told me. You guys should get out of here and I can stick with the food poisoning story. Any more random throwing up will set off weird signals."

"I want to say bye to Regan—we barely got to see him." Ember's eyes began to fill with tears, and it was clear she was feeling worse than I'd thought.

I put my arm around her shoulders and led her down the hallway. "It's okay, love. He'll understand eventually."

Ember turned to Willow. "Don't tell my parents, okay?"

Even though the girls shared a biological dad, they agreed a year ago to keep calling their parents *their parents*.

"I won't, but you better. Your mom has a keen sense about things. She'll know from across the country, you know she will."

"You knew the second you saw me, didn't you?"

Willow nodded. "What can I say? We're sisters." She winked and pulled Ember into a tight hug. "I love you."

"I love you, too." Ember wiped some tears off her cheeks and smiled broadly.

We said goodbye to Willow, and I sent a few texts. One to Regan, Yardley, and to Tyler to let him know we'd be returning to Concord a bit earlier than planned.

§

Once we retrieved our things from the hotel and were on the road, Ember fell asleep rather quickly. I hated leaving New York without a proper goodbye to Regan and Yardley, but clearly Willow's instincts about getting Ember back home were right. She was exhausted, and I knew she hated keeping secrets.

We were almost all the way through Massachusetts when Ember started to stir. It looked like she was dreaming, the way her hips and shoulders shifted from side to side. After a minute or two, it seemed like it was a bad dream. I shot a sideways glance at her and noticed that she was wincing.

"Ember," I called, reaching my hand over and touching her shoulder. She was giving off an unnatural amount of heat. "Hey, sweetie, wake up."

I kept my attention on the road, while turning every couple of seconds to look at her. Suddenly, she sat up, leaving her seatback down, and clutched her stomach. "Shit!" she hissed, folding forward.

"What's wrong?" My pulse pounded through my neck as I began to panic.

She shook her head, breathing heavily. "I don't know. It hurts. Bad." Her words were coming out in constricted spurts as her face turned red. "Ow! I need to get to a hospital. Something's wrong."

I swerved into the right lane, not paying attention to a single car on the side of the road. Leaving my hand on her back, I navigated to the closest exit, reasoning that a hospital had to be relatively nearby since we were in a densely populated area.

"Oh, God!" Ember's pain turned into a wail as she looked down. "I'm bleeding."

"What?" I yelled, my head spinning as I tried to navigate the roads of a town I'd never been in. I looked across the car and saw Ember studying the bright red fingertips of her right hand. "Shit."

"Bo, hurry. I'm scared." Her voice shook as it took on the timbre of fear itself. "Call Willow. Please. Call my sister."

I tapped the home button on my cell phone and spoke to the computer-generated voice asked me what I wanted.

"Directions to the nearest hospital." Speaking clearly while freaking out is incredibly difficult.

The phone beeped and the voice spoke back. "Did you say 'directions to the nearest IHOP'?"

"No!" I shouted back, then tried my request again, finally getting the answer I needed.

I don't know how long it took us to get to the hospital, because everything was loud and blurry. I remember pulling up to the emergency room entrance, leaving the car running, and yelling for help as calm nurses kept their professional faces. They moved quickly, maintaining steady voices as they asked me several questions that I could answer in just a couple of words.

"Thirty. Pain started about twenty minutes ago. She's a little over ten weeks pregnant. Please help..."

Ember's pain seemed to get worse as she writhed on the bed in the emergency room. I held her hand as tightly as I could, trying to remind her that I was there, since I knew she couldn't possibly hear my voice over her cries.

I didn't even think to pray...

CHAPTER Fifteen

Heavy rain falling on the porch

Ember

A ND THEN IT was all over.

I knew I was miscarrying the baby the second I woke up in pain. It was the kind of pain that tugged at my intuition and there was no escaping it. I didn't want to tell Bo while he was driving, though. I just wanted to get to the hospital and have it all be over.

My mind was spinning. Just days ago we'd looked at the baby's picture—a picture that still sat in my bag in the car—and heard the heartbeat. I heard it. Then it was gone.

I'd never thought much about miscarriages since I'd never been pregnant, and, before Monica, didn't have any friends who'd had babies. But, at the beginning of my own, I thought I'd be in a lot of pain, bleed a lot, and then that would be it. It hadn't occurred to me that I'd be *delivering* the baby. Of course I would. It was in there and had to come out somehow. I felt it when it happened, and then an emptiness surged into me, taking the place my baby had once resided.

The nurses were so kind. One in particular, Greta, stayed by my side during the whole ordeal, and did my vital checks throughout the night. I was grateful to have one person in the hospital to count on for the first several hours I was there. She was delicate in asking me if I wanted to see the baby. She explained that Massachusetts was one of the few states that allowed parents to decide how to handle the *remains* of a miscarriage. The emphasis on "remains" was mine. There was no other word, really. That wasn't her fault.

I told her I didn't want to see it, that much I knew for sure. I looked to Bo, silently asking if *he* wanted to see it. He clenched his jaw and looked down as he shook his head.

Bo.

I knew how scared he must have been, because I couldn't control my reaction to the pain I was in. He gripped the hell out of my hand and had whispered in my ear that everything would be okay. I couldn't look at him when the doctor confirmed what was happening. I'd selfishly avoided seeing the brokenness in his eyes that I knew would be there. I'd seen it before, and didn't think it would be this soon that I'd see it again.

When my eyes opened the next morning, I looked over to find an ashen Bo sleeping in the chair against the window. We opted to stay overnight, at Greta's strong suggestion, because of the amount of blood I'd lost, and we still had to make a decision on the remains. Looking around, I searched for signs of Willow. Even though I was in a pain medication-induced haze for most of the night before, I was certain she'd shown up before I fell asleep.

I sat up slowly, not wanting to wake Bo. I needed a few minutes in my own head to see how I felt. I needed to think about everything that happened yesterday. It was startling how *un-pregnant* I felt. I knew that I'd gone through the miscarriage yesterday, but I didn't realize how quickly that feeling would leave me. I'd have savored it more if I'd known how fleeting it would be. Sure, I hadn't felt any movement yet, as the baby was still so tiny, but I'd felt pregnant. I'd felt like a mother.

The door to my room slowly moved, and Willow slinked through, first eyeing Bo before turning to me. It was then that I noticed her coat draped on the chair next to Bo. She'd likely been here all night. Her eyes were tired and swollen as she met my gaze.

Willow held two Styrofoam cups in her hand, with tags from teabags dangling over the sides. She tiptoed to the chair next to me and put on a delicate smile.

"Morning," she whispered. "They were going to bring you some of their tea, but I insisted that crap wouldn't do."

She handed me my cup, and upon inspection, I found my favorite tea—which happened to be hers as well. "I'm sorry I always teased you for bringing your own teabags everywhere. This is perfection." I inhaled the calming aroma before taking a sip.

Willow's hand cuffed my wrist as I set the cup on my lap, still holding it. She met my eyes and offered a slight shrug of her shoulders.

"I don't know what to say, either," I replied to her unspoken words.

"How are you feeling physically?"

"Still drugged, I think." I so rarely took medication, that whatever they'd given me last night was still soaking my system. "When did you get here?"

"Around nine. You were kind of in and out. I'm sorry it took so long for me to get here. I had to rent a car and all that *shit*." Willow was frustrated.

I shifted over on the bed, patting the space next to me. "Come. Sit."

"Really?"

I nodded. "Please."

Willow adjusted herself next to me, and I put my head on her shoulder. "Thank you for coming. I needed you."

She kissed the top of my head. "I needed you, too."

§

It's funny how you don't realize you fell asleep until you wake up. My eyes slowly peeled open, and I realized Willow wasn't in bed with me, but I saw that Bo was awake. Still in the chair he was in earlier, but now he was watching me while he rested his elbows on his knees.

"Hey," I whispered as I rubbed my eyes. "Where's Willow?"

Bo sat up. "She went to get some lunch. Sorry I missed you when you woke up earlier."

This was the first time we were talking since I'd lost the baby. Neither of us could look the other in the eye.

"The nurse and social worker came in while you were sleeping and asked again about the..." Bo trailed off, clenching his jaw.

"Cremation?" I choked out, clearing my throat to avoid crying. I wasn't ready to cry yet. Not here.

He simply nodded. "They left the paperwork."

I hadn't been able to think about anything else since the option was presented to me. It seemed wrong, deep in my heart, to leave the hospital without the baby.

"I think we should," I suggested softly.

"Okay." Bo's tone was soft, but businesslike as he scribbled his signature on a sheet of paper and handed it to me.

I wasn't about to ask him if he wanted to talk about it further. It was clear he didn't and, really, neither did I. I signed where I was supposed to, and Bo left the room with the paper in hand. When he returned, he sat in the chair next to my bed.

"Everything's all set. The funeral home will contact us when...it's ready. Will be a few weeks." He held my hand, but it didn't feel right. It felt like a stranger's hand.

"Bo," I whispered, feeling the words build that I'd planned to save for later, "I'm sorry."

He dropped his head and brought our intertwined hands to his forehead as he took a deep breath. "Don't, Em. Don't apologize. This wasn't your fault, okay?" He spoke to the floor, and I could tell by the rigid set of his shoulders that he was holding back tears.

"I know." I took a deep breath and held the tears back. "Can Willow come home with us?"

Bo looked up, studying my face. "What?"

"I need her." I couldn't have explained it if he'd asked me to, but he didn't. He simply nodded.

"Of course, love. Whatever you need." He kissed my knuckles and rose to his feet. "Are you hungry? I want to grab some lunch."

I took a minute to decide if the emptiness was hunger or loss. Finally, I nodded. "Yeah, I'd love some food. I don't care what."

Just as Bo exited the room, Willow entered. They mumbled a tired greeting to each other. When Willow sat, I updated her on our decision regarding the cremation.

She sighed in apparent relief. "I'm so glad you're doing that. I was hoping..."

"Why?"

"I think it will make it easier to grieve. You can decide what—if anything—you're going to do with the ashes when you're ready. I'm proud of you." She leaned forward and kissed my forehead. Willow and I hadn't shown this much affection toward each other since I moved away in high school. It was exactly what I needed.

"You didn't call my parents, did you?" I winced at the thought.

Willow winced back, and I groaned.

"I'm sorry," she said. "It was a bit of an emergency. Once I got here and talked with Bo, we called them together. I'm surprised Bo didn't tell you..."

"We didn't talk much." I bit my lip and looked down. "I did ask him if you could come home with us."

Willow scrunched her eyebrows. "What?"

"I know you're busy and you have a job, but I need...I just need you for a few days. I don't know. I'm sur—"

Willow interrupted me. "Of course I'll come with you. I'll make some calls and rearrange my schedule."

"How'd you get out of the stuff at Grounded Sound yesterday?" I realized it would be weird for Willow to have to take off on a business trip.

She shrugged. "I told them there was a family emergency."

I stared at Willow as realization sank in. "Who knows about this?" I asked flatly.

Willow didn't hesitate in her answer. "Yardley and Regan. I didn't think before I said "family emergency," and Regan wouldn't let me off the hook. I spoke briefly with Yardley and let her know what was happening, and that one of us would get in touch with her in a couple of days. I wanted to make sure you had some space to get home and rest."

"Thanks for being my impromptu PR."

A few minutes later, Bo and a nurse entered the room at the same time. The kind nurse told me that I was welcome to shower at any time, and after I finished my lunch they would do my final vitals and process my paperwork to be discharged. Bo and I ate in silence, while Willow took care of some business on her laptop.

I knew what was coming after the shower. When it happened, though, it went smoothly. I held a tiny blanket in my hands. One the nurses had used to cover up our baby before taking pictures we hadn't asked for and sealing them in an envelope we didn't want. Well, didn't want *now*. Both Greta and Willow encouraged us to hang on to those things until we'd gotten through the bulk of the grief. Then we could choose to look at the pictures or not.

Not.

The grief was too thick to even know what a "bulk" of it would be. How long it would take. The blanket was soft, though, and I rubbed it between my thumb and forefinger as we drove.

Willow was following behind us in her rental car. I was given instructions to rest for the next few days, and then slowly return to normal activity.

I didn't know what normal even was anymore. Bo and I were dating, then suddenly we were married, then we had a recording contract, then I was pregnant, then I wasn't. There wasn't a single shred of "normal" as far back as I could remember.

"Is Tyler still at the house?" I asked after twenty minutes of silence on the highway.

Bo kept his eyes on the road. "He'll be back tomorrow, if that's okay with you. I told him what happened and asked him to go home and return tomorrow so we could have some down time. I'd have put the project on longer hold, but the snow…"

"No, it's good. It's okay." I put my hand on his leg. "The whole world doesn't have to stop."

I wanted it to, though. Badly. Even if just for a minute so I could find my bearings in this new world.

"Shit," I whispered.

"What?" Bo's voice was shaky.

"Monica…"

Bo swallowed hard. "I wasn't sure how you'd want to handle that so I haven't called her or Josh. I figured we'd wait till we got home."

Suddenly I was questioning how I was going to tell my still-pregnant best friend that I'd lost my baby. Just as quick, the thought entered my head that I didn't want to see her. I'd just send her the stuff I bought in New York.

My mind began to spin with the thousand tiny loose ends I'd have to tie up. In the meantime, I had to get home with the blanket of the baby that wasn't meant to be. The grief would come, and I wanted to prepare for it the best I could. It was like a freight train sounding its horn in the distance, and I was tied to the tracks.

§

It was too warm for a New Hampshire December. The whole drive back home I'd planned on asking Bo to build a fire in the fireplace in the living room and curling up on the couch in his arms. The further north we got, however, the harder it rained. It was a funny thing, the rain. It was so loud that I couldn't hear my thoughts, but each drop that hit the windshield took its time trickling down. But, I knew if I stuck my hand out of the window, it would feel like a million needles pricking my skin. It sounded hard, felt sharp, and looked beautiful. What a curious thing it must be to be a raindrop.

It was fifty-five-*fucking* degrees when we turned down the driveway. One thing I found to be grateful for was the rain; the sun would just have been mocking.

Bo put the car in park and exited, walking to my side and opening the door. I didn't always wait for him to open my door, but this time I did. We both needed it, I think. He put his arm around me and we hurried up the stairs to get out of the rain.

"Willow texted me a little while ago," I shouted above the rain. "She'll be here in about an hour. She pulled off for some food...probably to give us some time."

Bo nodded and unlocked the door. Stepping in was a bit jarring, because from the entryway we could see clearly that the wall had been taken down in the dining room. There was lots of thick construction plastic and plywood around, sealing the outside air outside where it belonged. It was a bigger hole than I thought it would be.

"Did you want to rest upstairs?" Bo went to take my hand, but paused when his fingers touched the tiny, soft reminder it held.

I shifted the blanket to my other hand and grasped his. "If it's all right with you, I think I want to sit outside for a few minutes."

The walls of the house felt just confining enough for me to crave the swing on the covered front porch.

Once again he nodded, the emotion of his eyes indecisive. "I'll bring in our bags from the car. Do you need anything? Tea?"

I wrapped my arms around myself even though it wasn't cold in the house. "Tea would be great. Whatever's in the cabinet. I don't care." I forced the corners of my mouth to twitch upward as I turned and headed for the door.

As I sat down on the swing, letting the momentum of my body carry me back and forth a few times before stilling, I watched the rain again. It was so heavy that it looked like waves were crashing through thin air. There was too much sensory input, so I closed my eyes.

For a few moments, I listened. Not only could I hear the wind and the sound of a million raindrops hitting the ground, but I could hear the slower ones, too. The drip-drop that splashed water onto my left elbow from the gutter that needed to be fixed. The rippling of water over the stones by the front stairs...

Slowly, I let my eyes open as I took three deep breaths. My eyes focused on the railing a few feet in front of me. It seemed as though the rain morphed into slow motion as I watched individual drops cling to the top beam of the porch before free-falling to that railing and splattering into ten new droplets of frigid water.

I knew I was clinging.

And I was ready to splatter.

As the long-awaited sob choked my throat, I clutched the tiny yellow blanket in my left hand and I ran. I didn't care about slipping on the repair-ready front stairs, and I sure as hell didn't care that I wasn't wearing a coat. Bo's head was buried in the trunk of the car as he dug around for our things. I splashed through an ankle deep puddle near the rear of the car, startling him.

"Ember!" he shouted. "What are you doing?"

I didn't answer, I just kept running. I shouldn't have been running. They told me to rest.

It hurts to run. It hurts to sit. It hurts to exist.

I knew I was still bleeding, and running would only make it worse, medically speaking. Emotionally, nothing was worse. I growled and screamed as I ran to the far corner of the property, where I found the giant willow tree.

Leaf-bare from a successful turning of the seasons, its branches hung in frightening patterns around the trunk. Skinless fingers all pointing in different directions. There was no hiding behind the lush green hug of Mother Nature.

Once I reached the base of the tree, where I'd fallen asleep more than once in more desirable weather, I collapsed to my knees, screaming unintelligible words and setting the tiny square of a blanket on a wet leaf. New Hampshire hadn't had a deep freeze yet, but the ground was painfully cold as I clawed at the dirt around the hundred-year-old roots.

"Ember!" Bo's voice was faint, but growing louder.

I had to get this done before he got here. He'd have an opinion, and probably one I didn't want.

I dug harder and faster, kicking dirt up into my eyes and mouth as I prayed for the ground to open up just enough. Once it looked like it was deep enough, even though I had no way of knowing what "enough" was, I picked up the blanket and pressed it into the cold, wet ground. I couldn't see anything. There was too much rain and far too many tears. My throat turned more raw with each scream I let out.

Before I let one handful of soil escape my hands to cover up the blanket, Bo raced to my side, throwing himself down on his knees next to me, and pulling my hands away from the dirt.

"What are you doing?" he cried as his raspy voice crackled through the rain.

As my eyes met his, I was pulled from my trance. My eyes fell to the sight of his hands wrapped around my dirt-smeared wrists, and I lost it.

"It's gone!" I screamed as I fell into his chest, sobbing with the force of hollowness threatening to swallow me whole. "Gone..." I trailed off into sobs once more.

Bo released my wrists and pulled me tighter into his chest, keeping one arm wrapped around me as his other hand stroked the back of my head. With my ear on his chest, I heard the scream brewing, and when he finally let it loose, it was the only sound all day that had cut through the rain. His chest shook with hard sobs as he rocked me side to side.

Once the shaking of his shoulders calmed, Bo rose to his feet. I felt him slide the rain-soaked blanket in his pocket as he slowly lifted me in his arms before making the long walk back to the house. I think the rain had stopped, but I can't be sure. Rainwater continued trailing from my hair down my neck, causing a surge of goosebumps over my skin with each drop.

Bo opened the door and kept moving up the stairs and all the way down to our bedroom, never once breaking his pace. I thought he was going to set me down on the bed, but he moved us into the bathroom, setting me down once we reached the tile floor.

"Can you stand for a minute?" His voice was shaking.

I nodded and he set me down. He pulled back the shower curtain and turned on the water, letting it run as he pulled my shirt over my head. Once it was off, I opened my eyes and met his. For the first time in twenty-four hours, we were staring at each other. It was almost too much to stare into the eyes that could have been mirrored in our baby. But I kept looking. For him, for us, and for my strength. I'd always found strength in his eyes, and now was no time to stop.

He brought his hands to my face and kissed me square on the mouth. Even his lips were trembling. I did the only thing I could do and kissed him back. I wrapped my hands around his neck and squeezed as hard as I could, needing to feel something other than emptiness.

"Thank you," I whispered. "I'll be out in a few minutes, okay?"

He pulled back his head slightly, looking down to make sure he was in my eye-line. "You sure?"

I nodded, leaning forward to give him a reassuring kiss on the jawline. I knew I was still bleeding some, and didn't want him to see it. It would be bad enough that I had to.

Bo kissed me once more and left the bathroom, leaving the door cracked behind him.

I finished undressing and stepped into the shower, where I turned the heat up as high as I could stand it. I wanted so badly to slink down the wall of the shower and sit in the tub, letting the scalding water pellet my skin. But, I stood.

For me.

Once I was under the covers and Bo had left the room, I stayed curled up on my side, and prayed.

"Hi," I whispered. "Um...we haven't really talked since the day Rae died. Sorry about that." I swallowed hard and clenched my eyes even tighter. "I don't really know who I'm talking to, honestly. Bo thinks you're one thing, and my parents say you're another. Either way, I just need you to be real. Please."

CHAPTER *Sixteen*

Job 3:26

Bo

EMBER FELL ASLEEP quickly after her shower. I'd met her in the bedroom with tea, a glass of water, and her prescribed pain meds. She took the pills and drank the tea before falling into a deep sleep before Willow even arrived.

Willow swooped in and ushered me from the bedroom and into the kitchen, where she made me a dinner that must have been from the co-op cookbook, because it had the flavor of all the meals Ember cooked.

"Just eat," she commanded as she fluttered around the kitchen, tidying up what little there was to tidy since we hadn't been home more than a few hours.

I never thought I'd see Willow flutter, or in any sort of caregiving role, but there I was, being taken care of by my wife's half-sister.

"What's with all the mud on the porch and entryway?" she asked as she sliced and diced vegetables, putting them in different containers and stashing them in the fridge.

I told Willow what I could remember from that horrific scene, though it came out in bursts. It was like my brain was already blocking it out.

"Where's the envelope of pictures and the little blanket?" She sat across from me with a steaming cup of tea.

"Shit," I grumbled, reaching into my pocket and letting the muddied square fall to the table.

"Calm down, it's okay. I'll clean it."

"No." I shook my head. "I should...right? I don't..." I sat with a heavy sigh. "I don't know what to do, Willow."

Willow rose with ethereal grace and floated over to me, setting her hand on my shoulder. "Sit," she commanded softly. "That's what you have to do. Then, when you've finished eating, go to bed."

"It's only six," I noted.

She cracked a small smile. "In emotional hours, it'll feel like it's perpetually two in the morning for a while."

I sat. She was right. I felt like I was in a drunken haze, but I hadn't had a drop to drink. Though, in that moment I would have killed for some of my dad's Scotch. I liked to savor that, though, since there wasn't much left, and if I drank anything now, savoring would be the last thing on my mind.

Willow cleared her plate and reached for the blanket.

"What are you doing?" I asked, stupidly.

"Cleaning it." She spoke softly with well-crafted sympathy.

I nodded, unable to swallow my food past the lump taking over my throat. As Willow stood at the counter, seeming to study the stains, I dropped the food from my hands and let my head fall to the table.

I tried to cry again, and I couldn't.

I replayed the scene of a feral-looking Ember clawing at the dirt in the rain, screaming in primal agony as she pressed the only blanket of our unborn child into the semi-frozen ground. It was like something out of a horror movie, and I could only see it in flashes—one movement and then the next—as if my heart wouldn't let me see it all at once.

I'd felt like a dad. For a few days I felt like a father, and had hope that I'd see the same glimmer my mom had in her eyes, or the dimple my dad had in his right cheek. For a split second of time, I thought maybe I'd feel the spirit of my sister as I held my newborn. Above all of that, I thought I'd rock to sleep in the middle of the night the human embodiment of my love for Ember, and hers for me.

That was all gone, now. And there was nothing I could do. There was no way I could have acted faster. There was no acting to be done on my part. I was just as helpless then as I'd been when Rae mounted that horse, or when my parents had left that restaurant.

Slowly, I rose from the table and trudged up the stairs. All I wanted to do was curl up with Ember and hug the pain away from her. I knew I couldn't, but I needed to try. *Maybe more for me than for her at this point.* It wasn't her fault I felt helpless.

I pushed the door open and found Ember in the same place she'd been when I left. Curled on her right side, her back was to me and her hair was tied in a loose bun on the top of her head. As she breathed, I watched the minuscule rise and fall of her shoulders. From this vantage point, you'd never know the living hell she'd been through in the last twenty-four hours.

I crept over to the bed and slid in fully clothed, not wanting to waste time undressing when I needed so badly to hold my wife. She didn't move an inch when I wrapped my arm around her—the pain pills were pretty strong, especially for someone who doesn't often take medication. For a few moments I got to listen to the wondrous sound of her breathing, thanking God that I had this woman in my life.

God.

As soon as the prayer of gratitude swirled through my mind, it was replaced by a gut-punching sense of anger and betrayal. I took several deep breaths, wanting to excuse those thoughts from my mind while I focused on holding a sleeping Ember.

Several minutes later, the rage was too much, and I felt like my skin was on fire. I tossed the blanket from me, careful not to disturb Ember, and I left the bedroom as quickly as I could, barely able to stand being in my own body.

Leaving the house, I stomped down the front steps. The rain hadn't let up yet, and I didn't know if it ever would.

"Hey," Willow called after me as I reached my car. "Where you off to?"

"Just have a few errands to run," I lied. "I figured I'd get them done before I crashed. Need anything while I'm out?"

I *hated* lying.

Willow looked up in thought. "No," she answered. "I'm good. I'll text you if I think of anything."

She closed the door and I got in my car and closed mine, driving away with only one destination in mind.

§

The temperature hadn't dropped below fifty all day, which I was thankful for as I ascended the stone steps of the church. With all of the water, it would have been an ice skating rink if it were much colder. Despite the anger coursing through my veins, I was glad that this church—the church that hosted the funerals of my parents and Rae—had an open door twenty-four hours a day.

Entering the expansive, marble-floored space, I walked to the flickering votives on the left. As a matter of habit, I lit one candle each for Rae and each of my parents. I was ready to walk away, and then I remembered one more candle I was now forced to light. The one for the baby we'd lost just yesterday.

As the flame ignited on the virgin wick, my back teeth ground into each other with so much force I thought they'd crack. I dropped the matchstick and walked slowly down the center aisle of the church.

I reached the altar and closed my eyes for a moment, listening intently for the sounds of people lingering around. I turned around and opened my eyes, scanning the back of the church once more.

Silence. Emptiness.

Turning back around, I faced the wall just to the left of the altar, where a large cross was hanging, lit from below.

"You," I sneered, pointing a shaky finger at the tattered wood. "You!" I shouted a second time, bouncing my voice off the marble that surrounded me. "Come and get me, you *coward*."

The echo of my words seemed to linger. I waited for some kind of response, but felt nothing. Nothing but spite.

"The loving arms of a father, my ass. It wasn't enough for you to orphan me. No, you couldn't stop at snatching my parents from me in the middle of the night. *Thief.* What? You didn't delight in killing my baby sister, either?" My skin heated as my breathing grew ragged. "Didn't get off enough on that, did you? I guess not. You are so cowardly in your hatred toward me that you thought nothing of stealing my first child. Why did you have to take Ember down with me on this one? Huh?"

I paced erratically across the front of the church, waving my hands as I spoke. I knew I wouldn't have all night to be alone in here. I didn't need all night anyway.

"Whatever grudge you have against me, Ember didn't deserve that. She didn't deserve whatever it is you're doling out to me." I took a deep breath, and with a broken cry I screamed, "What did I ever do to *you*? Have I not been kind enough? Loving enough? Charitable enough? Did I not praise you loud enough after you stole my whole family? Is that it? Should I have fallen to my knees in thanks?"

On my own command, I threw myself to my knees on the marble stairs, not even wincing at the pain as it shot through my body. "Thank you!" I screamed as sweat dripped down the back of my neck. "Thank you *so* much for murdering almost everyone I've ever loved." I bowed my head, breathing deeply, knowing that what I was doing was sin at its finest. And caring not one bit.

Slowly raising my head, I continued through gritted teeth. "Don't you dare touch her again, you spineless bastard, do you hear me? You leave Ember out of this. You have a problem with me? Take it out *on me!* I have no interest in playing the part of Job. If that's your plan for me, strike me dead right now." I threw my head back and stretched out my arms, still on my knees. "Do it! I beg you! Take me now and be done with me. I don't want to play anymore!"

After a few seconds of silence, I opened my eyes, once again eyeing the cross. "That's what I thought."

I rose to my feet, wincing at the agony searing through my joints. Feeling weak and drained, I trudged back down the hypocritical aisle, stopping only when I reached the back door. I turned once more to the altar, taking one final look.

"I have no peace, no quietness," I began quoting the Bible through thick tears. "I have no rest, but only turmoil."

As my mouth formed the last word, my tears dried, and a bitter emptiness crept through the place my soul once rejoiced. I put my hand on the cold handle, curling my lip as I spit on the floor in front of me.

"We're done here."

CHAPTER
Seventeen

One day at a time

Ember

THE NEXT FEW weeks went by slowly...if a whirlwind moved slowly. First, there was the bouquet of flowers sent from Grounded Sound, then the well-wishing cards and emails from our colleagues at both GS and DROP. Willow stayed for two weeks and helped manage the influx of mail and phone calls. The calls from my parents, though, I'd handled. They checked in almost daily, but this week it had moved to every other day.

Willow was able to do some work both in our studio, and from her computer, so she didn't miss out on work completely. Though, she insisted she wouldn't care if she had missed work. For the first several days, until I was back on my feet, Willow cooked and cleaned a lot. We didn't directly talk about the baby, except when she'd told me about cleaning the blanket I'd tried to bury. She'd placed it neatly on a shelf in the livingroom instructing me to just leave it alone for a while.

Then, there was yoga. Lots and *lots* of yoga. It was the easiest way for Willow and me to communicate without words, and it helped bring the tears and the healing I so desperately needed. I wasn't healed, but the practice helped.

Since my prayer the night I'd come home from the hospital, though, I was filled with a strangely serene peace that I couldn't describe—only feel. I'd felt, somehow, that if I continued putting one foot in front of the other, that everything would eventually settle back into place. I'd spent days upon days sifting through "Life after miscarriage" forums and reading about grief and loss. I finally decided I needed to trust the hope inside me, slowly mourn the loss of my baby, and accept that it was never meant to be, while looking toward the future.

Eventually, though, Willow *did* have to get back to California. Celtic Summer had finished recording their tracks, and she was vital for the production of their album. Also, she needed to get back to her life. We all did. The change in my relationship with Willow was massive. It had happened just below the surface, but it brought us to a level neither one of us could have anticipated. We didn't spend hours crying or braiding each other's hair, but spending day-to-day life with each other in the wake of what had seemed like a bottomless loss, had brought us to a place of reliance on each other.

I did cry when she left, but promised I'd come to California the first chance I got. She winked and said she'd likely see me in New York first, for album things.

On my first day without Willow, I anxiously awaited Tyler's arrival. The bones of the addition were up, and painting in the dining room was to begin. He was going to take me to a home improvement store to pick out hardware for the kitchen and cabinets, since we'd decided to reface them to match the flow of the dining room and sunroom.

"You're looking really good, Ember," Tyler said as we navigated down the highway to the store.

I smiled. "I'm feeling much better, truly. There aren't whole days where I'm sad right now, and fewer moments during the day."

"How's Bo?"

"I don't know. He seems fine, I guess."

"What do you mean?"

I sighed. "He's been great..."

"But..." Tyler filled in.

"Something seems a little off. Since the morning we got back from the hospital. I don't know, maybe it's my own paranoia? He's not really behaving any differently but something just... *feels* different." I didn't tell Tyler that I'd noticed a slight greying of Bo's eyes over the past couple of weeks, or that he *hadn't* really "been great" as I'd asserted. I felt lonely.

Tyler shrugged. "Grief manifests differently in people, right?"

"I don't know..." I looked out the window briefly, knowing I should be discussing this with my husband, and not the friend he had a weird history with. Still, Bo didn't seem to want to be processing anything other than how *I* was feeling, and barely that at all. "After Rae died he cried...a lot."

"Then what happened?"

"He kicked me out," I snorted as I said the words.

Tyler let out a loud laugh. "What?"

I took a few minutes to explain, through many eye rolls and some laughter, the sordid, bizarre summer Bo and I had back when we first met.

"So you were going to get back together that night, if Rae hadn't had her accident?" Tyler turned into the large parking lot and quickly found a place, being that it was a Tuesday morning.

I shrugged. "I'm not sure. I think that was the plan. Rae had told me to be there for the open mic night...all I can assume is he was going to woo me back with a song."

"You never asked?" Tyler's eyes widened.

"Honestly, I kind of forgot. And, by the time I remembered, I figured why look a gift horse in the mouth? If he was going to put a final end to things that night, I certainly didn't want to remind him of it."

Tyler shook his head. "Rae wouldn't have set you up for that."

"I know," I agreed. "I guess by the time the dust settled it didn't really matter what he'd intended. We were together. That was it." I exited the car, not fully admitting to Tyler that it took a while for me to let go of what it was Bo had intended for me that night.

"Your self-control is better than mine. I'd have wanted to know every detail. Play-by-play." Tyler linked arms with me as we walked into the store.

I arched my eyebrow in his direction, but thought better of asking my own burning questions of him. This morning's focus was drawer handles and cabinets. And that was it.

§

I'd been given no warning about the sheer amount of choices in the hardware store. None. After far too many hours than one should ever spend in a home improvement store, Tyler and I were back at the house, wandering through the living room.

"We can do color and furniture changes in here, if you want, but anything else would require thinking around the built-ins, or removing them."

"No," I snapped playfully. "The built-ins stay. I like this room the way it is."

Tyler nodded. "I agree. If I'm not mistaken, Spencer and Vivian worked on it before they died. They painted it, or something, and then Bo bought the furniture..." Tyler's eyes went somewhere else as he ran his hand along the oversized mantle.

"Uncle," I said flatly.

Tyler whipped his head around. "I'm sorry?"

I sat on the large chocolate-colored leather sofa and patted the cushion next to me. "Sit."

With a curious look on his face, Tyler sat carefully.

"Now," I continued softly, "I want to know what happened between you and Bo."

"Ember..." Tyler growled as he ran a hand through his hair.

"Please?" I begged. "I just...feel like I'm missing something with him. It's like he's here but he's not and, I don't know... maybe your story with him can help shed some light on what's going on here?"

Tyler bit the inside of his cheek. "I doubt it. Look, Ember. Neither Bo nor I look good there. Especially me."

I leaned my head on his shoulder, playfully batting my eyelashes. "Please? I already know the ending of the story. You two are speaking and you're working on this huge project."

"Okay," Tyler finally conceded. "But when I tell you this story I need you to keep your head on my shoulder."

"Why?" I questioned.

"I can't watch your face," he said bluntly. "And if you pull away it'll just remind me of the worst of it."

"I won't move," I promised, my heart beating rapidly.

I heard Tyler swallow and my head rose under his large breath.

"You know the first part of our story. Where Bo was the hero that saved my skin with the football team and stood up for what was right..."

I nodded.

"As I also told you before, Bo went to UNH and I was at Pratt. We talked as often as we could, but you know how it goes when you get to college. I was hanging out with a lot of my design friends, and he was in a CEO's paradise. It got to the point where we just knew we were friends, but didn't spend a lot of time talking with each other, and even less time together when we were both home on breaks."

"Okay..." There hadn't been anything in his tone to suggest the ominous turn the conversation was about to take.

"Early on in college I got hooked on drugs," he blurted out.

"Wow," I answered, fighting the urge to lift my head and look in his eyes. It was unnatural for me not to make eye contact with people while they were talking.

Tyler cleared his throat. "At first I experimented with anything I could get my hands on. Nothing really *took* except for the pills. It was perfect, really, one pill to wake me up, and another to make me sleep. I was on that cycle for weeks. When I came home for one Thanksgiving break, there was a killer party at a high school friend's house. Rich kid like Bo and me...huge house. I'd planned to make some serious cash from pills I'd bought in the city. I knew kids in town didn't have the same access to these pills as I did, so they'd pay whatever I charged them."

"Jesus," I mumbled under my breath.

"Yeah." He sighed. "Anyway, I knew Bo wasn't going to be there. He'd already told me that he didn't approve of what I was doing to myself."

"How'd he know?"

Tyler shrugged. "My attitude when we talked, behavior... he's wicked perceptive, you know."

"Yeah," I chuckled. "I know."

"Anyway, by the time the party got really underway, and I was high as hell, a group of high school kids showed up."

A knot began to form in the pit of my stomach at his words.

"They weren't invited, of course," he continued. "But, in a town like this, word gets around fast. Before I knew it, I saw Rae Cavanaugh drinking with her friends in the living room."

I swallowed hard as my chin began to quiver. I knew pieces of this story, but not from this angle. Not from this character. I wasn't sure I wanted to know.

"You sold her drugs?" I whispered.

Tyler sighed. "I knew it was wrong. This was my old friend's little sister. I didn't sell her pills that night. But...she got them somehow. I think by then she'd already been dabbling in the scene."

"So how..." I started, not knowing how to finish.

Tyler picked up where my invisible question left off.

"By the time I came home a month later for winter break, she was a full-blown addict, and so was I. The next party I ran into her it went way beyond me selling her anything."

I wrapped my arm through Tyler's, squeezing slightly to give him the best hug I could from this situation. "Beyond?"

"That whole break we did drugs together every couple of days. Drinking, swallowing pills...sometimes snorting them..." Tyler cleared his throat as his voice cut off.

"God..." My stomach churned with the thickest nausea I'd felt in a long time.

"So," he sighed, "I went back to school. She kept partying and got really sick. Had to go to rehab...I'm sure you know all of her side of the story from there."

I nodded, unable to find anything useful to say.

Tyler cleared his throat again, straightening his shoulders as he talked. "When she was in rehab, she opened up to Bo, talking about all the times and ways she got drugs. My name came up more than once in her recent history."

After a brief pause, Tyler nudged me forward. "You can sit up now. I kind of *need* to look at someone for this part."

"K," I sat up and found Tyler sitting with a tight-set jaw and wet eyes. "What'd Bo do?"

Tyler looked me square in the eyes. "He tracked me down in my dorm room at Pratt and kicked the shit out of me." His tone was flat and chilling, the way it had been when he talked about how Bo had reacted when their friends bullied Tyler.

"Like...bad?" I knew I sounded like a child, but I couldn't believe what I was hearing on a number of levels.

Tyler nodded. "Not enough to put me in the hospital, but enough to make it clear that we were done. He called me a worthless human being...the scum of the earth. He said he would have let the football team do what they'd wanted to with me in high school if he'd known I was going to nearly kill his little sister." Tyler exhaled roughly, puffing out his cheeks.

"She'd already done drugs though, before she met you. I know that doesn't make it better, but...it's..." I shook my head, trying to make sense of this situation.

Tyler shook his head. "You don't sell drugs with your best friend's little sister. You just...don't."

"Wait," I questioned. "Bo has always been very open with me about Rae's addiction. Talking to me about the disease, and everything. You were an addict, too."

Tyler sat forward, resting his elbows on his knees. "It's hard to see clearly when you're scared. Also, he didn't always view addiction as the disease it is. That didn't happen until he was knee-deep in founding DROP. When his parents died, I tried to connect with him. I was already up to my neck in twelve-step programs, and was trying to reach out. Though I was all the way back at step four and was trying to smack him over the head with step nine." Tyler chuckled. "I wasn't ready to be reaching out to him, and he certainly wasn't ready to hear me."

I smiled and gripped Tyler's hand. I wasn't as well-versed in addiction as I probably needed to be for someone married to the director of an anti-drug program, but I knew the basics.

I took a deep breath and looked around. "So how did you two finally end up...here?"

"God," Tyler said matter-of-factly. "We both went through a lot of healing and contemplation and received a healthy dose of forgiveness and grace. It all sort of happened at once. We were both in therapy and I was further along in my step work by then, but we just started talking again. And, I had a chance to make my amends with Rae as well, which was wicked important to me."

I sat back, feeling out of breath. "Just like that?"

Tyler twisted his lips. "Hardly. It took years. Like I said, we were both in *lots* of therapy. I still am. I think I'll always need to be, but I just focus on today, really."

"Do you still go to meetings?" I questioned, not sure if that was something I should be prodding into.

He nodded. "At least three a week, more if I can work it into my schedule. Being healthy, for me, means working at it every single day. I can't ride on a chunk of therapy I received five years ago. I'd have depleted that account my first day out on my own."

Suddenly my face felt flush.

Tyler put his hand on my shoulder. "Are you okay?"

"Yeah. That was just...a lot of information. I..." My eyes began to water with tears that, for the first time in weeks, had nothing to do with my miscarriage.

"Ember, what is it?" Tyler spoke softly.

His gentle tone speared me in the chest, and I let a few tears fall.

"Bo mentioned to me that he was going to make an appointment with Dr. Bittman. But, that was the day I told him I was pregnant, and then we went to the OB appointment instead, and then...the miscarriage...I don't know if he's been to her, and I..." I covered my mouth with my hand.

"Has he gone back?" Tyler sounded practical in his questioning.

I shrugged.

"Have you gotten any therapy yet? I don't really know the... rules there."

I sniffed. "I talked with the social worker in the hospital, but when my sister was here we worked through a lot of things and she gave me some good yoga and meditation exercises for healing."

Tyler smiled. "I still can't believe Willow is your sister! Talk about the genetic lottery you two won, huh?"

I laughed, grateful for the lift in tone. "You couldn't stop staring at her. You're gay, Tyler!"

"And, again, *Ember*, I'm not blind. I'm a designer, for Christ's sake. I know beauty when I see it. I've asked her to model for me. Just to have a strikingly beautiful woman in my stellar design portfolio."

I grinned. "She told me. She's gonna do it, I think."

"Yes!" Tyler lifted his fists in the air. "All right, Ms. November Blue, it's time for me to hit the road. My other clients are about to get jealous."

I stood and walked with him to the front door. "One of these days we need to sit around with a huge bottle of wine—oh," I corrected myself, "sorry."

Tyler laughed. "It's all right. The way I see it is, we're all born with a certain number of drinks, and I've already had all mine. I'd love to sit with you while you show a bottle of wine who's boss, though. Something tells me that'd be a trip." He winked and slid on his coat.

"Great," I grumbled. "How about I get drunk and tell you my feelings about Ainsley Worthington in a series of interpretive dances?"

Tyler laughed loudly, throwing his head back in carefree joy. "I can't wait. That tightly wound music-box doll has always had a serious boner for Bo."

I arched my eyebrow. "No shit, right? Like, get over it, Lady!"

Tyler leaned in and kissed my forehead. "Thanks for listening. Look, I didn't tell you all of that for Bo's benefit. It was for mine. I don't want to live a life of secrets and shame anymore."

I kissed his chin. "I know. Thank you. See you tomorrow."

Tyler left, and Bo would still be at work for a few more hours. While my soul thrived in the healing minutes of alone time, I was excited when Monica's knock on the door interrupted my gaze out the kitchen window.

I flung the door open and squealed. "Hey you!"

Monica bounced into the house and threw her arms around my neck. "Hey, gorgeous! I've missed you."

Monica and I had only seen each other once since my miscarriage a few weeks ago. She came up for the afternoon after I'd been home for a few days. She curled up in bed with me and cried on the same pillow that held my tears. We comforted each other in those precious few hours. I told her, and meant it with every fiber of my being, that I wanted to be as involved with her pregnancy as I would have if I'd never been pregnant or if I still was.

"Did I miss Tyler again?" She pouted as she walked into the living room.

"Sorry," I pouted back, "we spent far too many hours picking out drawer pulls and handles today."

Monica turned in a circle in the middle of the expansive room. "Where the hell is your Christmas tree?"

"My wha—oh shit! Seriously?" I threw my head back and pulled my phone out of my pocket to check the calendar. Sure enough, Christmas was a week away and the Cavanaugh residence was sans Yuletide decorations.

Monica sighed. "Ember. I didn't spend four years at Princeton coaching you on the societal norms of this holiday to have you throw it all away your first year in this gigantic house that *aches* for festive attention."

I never celebrated Christmas as a child. I knew it existed, of course, but it wasn't on my radar. Sure, I'd been familiar with the customs, as most people are, but every year it seemed to sneak up and wiz past me much like Groundhog's Day does. Moreover, even though the houses and shops around Concord had been well lit since before Thanksgiving, the minor stumble into depression I'd taken warped my sense of time. Now that I was climbing out of the hole, I needed to get my act together.

"Shit," I grumbled. "Help me."

Monica shook her head. "I figured as much, that's why I brought Josh's truck. I was going to help you get a tree, since I was certain you hadn't bothered, but looking at this ceiling...I think we're gonna need a bigger truck."

"I wonder why Bo hasn't mentioned it," I said passively as I stared at the space in front of the oversized picture window that would be the perfect frame for a tree.

"Well," Monica encouraged, "DROP has that gi-*normous* end-of-the-year gala coming up in two weeks. I'm sure he's just wrapped up."

I swallowed hard. "He hasn't mentioned *that* either."

Monica shrugged. "Maybe he doesn't want to bring his work home?"

I narrowed my eyes at Monica, and she sighed as she sat on a nearby chair. "How much have you guys been talking about the miscarriage?" she asked.

"None," I admitted.

"None?" Monica's eyes bugged out.

"We did a little bit that first week, but then it was like a switch with him and he was back to business as usual. I figured he'd maybe started seeing Dr. Bittman, like he'd wanted to before he found out I was pregnant, but now that you reminded me about that damn gala, I know for sure he hasn't had time to squeeze in an appointment." I spun through our interactions over the last few weeks. They'd been standard. Always loving, but nothing of any significance to note. Good or bad.

Monica twisted her lips. "Is he checking in with you?"

"Yeah, but, I mean…shit. I've been doing all of that yoga and meditation stuff that Willow and I worked on, and…I don't know, do you think maybe he feels like I'm pushing him away because *I'm* not the one talking about it?" My eyes flickered up to the small, loud blanket resting on one of the bookshelves behind Monica.

"Maybe," Monica agreed. "It's not like either of you to not be talking about something…ad nauseam," she added with sarcasm.

"Ugh," I groaned and plunked next to her.

I'd spent so much time working on myself with Willow, and in hour-long phone calls with my mom, and even talking with Tyler, that I'd failed in working on the loss with Bo. It wasn't intentional, by any means. And, as I'd told Monica, he *had* seemed to be taking it really well. It just...didn't occur to me. And I felt awful about it.

Monica perked up. "Well, let's go get that tree. We can stalk Tyler down and have him come help us string the lights on it really quickly, since it'll be a monster tree. When Bo gets home tonight you can kind of give him the tree as a gift, and that'll open up the lines a bit?"

I smiled. "Brilliant! I'll text Tyler and ask him where the giant trees are, and see when he can meet us."

As Monica and I drove to the outskirts of Concord, I was filled with fresh hope at falling back in step with my husband once again.

CHAPTER *Eighteen*

Asshole

Bo

"MAN, IT'S BEEN a hell of a couple of weeks. The team's done an excellent job, though." David Bryson sat on the stool next to me at McCarthy's as we relaxed after a killer week.

I nodded as I sipped from my pint. "You're not kidding. I almost forgot how much day-to-day work went into the gala. Remind me to give everyone a huge gift at the end of the year to make up for the one I wasn't home for last year."

He chuckled and sipped his own drink before eyeing me seriously. "It's been an even rougher few weeks for you, though. How are you holding up? How's Ember?"

"She's tough as hell, David. You know that." I tried to make light of the situation I didn't want to think about.

David shook his head in the frustrated way my dad used to when I'd said something outlandish. "She is, but she's also one of the most human people I've ever met, too. So are you, for that matter…" He trailed off and raised his eyebrows the way my dad did when he was waiting for a more substantial answer than the one I'd given him.

"What do you want me to say, David?" I ran my tongue across the front of my teeth and looked down at the bar.

David put a firm hand on my shoulder. "I want you to tell me that you're taking care of her *and* that you're taking care of yourself."

"That's all I've done for the last several years—take care of myself," I grumbled smugly.

"Son, I'm only going to say this once." David took a long pull of his beer. "Don't screw this up. This test you've been given. In sickness and in health? You're being called to the carpet on that right now. It doesn't just mean making sure your wife is okay. You need to make sure you're healthy enough to be the man she deserves. Someone she can count on."

I swallowed hard, finding it hard to meet his eyes. "I get it," I murmured.

"Good." David slid off his stool and patted me on the back. "See you tomorrow."

Once he left, I took a deep breath and reveled in being alone at the bar. There were several DROP employees that had come to the pub after we closed up for the day, but most were sitting at tables eating dinner.

The solitude was gratifying. Putting on the smiling face at work, only to have to plaster the same one on at home, was becoming a fulltime job in itself. The feeling of emptiness would go away, I'd reasoned to myself. I just had to push through. Fake it until I made it. After the rush of the holidays and the gala, it would be time to amp up promotion for the album and get ready for the tour. If I could make it until then, I knew I'd be okay.

"All alone?" Ainsley perched her petite self on the stool David had vacated.

I smirked. "Not anymore."

She put her tiny hand on my arm and laughed. The diamond from her oversized—and under-quality—engagement ring sparkled in the light. "You're so funny."

I raised my eyebrows for a fraction of a second. "I try."

"Seriously, though," she cooed. "How are you doing?"

If one more person asks me that...

I couldn't tell if she actually cared. I never could with Ainsley. Her motives were as murky as a bog.

"It's been tough, but we're getting through it." I was as honest as I felt would be safe with Ainsley.

She tilted her head to the side and cleared her throat. "And how is Ember?"

To be fair, all of DROP's employees were good to us immediately following the miscarriage. Ainsley included. They arranged for some food delivery, sent flowers, and managed my position for the few days I was out of the office. It's not like the miscarriage was a secret, but it also wasn't a secret to Ainsley that I rarely brought my personal life into work. Not since I'd gotten together with Ember, anyway.

"She's good, Ainsley. Thank you for asking." I was polite. Ainsley hadn't done anything wrong.

I know it's unwise to keep ex-girlfriends around for any length of time, but the fact was—Ainsley was stellar at her job. Sure we'd had that one snafu back during my break-up with Ember, but after that things went back to business-only.

"Well," Ainsley said with a bored tone in her voice. "I'm going to get on my way. Preston is waiting for me at *Mast*."

Mast was a *very* swanky five-star dining experience that had opened in the past two years. Ainsley had found a true mate in Preston Kentfield—one who wanted to throw enough money around to make it look like they had more. I didn't envy that life one bit, and was suddenly filled with desperation to get home to my wife.

A woman on solid ground who didn't care one bit what was written on the bottom line of my portfolio.

I ordered one more pint before heading home though, because I didn't deserve her. Over the past year, and even more so since the miscarriage, Ember had settled into her own skin more than I'd ever thought was possible. Drawing on the strength of her childhood and her family—especially with her burgeoning relationship with Willow—each time Ember took a deep breath, it seemed like she breathed in more strength, and exhaled a million shards of weakness.

I teetered to the car, knowing I'd been letting her down. Pushing her away because I couldn't shoulder the challenges God had laid before me, while she seemed to be rising from them even stronger than before. I was supposed to take care of her, protect her, and love her with reckless abandon.

As I navigated the car carefully home, I feared I was failing on all accounts.

§

Pulling down the driveway, I had to adjust my eyes at the sight of a brightly lit Christmas tree in the front window.

Shit, one more thing I fucked up.

Sure, I'd been busy with the gala, but one thing Rae and I always demanded of each other after our parents died was that the house would be fully decorated all holiday season. It brought warmth and comfort. Seeing it in the window flooded my chest with love, and immediately following that was a surge of regret.

I parked the car and raced up the front stairs. I opened the door and turned right, and the sight of Ember standing in front of the white glowing lights took my breath away. It was like our wedding night, only more fulfilling. This time she *was* my wife. Standing in our house. Our *home.*

"Hey," I whispered. I was certain she'd heard me come in, but she looked so peaceful, I feared I'd startle her.

Ember turned slowly toward me, and I saw a glistening in her eyes that lurched my heart into my throat.

"Hi," she whispered back through a beautiful smile.

"You did this?" I gestured to the tree as I walked into the room and stood next to her.

She nodded. "Monica and Tyler helped, but, yeah."

"I'm sorry," I stammered as I put my arm around her waist, enjoying the view of the ten-foot tall tree. "Work...the gala."

Looking down at Ember, I watched her eyebrows scrunch in confusion. She lifted her chin and met me with a fierce gaze.

"You've been drinking."

I shrugged. "We went to McCarthy's after work. It's been a long couple of week—"

"Has it?" she snapped. "Has it been a long couple of *fucking* weeks? Did it ever occur to you that I might want to get out of the house, too?"

Her nostrils flared and I took a self-preserving step backward.

"I haven't told you that you couldn't...you have your own car..." I tilted my head trying to understand where this was going.

"Ever since we lost the baby you haven't taken me anywhere. We don't go out to dinner anymore, you don't ask me for lunch at your office..." She paused long enough to burst into tears. "And you didn't even tell me the details about the gala. I know I let you down, Bo. I'm *sorry*. I'm sorry I lost the baby!" Her face turned bright red as she shrieked and walked out the back of the room and into the kitchen.

"Ember!" I called after her. "What the hell?"

Entering the kitchen, I found her pouring a glass of wine. She closed her eyes, took a deep breath, and brought the glass to her lips.

"Yeah, *I've* been drinking." My mocking tone arched her eyebrow all on its own.

"Look at the counter, asshole. There's a glass here for you, too. Only, that was poured two *hours* ago when you were supposed to be home. No call. No show. That's your M.O. the past two weeks, isn't it?" Her eyes never left mine as she set her glass on the counter. She finally broke my gaze when she turned and walked through the dining room and headed for the stairs.

She'd never called me an asshole before. In my anger, I was scrolling through my brain in futility to remember if we'd ever sworn *at* each other...outside of any instances where Adrian Turner may have been present.

"Asshole?" I said more to myself than her as I ran to catch up with her on the stairs. "Did you call me an asshole?"

Ember whipped around mid-step. "Yes," she hissed. "I did. You're an asshole. All day I've felt like complete *shit* because I thought I'd been selfish over the last several weeks. Spending so much time with Willow and on the phone with—you know what? It doesn't matter. The point is I knew we were off-kilter, and I was trying to make it better. I thought I'd at least get a *fucking* tree since you don't seem to think I'm even worthy of having this tradition with you!" She gripped the railing and turned back for her ascent.

"Off-kilter? We've been fine! You've been working with Tyler and I've been at work. What the *fuck* do you want from me?" I shouted as she reached our bedroom door.

I was halfway down the hallway when I said that, and Ember turned on her heels and walked with rage-filled speed to meet me where I stood.

"What I *wanted* from you," she started in anger, "was to hold me. Cry with me. Scream—" Her voice cut off as it turned to sobs. "I wanted you to scream with me about our baby that we lost and to talk with me about what we might want to do with the ashes, Bo! I wanted you to walk through this with me! Instead, you go off on your merry way to work and pretend none of this ever happened!" She stood toe-to-toe with me and pushed me with all of her might, causing me to stagger back two or three steps.

Ember's sobs carried her back to the bedroom door. I met her there, grabbing her arm and spinning her around.

"Don't touch me!" She thrashed like a wild animal as she screamed.

"Calm down!" I shouted back.

"Fuck off!"

I dropped my hands, and with it, my tone. "Don't you *dare* tell me I'm walking around like *nothing happened*. You have *no idea* what's *happening* in my head."

Tears poured freely from her stiff eyes. "Because you won't talk to me. This is a partnership, and I'm the only one sitting at the table." She walked through the door and over to our bed, climbing onto it and moving to her side. "Get out."

I shook my head. "No. It's my house."

"*Our* house," she cracked mockingly.

I stood my ground just inside the door.

Ember's hands clenched around the perfectly white comforter. "Bo, I swear to God if you don't get out—"

"What?" I challenged. "Are you going to push me? Again?"

She slid off her side of the bed and walked around it until we were once again face-to-face. "No. But if you won't leave, I will." She spoke with unfaltering confidence.

I clenched my teeth and stepped to the side, gesturing my hand to the door.

Ember huffed. "You just love letting me go, don't you? I'm tired of the game, Bo."

"What fucking game?"

She held out her hands. "I thought we were soul mates. I thought we took *vows* to protect *us* from this shit. Where are you? Where'd you go? Is this how it is when shit gets rough? Bo Cavanaugh puts on a suit and a smile and drinks a quarter of his weight in beer?"

My breathing was still rough, but my tone was calmer. "The only one playing a game here is you. Threatening to leave? How is that virtue? How is that honoring and cherishing?"

"We lost our *baby*, Bo..." Her eyes filled with fresh tears that I could bear no longer.

"I know we lost the damn baby! I know! I want to stop talking about it. I do! I want to stop adding to the list of shit that I've lost." My voice cracked as a few tears slid down my cheeks.

"No," Ember demanded. "You don't get to start crying. Not now. Not after weeks of abandoning me." Her voice was scratchy from yelling, and shaking from the tears.

I meant to tell her I was sorry. That it wasn't her fault that she'd lost the baby. I wanted so badly to tell her that God was the one we should be mad at, not each other. Instead, I watched her walk out of the room and slowly down the hall. She reached the door to my old bedroom, and as she touched the handle, she addressed me while still staring at the door.

"In two weeks I'm going to the DROP gala with you. We'll play the part of the happy couple because I refuse to sit hidden in here anymore like I've done something wrong. Until then, I'm sleeping in here." Ember walked through the door and slammed it shut before I could respond.

Once I heard the click of the lock, I slammed our door and crashed onto the bed. Just then, my phone buzzed with a text. It was from Yardley, and sent to me and Ember in a group message.

Yardley: Hey guys! Just wanted to firm up with you that we're going to do some promo stuff in California mid-January. We'll do some still and video shots of you all performing in the sand, similar to the idea we did in the studio in NY. Pack your bags! You'll fly out January 12. I'll call you both after Christmas. Enjoy the holiday! Xo

Ember texted back almost immediately.

Ember: Sounds great, can't wait! Merry Christmas. :)

I took my phone and chucked it across the room.

"Great!" I shouted so loud I was afraid I damaged my vocal chords. At least I was pretty sure Ember heard me.

CHAPTER

Nineteen

Say something

Ember

1:00 AM.

IT WAS THE longest Bo and I hadn't spoken since we'd gotten back together. It was the only major fight we'd had as husband and wife.

And, I couldn't sleep.

I'd snapped. It came out of nowhere, and by the time I was several minutes into yelling, it was too late to do anything but see it through. I hadn't acknowledged the pressure I had been feeling inside, and when it broke free, I'd said things I didn't even realize I'd been resenting, but had to acknowledge.

Now it was one in the morning, and I was angry, sad, and ashamed. About everything. Christmas was next week, the gala the following week, then two weeks later we'd be flying to California to face our first PR firing squad. To sell a CD sung by two total different people. Ones who were on the same wavelength. Ones who wouldn't have ever said the things we'd said to each other.

I lay restless in Bo's old bedroom. I didn't even try to sleep. Tossing and turning, I fought the urge to race down the hallway to our bedroom. Would I yell? Would I apologize? I had no answers, so I stayed put.

I buried my face in my pillow and screamed and cried as loud as I could. My throat hurt, and I was thankful we'd already finished recording the album. This wasn't how it was supposed to go. Any of it. Bo and I were soul mates. Weren't we? I cried harder at the question that never should have swirled through my mind.

While I'd spent weeks working on my spiritual healing, there was an empty hole inside my heart from the connection Bo and I used to have. Until I'd lost our baby. I knew it wasn't my fault, but it kept me awake some nights knowing that I couldn't help the instant vacancy in Bo's eyes when the doctor confirmed the miscarriage.

During an intermission from the tears, there was a soft knock on the door.

"Ember?" Bo's voice was hoarse and raspy, but came out in a whisper. There was brokenness scraping away at his throat that stung my eyes.

I sniffed as I sat up, weighing if I should go to the door or make *him* go away. I couldn't trust my actions as evidenced by our heinous fight hours earlier. I didn't want to hurt him any further. And, I didn't want to hurt *us* any more, if that was even possible.

"Em," he pleaded. "You're crying and I can't...just *please* open the door."

As I rose to my feet, I wiped under my eyes, feeling how swollen they were from the uppercuts of a thousand tears. I straightened my shoulders as I opened the door, but that did nothing to steel myself from the sight of him.

Bo's head leaned against the doorframe, and he was picking at his fingernails. When he looked up, my chest hurt at the sight of his tear-soaked cheeks and pained eyes. Everything about him looked grey. His eyes, the skin under them, and his frown. Drained to a level of lifelessness I hadn't seen since Rae died.

We stared at each other for three of the worst seconds of my life. Bo moved away from the doorframe and stuck out his hand. Instinctively I took one step back and turned my head. I couldn't bear his touch if it would feel anything like he looked.

"Can I come in?" he asked as he stuck his hand in his pocket.

I nodded and walked back to the bed, sitting gently and curling my hands around the edge of the mattress. Bo sat next to me, his leg brushing against my wrist and staying there. A churning pain in the center of my chest worked its way to my throat and up into my eyes as I looked to the floor.

Bo sighed heavily and put his hand on the center of my back, moving his thumb up and down a few centimeters at a time. I was frozen solid, knowing I was about to explode from the fuel of every emotion I was feeling, and I didn't think I'd survive it.

"Hey," he whispered because I think that's all the voice he had left.

I looked to the floor and shook my head. My tongue was swollen with sorrow and anger.

"Em," he continued. "Say something."

The urgent insistence in his voice broke the dam in me. As I exhaled, tears fell from my eyes and landed between my feet on the hardwood floor. The garbled moan soon followed, and Bo whispered, "Jesus," as he wrapped his arm around my shoulders and pulled me to his chest.

"I..." I started to say *something* but I couldn't.

"Shh," Bo replied. "It's okay. Jesus, Ember, I'm so sorry."

"No!" I yelled over my cries as I pressed my face into his chest. "I'm sorry. I'm sorry I screamed at you, I'm sorry I pushed you, and I'm sorry I lost the—"

"Stop." Bo gripped my shoulders and urged me to sit up. "It's not your fault. It's not *anyone's* fault." His chin shook as he cried through the rest of his words. "It just *happened* and it's no one's fault, okay? I didn't even realize you thought it was your fault."

I wiped under my eyes, but I couldn't keep up with the tears. "That's because you wouldn't talk to me about it! I... you just wanted to get back to normal and didn't even..." I couldn't finish a single sentence. The tears made them want to come out all at once.

I took a deep breath and continued. "Maybe it's because I kept the pregnancy a secret from you for too long. Maybe I didn't want it bad enough." I hung my head and cried even harder.

"Ember, please," Bo begged. "Stop beating yourself up." He lifted my chin and looked me in the eyes.

"How am I supposed to feel? You dove right back into work and stay out drinking with your colleagues at least two nights a week."

Bo dropped his hand from my face and covered his mouth, taking a deep breath as he closed his eyes. When he opened them, he shook his head and shrugged. "I'm a total fuck-up. I'm sorry. This isn't—"

"How marriage is supposed to be," I cut in. "What's happening to us right now?" I lay back on the bed, curling up on my side because I was too tired to even sit.

Bo sniffed and cleared his throat. "Can I lay next to you?"

I nodded, and Bo curled his body against mine, wrapping his arm around my waist. Instinctively I took his hand, lacing my fingers through it, and gripped tightly. In the heavy silence of my open-ended question, our bodies clung to each other for dear life.

Bo kissed the top of my head and rested his chin there for a moment before he spoke. "I'd like us to see Dr. Bittman. Together, if that's okay with you."

"I'd like that," I responded as my tears slowed and my eyelids grew heavy.

"Ember?" Bo said after a few minutes of silence.

"Yeah?"

"Would it be okay if stay in here with you tonight?"

My heart broke at the tired hope in his voice.

"Please," I whispered. I didn't know what tomorrow would bring, but I needed the comfort of the man I knew was still inside his embrace.

Just as I drifted off into sleep, I heard Bo say, "I'm never letting you walk away again."

I prayed we were strong enough to hold up to that promise.

§

Dr. Kathryn Bittman was able to see us the next afternoon. Bo had told her some of the shit we'd been going through over the last few weeks and she granted us top billing in her emergency slot. I felt like a bit of an interloper in her office. I'd heard her name several times over the last couple of years, and I knew some of the most intimate things Bo had shared in these walls.

"November, it's a pleasure to meet you, finally." Dr. Bittman had a sweet smile as she shook my hand. She was younger than I had assumed she'd be.

As I did the math in my head, it seemed possible that Bo was one of her first patients when he came to her after his parents died. She certainly wasn't close to forty and I don't know if I could put her much over thirty-five. Her jet-black hair was cut into a severe reverse bob that I'm certain only a therapist could pull off. She had olive skin and dark almond-shaped eyes.

Instinctively I was uncomfortable, but had to make the split-second decision to get the hell over it if I was expecting her to help us.

"It's nice to meet you, too." I smiled back, my eyes still feeling swollen from the night before. I did my best to make myself look presentable, but I didn't put on makeup before the session. I figured I'd cry it off anyway, so I made sure my hair and clothing were nice to make up for the puffy disaster that was my face.

Dr. Bittman gestured for us to take a seat. I looked at our options. There was a rocking chair, two armchairs, and a couch. The rocking chair looked nice, but Bo went for the couch and motioned for me to sit next to him. I thought it would be in bad taste for me not to sit next to the husband with whom I was trying to mend a relationship, so, I took my seat and he took my hand.

Dr. Bittman sat in one of the armchairs across from us and crossed her legs, folding her hands in her lap. "Before we start, I do want to say how deeply sorry I am for your recent loss."

Bo's hand tightened over mine. I didn't look at him, but I smiled at her. "Thank you," I managed without falling apart.

"So," she continued. "Why don't the two of you try to give me a general idea of why you're here and what you think you need to accomplish?"

Dr. Bittman nodded her head, taking deep breaths in some parts, as Bo and I caught her up on the last year of our lives. Mainly the last couple of months—since those were causing the most upheaval at the moment.

We took turns telling the story—the story of us. I started with the way Bo proposed, he jumped in with details of our great adventures on tour, we told her about the weekend we were offered our contract, and she smiled. We were talking a hundred miles an hour as we flew through the exciting details.

I slowed down as we covered the pregnancy and miscarriage. Bo's thumb grazed back and forth across my knuckles as I choked up.

"I knew what was happening the second I felt the cramps. They were so painful." I bit my lip and looked down as I wiped away some tears.

"You knew?" Bo's thumb stopped moving. "Why didn't you say something?"

"It doesn't change anything, Bo. I wanted to be sure. And you were driving and I didn't want to scare you any more than you already were." I sighed as I faced the truth of my intentions. I looked at Bo as Dr. Bittman seemed to fade into the background. "I didn't want to be the one to say it."

Bo's eyes closed and he took a deep breath. I refocused my attention on the doctor and quickly told her about the weeks since we'd been home. I tried to stay away from attaching adjectives to all of my feelings since I knew she just wanted an overview. There would be plenty of time to delve into my feelings of abandonment. And helplessness.

"Okay," Dr. Bittman took a quick breath. "Before we discuss those things, can you tell me why it is you're here with me today? What do you hope to achieve?"

Bo shifted in his seat and let my hand go, wiping his sweaty palms on his pants.

"I don't want to lose her," he stated bluntly.

"And you're afraid that will happen because—?"

Bo cracked his knuckles, which I'd never once seen him do.

"I've been a complete asshole."

Hearing it spill from his lips filled me with regret that I'd said it to him at all.

"No, you haven't—" I started, but he cut me off.

"I've let you down," he insisted.

Dr. Bittman stopped us both. "Let's back up for just a second. We'll have time for that. Ember," she smiled softly at me, "why do you want to be here?"

I put my hand on Bo's leg and gripped his knee. "I don't want to lose *us*. I'm sure I could keep him forever, but if we're not communicating and loving each other like we should then there's no *us*. It would just be two people who tolerate each other until one of them dies."

She nodded. "And why do you feel your *togetherness* is in flux?"

"There's all this *stuff* about him emotionally that I don't know. Sure we haven't been together *that* long but we're so in synch most of the time. There's lots about the time in his life before his parents died that I don't know a whole lot about. It makes me feel like I don't have the full picture." I thought back to my conversations with Tyler, and immediately realized that I shouldn't have said anything. Because now Bo would know. That was followed by the realization that inside a therapist's office was exactly where we needed to be if I was nervous about telling him I knew.

Bo turned his head toward me. "What stuff?"

I shot a glance to Dr. Bittman, who nodded once. Carefully and slowly as if she were telling me to proceed as she prepared the emotional gurney for standby.

I cleared my throat. "Stuff. With Tyler."

"You told me about that," he asserted.

"Right," I agreed. "I was the one to tell you about that huge part of your high school history. You never did. Tyler had to. And then the stuff from college—" I stopped myself as Bo's eyes widened.

"He told you that?" Bo's voice raised a few decibels.

I nodded. "He only told me his side. It is his story too, you know."

"Damn it," Bo whispered under his breath.

Dr. Bittman put up her hand. "Am I to assume we're speaking about Tyler Madison?"

Bo nodded. "Ember met him several weeks ago. He's in charge of the remodel on the house."

Dr. Bittman's eyebrow lifted just a hair over the accepted level for a professional setting. "Why didn't you want Ember to hear this story, Bo?"

I couldn't tell if Dr. Bittman wasn't asking us for details because they weren't relevant or because she already knew them. I quickly decided by the looks on both their faces that it was both.

"Because," Bo huffed. "It's ancient history."

I held out my hands. "It's *your* history."

"Right," he snapped. "And I look like a self-righteous asshole with fists quicker than my brain! You were never meant to see that side of me, Ember. I never wanted you to know it existed."

"Sure," I rolled my eyes, "you didn't want me to know it existed until you were out drinking last night while I was home alone...again. Never mind that you grabbed me in the hallway."

Dr. Bittman's eyes widened.

Bo's jaw dropped. "You pushed me and then ran down the hallway!"

"Okay, okay, okay," Dr. Bittman cut in. "We need to slow way down again. What happened last night?"

Bo and I started to speak at the same time, but he conceded, sitting back and holding out his hand to let me tell my side. When I was through, Bo filled in his own details, from his day at work up until we got the text message from Yardley about our upcoming trip.

Dr. Bittman took an exaggerated breath before eyeing us both. "First rule from here on out, no touching each other in anger. Got it?" Her voice was sharp and terse. "What happened last night doesn't seem like a big deal, but it sounds like both of you have pretty hot tempers. When you add in a physical component, things can escalate quickly. Hands. Off." She eyed Bo as her nostrils flared.

"Sorry," I whispered.

"Me, too," Bo echoed back.

"Now," Dr. Bittman composed herself and offered a small smile, "each of you tell me in three words—no more or less—how you're feeling right now. Write them down on this paper. When you're done I want you to switch and read the other out loud."

About three *hundred* words flashed through my brain before I settled on the required number. I looked down and wrote the first three words that had come to mind: *abandoned, confused, scared.*

Bo folded his paper, handing it to me as I did the same with mine.

"Ember," Dr. Bittman started, "you can go first. Read Bo's feelings out loud."

I nodded and slowly unfolded the paper. My eyes watered as I read his words.

"What do they say?" the doctor encouraged.

I cleared my throat. "Scared, angry, and confused."

"Bo," she said, without processing my reaction.

Bo unfolded my paper and his eyebrows drew together as he read my words aloud. When he was through, he set the paper on his lap.

"Well," Dr. Bittman smiled, "it looks like we have a good place to start."

I reached for Bo's hand, and he reached for mine at the same time. We grinned when our hands collided in mid-air, and we settled them on the space between our legs.

"What I want the both of you to understand at the outset is that you're about to embark on a very public, very stressful life. Just because you live in New Hampshire won't absolve you from tabloid scrutiny or other gossipmongers. The entertainment industry requires thick skin." She eyed both of us, and we nodded in agreement. We both knew this, but hearing it from someone else felt a bit more ominous.

"Also," she continued, "while it's not uncommon for people in the entertainment industry to be married to each other, your circumstance is rather different. You two aren't just in the music industry, you're performing together. You're one act. The schedules are the same, the stresses are the same, and you're going to be dealing with the same pressures. There isn't a time when one of you will be busier or less busy than the other. The good news is when you have a break, you'll have it together, so long as you're performing together.

"What I'm going to help the two of you do over the course of the next few months is to get back on track, strengthen yourselves, and strengthen your bond. By the time your album releases and it's time for your tour, you don't just need to be on the same page, you need to be *together* in every aspect of the word. You need to be stronger than you even thought you were before all of this happened, because while the miscarriage was a devastating event, there will be other stresses that *feel* earth shattering. There will be rumors of discontent, accusations of affairs..."

Bo and I took a deep breath at the same time.

"Now," Dr. Bittman continued. "Let's talk about the confusion you feel, Bo, and the abandonment you feel, Ember. Who wants to go first?"

I nudged Bo. "I've been doing a lot of talking…you can go."

Dr. Bittman smiled. "Bo?" she encouraged.

"Well," Bo let go of my hand and leaned forward, clasping his hands in front of him, "I wrote confused because I really *was* confused about what I was feeling. When I read Ember's paper, though, it hit me. I feel abandoned, too."

I scrunched my eyebrows, a sinking feeling growing in my stomach as I contemplated the ways in which I may have abandoned him over the past few weeks.

"How do you feel abandoned?" Dr. Bittman asked.

Bo lowered his head into his hands and I watched his shoulders tighten. Tentatively I rested my hand in the center of his back. It was as hard as a rock.

"By God," he whispered.

Chills shot through my spine at the emptiness in his tone. The helpless way in which his voice seemed to collapse as he spoke.

"Go on," Dr. Bittman said.

Bo took a few deep breaths and sat back, wiping his hands against his jeans. "I'm angry with Him because I feel like I don't matter to him. I've lost almost everything and I've been faithful through it all. Ember's miscarriage was the last straw. The night we got home from the hospital I drove to the church when Ember was sleeping."

"You did?" I cut in quietly.

Bo nodded and then addressed me. "I stormed in and screamed at Him…God." His eyes filled with tears as he choked out the rest of his words. "I told him I was tired of playing his games…and that we were done. I was done. With Him."

My jaw swung open as I stared at Bo with wide eyes. "You've been different since that day, and I thought it was just from the miscarriage...I...you didn't tell me, Bo. Why didn't you tell me?" My cheeks burned as I waited for his answer.

"I'd failed in my relationship with God, Em." He shrugged. "I didn't want to fail with you, too. I thought if I stopped relying on God that I could make myself a better man. One that wasn't at His mercy."

"Ember," Dr. Bittman cut in, "you look shocked."

I turned toward her, my throat having run dry. "I'd never prayed in a church before the day that Rae died," I admitted. "Bo's faith through everything is something that I've always admired."

"It is?" he asked.

I nodded then continued. "I prayed, too, the night we got home the hospital. I talked to God about how certain you were about His existence. I wanted that. I felt okay when I fell asleep that night." I sniffled as my throat tightened. "I never felt God before that night. Ever. But I felt *something* around me as I slept that night...then the next day it felt like you were a stranger." I wiped under my eyes, feeling some of the confusion that Bo had written on his own paper earlier.

Dr. Bittman checked her clock. "This is a good place to stop for today. I want you two to go home and be gentle with each other. No yelling. If one of you wants to yell, get up, walk out of the room, and go scream in the pillow, another room, or the freezer for all I care. No yelling *at* each other. Let's meet again in ten days so we can get through Christmas, okay? Today, I want you to talk about the baby." She paused as she waited for it to sink in. "Talk about what you'd hoped and what you felt when it was taken away. Remember to use *I feel* statements, okay?"

"Okay," we answered in unison.

The drive home was as silent as the thick snowflakes falling around us. Heavy and cold, but somehow peaceful. As I watched the wind whip the snow into frozen circles above the sidewalks, I felt lost. I'd failed in my understanding of my husband. He'd had a major falling out with God and I hadn't had the faintest clue. Instead, I spent the following days taking it out on him and myself, thinking he was being cruel when, really, he was as lost as I felt.

"I'm sorry," Bo seemed to be answering my thoughts as he placed his hand on my leg, running his thumb over my knee.

Not wanting to tease out his apology in the car, I nodded and placed my hand over his.

"I am, too."

Now, the work was to begin. We had get back to a place of *us*. We had to be Bo and Ember again.

CHAPTER *Twenty*

Every time a bell rings...

Bo

WHEN EMBER AND I arrived home and I turned off the car, she remained still for a moment. The wind was howling outside as winter finally decided to make its appearance.

"How are you feeling?" I asked as I studied her profile. Through this entire ordeal, the color remained in her face... the life in her eyes. She was incredible, and I was undeservingly fortunate.

"Can you start a fire in the living room when we get inside?" she answered softly.

"Of course." I exited the car and walked to her side. She'd remained in her seat while I made the walk around the vehicle.

I knew she often felt uncomfortable about waiting for me to open the door, but I was grateful she let me do it. My father always did it for my mother, and I remember asking her in high school why she sat there and waited because it sometimes seemed to make her uncomfortable, too. My mother looked back at me and smiled. *"Because it means more to him than it does to me,"* she'd answered.

272

Once inside, Ember put a kettle of water on the stove and pulled tea down from the shelf above the sink.

"Tea or coffee?" she called as I started the fire.

"Tea's fine," I answered back as I adjusted the flue, thankful I'd had the foresight to have the chimney cleaned before we arrived back in New Hampshire.

Once the kettle whistled and the flames were taking hold, Ember appeared with two steaming mugs of herbal tea.

"Thank you." I took my mug and followed her to the couch, where she waited with a soft and oversized blanket.

I climbed under the cover with her and watched her face as her eyes fixated on the orange flames. I sat there for a moment in silence, appreciating the peace she brought to my life. Ember took a careful sip of her tea, and eyed me for a moment as a melancholy smile pulled at her lips. She rested her head on my shoulder, and in her next breath, she spoke.

"I'm sorry I didn't tell you about the pregnancy right away," she started. "I was freaked out, and I wanted to be sure because I didn't want to throw a monkey wrench into anything unless it was real."

I squeezed my arm around her waist. "I get it. It's okay."

"I feel like I cheated you out of...time, or something."

"Time?" I questioned.

She nodded. "Like, time with the baby, even though it was inside me. I kept it to myself longer than I should have."

"Oh, Ember," I sighed, "you had no way of knowing..."

"Still," she replied.

After another few minutes of silence, I gathered the guts to speak.

"I'm sorry I wasn't there for you. I was so *angry* with God, and I took your sister and parents for granted. I knew I was being a shit, but knew I wasn't leaving you with *no one* to talk to. I can't believe I wasn't there for you...I never meant for that to happen. Shit..." I rested my chin on her head.

"Bo," she sat up and set her mug down, facing me with pure intensity, "neither of us knew what was going to happen, but we were emotionally unprepared. We both went into our own corners to lick our own wounds when we should have been doing that together. I feel like you pushed me away, while I did the same to you by not demanding that you do something for me. I had no idea what to even ask for...or how to ask for it."

"Where do we go from here?" I asked, looking down.

"We need to talk about what Dr. Bittman said." Ember's voice shook as she continued. "I really did want that baby, you know. I felt like a mom." Her mouth formed a perfectly horrible frown as she looked down and let her tears fall freely.

"You looked like a mom," I admitted as my own tears took over. "It was the most beautiful I'd ever seen you, knowing you were carrying our baby inside of you."

Ember's head collapsed against my shoulder as she fell into heavy sobs. "I'm so sad, Bo."

I held her close and closed my eyes. "Me too, love. Me too."

She pulled back, wiping under her eyes. "And here I was clinging to this spiritual lifeguard you introduced me to, and at the same time you were, like, breaking up with it. Why didn't you tell me? Do you really believe all the things you yelled at him? God, I mean."

I felt like my nerves were going to claw their way through my skin. I'd never felt more watched in my life. And, not just by Ember in that moment.

"I just don't understand," I confessed as I rested my forehead on her shoulder. Her arms draped around me as her fingers clenched the fabric of my shirt. "Why? Just...why? My parents, Rae, our *baby*. I don't know how to make sense of it. Any of it." A low growl started deep in my soul and pushed its way out into a full yell as I screamed into Ember's shoulder. I yelled out until my voice cracked and the sobs took over.

"I don't know if there's a sensible reason for everything," Ember whispered as she rubbed my back. "But I know that I love you with every fiber of my being. More than that, I know that when I prayed to the same God you disowned, I felt hugged, Bo. I felt like someone put a bandage on my heart and told me it would be okay."

"I've felt like that before," I admitted as I sat up. "When my parents died. After Rae died, it was a little harder to get there. A few weeks ago...I just...I couldn't take it anymore. How much am I supposed to shoulder?"

Ember's eyes stayed on mine for a few moments, as she seemed to be weighing her answer. "As much as you're given," she stated definitively. "No matter where you and I are on what we believe and who we believe in, and all of that, I believe we are to take what we're given and go with it. All of those things happened, Bo, and wouldn't you say you got through them in much better shape with God than you would have without him?"

I nodded as more tears rolled down my face. "I said some really awful things in that church, Ember."

She shrugged. "I've said some really awful things to my parents...to you. But all of your love for me hasn't changed, has it? I called you an asshole last night, for God's sake. Did it make you love me less?"

I shook my head.

"And," she continued, "what I believe aside, don't *you* believe that God is like a father?"

I nodded again.

"Then," she sighed, "can we agree, for tonight at least, that you and God just kind of...had a fight?" She shrugged and looked at me with hopeful eyes and a comically twisted mouth.

I chuckled. "It was kind of a one-sided knock-down drag-out. I lost."

Ember shook her head. "You don't lose until you give up. Have you given up?"

I looked down and realized that the longing in my gut showed me I still had hope. Still had a need—a desire—to be taken care of beyond what I could do for myself. The couple weeks I tried to do it myself ended up with my wife and me in a disastrous mess on a therapist's couch.

"No," I answered. "I haven't given up."

Ember sighed, seemingly in relief, as she leaned against the arm of the couch and opened her arms, encouraging me to lay on her. It wasn't often that we took this position, but I realized in that moment that's exactly what I needed.

To just be held.

§

"God," Ember grumbled in frustration. "Only *you* could make yoga stressful. Relax, damn it!"

I broke into laughter as I bent forward, trying to touch the ground. "Is that how a yoga instructor talks?"

"What is with your shoulders?" She ignored my question as she stood to my side and pushed down on my shoulders. "Get them away from your ears. What the hell?" She broke into laughter.

"Come on, Ember! Help me!" I laughed some more, and it felt good.

It was Christmas Eve, and Ember and I had spent the past week doing exactly what Dr. Bittman had asked—being gentle with each other. After our night by the fire, where Ember had soulfully encouraged me to find my peace again, I promised her I'd try. Today, though, I asked her to show me hers.

I'd known for years that yoga was Ember's go-to therapy. Through our time in California, I'd gotten used to seeing her in every pose. Headstands in the sand as the sun rose were her favorite, though she told me I wasn't allowed to try that yet.

"Okay," she composed herself, "time to get serious." Ember closed her eyes, took a deep breath, splayed out her fingers, and exhaled. I swear I could see all of the wild energy leave through her fingertips.

"Wow," I whispered. I'd intended for it to be in my head, but it flew out of my mouth while I watched her physically relax.

"Now," she spoke quietly as she slowly opened her eyes, "let your arms hang by your side, palms forward, your feet hip-width apart. Good. Breathe in through your nose, filling your toes all the way up to your mouth. Then," Ember closed her eyes as she once more demonstrated her impeccable exhale, "let it all out."

I did as instructed, remembering to keep my shoulders away from my ears.

"Excellent." Ember's voice sounded like she was narrating a guided meditation. I'd buy that CD. "This is Tadasana. Mountain Pose."

"I'm doing a pose?" I said a little too excitedly.

Ember simply nodded, keeping the slightly drunken smile on her face. I knew this to be her "ohm" smile, and I wanted to wear the same one.

"Now just watch me once," she continued. "So you can see what I'm doing and the language I use. We're going to do a full sun salutation."

I nodded and simply watched and listened as my wife flowed through the most beautiful set of movements I'd ever seen.

Her voice never went above a meditative hum. "Urdhva Hastasana, Uttanasana, Ardha Uttanasana..." She got slightly quieter as she lowered herself to the ground in a pose that looked exponentially harder than a push-up, but her breath never changed.

The muscles in her arms and shoulders rippled beautifully beneath her skin as she flowed into what I knew was downward-facing dog, and back up through the reverse of the same movements until she was once again standing in "Mountain Pose."

Ember took a deep breath and opened her eyes. "Ending in Tadasana..."

"Jesus," was all I could say as I stared at her flushed cheeks and completely relaxed aura. It was the first time I could see an aura, and it was stunning as it blended with the lights from our Christmas tree. A soft glow that came from somewhere inside her bordered the edges of her body. When she smiled, it got brighter.

Ember drifted toward me. "Okay, you try. I'll explain what you should be doing as we go through it. Your job is to keep breathing deeply, okay?"

I nodded.

She tugged on my shirt. "You might want to take off your shirt."

"I'm not doing yoga for your pleasure," I teased. It had been a long time since we'd goofed off with each other, and it felt good.

Ember rolled her eyes. "Do you think I do yoga for *your* pleasure? Ever notice how tight my yoga clothes are?"

I grinned and wiggled my eyebrows.

She smacked my arm. "Pig. That's because I spend half my time upside down and don't want my clothes in my face."

Suddenly, yoga clothes made perfect sense beyond my visual gratification. I removed my shirt and Ember took a step back, visually assessing me.

I tossed my shirt at her. "Liking what you see?"

"Mm-hmm. Now, take a deep breath, and listen to my words."

Within seconds, our playful banter was transformed as Ember's voice dropped half an octave lower.

She took exaggerated breaths to remind me when I was supposed to breathe.

"Now," she hummed, "Ashtanga Namaskara and flow to Urdhva Mukha Svanasana..."

I opened my eyes to find Ember demonstrating that push-up like position. I moved overconfidently into that position. Once I was in it, my triceps were screaming.

"God!" I grunted. "What kind of demonic push-up is this?"

Ember ignored my cries for mercy. "Stop holding your breath. Move right into Adho Mukha Svanasana."

I was breathless. "That's downward dog, right?"

Ember chuckled. "Right."

"Yes, I got one!" I exhaled and moaned in ecstasy once the burning in my arms ceased.

Ember guided me calmly through the rest of the sequence, until once again I was standing in Mountain Pose, feeling rather victorious.

"Take three deep breaths before opening your eyes." Ember slipped into the exaggerated breathing that sounded like the ocean waves.

"What's that kind of breathing called again?" I asked as I took my last required breath.

"Ujjayi. That's Sanskrit for 'to be victorious.' My mom always calls it 'ocean breath' though. You can open your eyes now."

I smiled as I looked at Ember, who seemed to be studying me curiously. Her head was tilted to one side and her eyebrows were drawn in slightly.

"What?"

"I want to try something on you."

Ember slowly sank to her knees and moved into a position I'd seen her in several times over the last month. Often in the morning, when I'd walk by her and Willow on my way to make coffee in the days following the miscarriage, they were in that position.

She stayed on her knees, and stretched her arms out in front of her, folding the top half of her body onto her thighs. Her forehead rested on the ground.

"Do this," she whispered. "Next to me."

I moved, as instructed, and found that the pose was a bit harder than it looked, but I was able to get there.

"Remember," she continued, "shoulders away from your ears."

"K," I whispered.

I sank into the position and started breathing deeply. On my third breath, my eyes were clouding with tears and it wasn't from pain. Muscle pain anyway. Searing through my chest was a deep ache I'd only felt a few times in my life. I sniffed.

"Weird, right?" Ember sniffed back.

"What...what the hell?" Tears were falling hard, and yet, I felt okay.

"Don't fight it."

"What is *it*?"

Ember's voice was heavy with her own tears. "Willow and I cried in this position almost every morning for two weeks. Certain yoga poses unlock certain emotions."

"What's this one for?" I asked, sniffing between every other word.

"Softening grief. Balasana..."

"What is that in English?"

Ember was silent apart from a few soft sniffs.

"Ember?" I asked again. "What is this called in English?"

"Child's pose," she whispered.

I took a deep breath. "Oh..."

A second later, Ember's hand touched my arm, and her fingers worked their way down my skin until they found my hand. I gripped it for dear life.

"Just a few more breaths, k?" Her voice was strong and reassured.

For three deep breaths, I begged for my grief to be *softened*. I felt like I was being wrung out. With each breath I took, the grief was squeezed a little harder out of me, from places I thought I'd already wrung it from. It killed me to know that for two weeks, as I guzzled coffee and checked emails before heading to work, my wife was on this very floor with her sister, wringing out her own grief—and I'd had no idea that's what she was doing.

Ember spoke again. "Slowly move into Shavasana to close it out, okay? We'll hold that for a couple of minutes."

"Thank God," I mumbled. Shavasana was the first yoga pose I'd learned. You just lay back and...lay there.

Ember's voice took on her instructor tone again. "Let the earth hold you, remember. Give yourself some space to process the feelings from the last pose."

When our time was up and Ember said "Namaste" to me, more out of habit than anything else, we sat cross-legged on the floor, staring at each other.

"You made me cry," I said as I wiped under my eyes, still not dry from all the wringing.

Ember shook her head. "Balasana did."

"You made me do it."

She shrugged. "I wanted to see if it worked on you."

"Sorcery. First that tortuous push-up nonsense, then that?"

Ember gave a soft giggle before pulling the elastic from her hair and raking her fingers through her thick waves.

"I'm sorry I wasn't there for you," I blurted out as I watched her tie her hair back once more.

Her eyes shot open and moved rapidly over my face. I watched her shoulders rise slightly as she swallowed, her eyes starting to glisten with fresh tears. There had been so many tears, I wondered when either one of us would dry out.

Ember crawled over to me and pushed my knees apart, curling her body into mine.

She kissed my chin and rested her head on my shoulder. "I'm sorry I wasn't there for you. It was *our* loss. Not just mine, and not just yours. Ours. We've never grieved together, and this loss was so..." Her voice broke but she recovered quickly. "Much. I know I don't know what it's like to lose a parent, or a sibling..."

"Hey," I cut in, rubbing my hand across her shoulders. "This *was* big. Deep. Like nothing I've ever felt. Listen...I've got something for you." I nudged her forward and stood, walking to the backside of the Christmas tree.

I reached up as high as I could, feeling around for a minute before grasping the box and pulling it gown. I ran my thumb over the textured gold wrapping as I walked back to Ember and sat across from her on the floor.

"What's this?" she asked as she took the package from my hand.

I laughed. "You always ask that. Just open it."

She was careful as she separated the tape from the paper, taking care of the wrapping as if it were the gift itself. Removing the small square box from the paper, she eyed me.

"Go ahead," I encouraged.

Slowly, Ember lifted the lid off the box. She gasped and covered her mouth with her fingers.

"Bo," she whimpered as her head tilted to the side.

She looped her finger through the thin string and held the ornament in the air between us. It was a set of silver angel wings I'd found in a store in the center of town earlier that week. I was in there looking for something else for her for Christmas, and when I spotted the wings hanging behind the cashier, I discarded what was in my hand, and purchased the wings.

I cleared my throat. "I want you to know I felt it too. The loss. I miss the baby, too, Ember. These wings will remind us that the baby is always going to be a part of us, and is watching over us. My parents and sister, too."

Ember nodded as tears rolled down her cheek. Still holding the ornament, she shifted forward and wrapped her arms around my neck. "Thank you," she whispered.

She stood and placed the ornament front and center on the tree, then stepping back to admire it.

"It looks good." I wrapped my arm around her waist and pulled her close.

She nodded. "I want to keep it out year-round. We'll find somewhere to hang it when Christmas is over."

We stood in silence for a few moments, our eyes grazing over ornaments my sister and I had made as kids, and ones that my parents had exchanged with each other.

"I've never had a Christmas ornament before," Ember said, as she remained focused on the tree.

The past couple of Christmases we'd exchanged gifts, but we'd been on the road, and never had a tree of our own.

"Well," I sighed, "we'll have plenty of time to fix that, won't we?"

"We will," she agreed. "I have something for you, too. But, we have to drive there."

"Ember," I grumbled teasingly, "why would you buy me a house? We have one right here."

She pulled her head back and pursed her lips. "Yoga makes you weird. Put your coat on—we don't need to change."

Once we had our coats on and braced the bitter three-second walk to the car, Ember beat me to the driver's seat. "I want it to be as much of a surprise as possible."

I shrugged and got in the car, buckling my seatbelt as Ember pulled out of the driveway. As we rolled through the center of town, I took a few moments to enjoy the quaint shops that were decked out with perfectly placed lights and lush garland.

My idle enjoyment quickly turned to anxiety as Ember slowed down in front of the church. Without moving her eyes from the road, Ember drifted to a parking space directly in front of the steps, put the car in park, and cut the engine.

Neither of us moved for a solid fifteen seconds.

"What are we doing here?" I planted my elbow on the rounded edge by the window and rubbed my chin.

"It's between Christmas Eve services," Ember said plainly. "We probably won't be alone, but it'll be okay." She placed the keys in her pocket and exited the car. I left my seatbelt on. Ember walked around to my side and opened the door. "It's not polite to ignore me. It's Christmas."

My palms began to sweat. Not wanting a fight, I unlatched myself and stepped onto the frozen sidewalk. "Ember..."

She held up her hand and cut me off. "Bo, if you really don't want to go in, we don't have to. But, I want you to try. Trust me."

"How long have you been planning this...whatever this is?"

Ember took a deep breath. "A few days, but," her eyes watered, "after you gave me that gift I knew I had to do it *now*."

She held out her hand, and I took it, walking one step behind her as we ascended the stairs. I kept my head down as we walked through the doors, just grateful that the building didn't crash around me.

Ember didn't stop walking until we reached the front. She pulled me to the left and sat in the front pew. You mean business if you sit in the front pew.

I sat next to her, my chest tightening as the rest of me began to sweat. I felt like I was going to explode.

"Look up," Ember whispered.

I shook my head. "No."

I'd seen it before.

Ember was quiet for a moment, gliding her thumb across my hand. "Bo," she said again. "Look."

Lifting my head, I was greeted with the same cross I'd screamed at weeks earlier. There was nothing different about it this time. Except everything.

"What?" I questioned. "This is what you're giving me?"

Ember nodded.

I shook my head, shrugging. "I don't get it."

My throat tightened as I fought to look away from the striking wood. I couldn't.

Ember cleared her throat and wiped under her eyes. Her voice maintained a steady whisper. "Once upon a time, an angry, scared, and sad girl walked away from her dad." Her lip quivered as bulbous tears fell. "On the second to last page, that girl and her dad made up...because her hero brought them together."

I coughed as the pressure from my chest released through my eyes.

"You see," Ember continued, tears falling more rapidly than I'd ever seen. "If the second to last page hadn't been written, neither, then, would the last page."

"What happened on the last page?" I tried to keep my voice quiet, but I never was skillful at talking through my tears.

Ember moved her hands to my face, looking me straight in the eye. "She got to live happily ever after."

She pressed her forehead into mine, the way we'd been when I'd asked her to marry me. "Come," she said. "Live happily ever after with me."

A loud sob leapt from my throat. "I'm so broken, Ember..."

She smiled. Even through those tears, her smile was the most beautiful thing I'd ever see in my life—I was sure of it.

"Me too. Let's be broken together."

I stood from the bench and squeezed Ember's hand. I knew that in order to be the man she needed, I had to do this part alone. I moved to the same marble stairs that I'd crashed onto weeks before, but this time—when I crashed—it was in humility rather than anger.

Immediately, thoughts and prayers whose words were numbered enough to fill volumes of books filled my mind. I couldn't speak a word. All I could do was bow my head and beg for forgiveness and strength through salty tears.

"She needs me," I whispered. "I need you."

A soft hand touched the back of my neck, and Ember knelt next to me. "You've given me faith, Bo, even if I'm not sure what I believe or where it fits," she whispered. "The least I could do is give it back to you."

There, on the cold marble stairs of a building as old as the town itself, Ember and I held onto each other as the church bells rang. And, I knew we'd be okay.

CHAPTER

Twenty One

California dreamin'

Ember

As Bo and I cruised at thirty thousand feet somewhere over the middle of the United States, he started humming "California Dreamin'."

"Seriously?" I grinned and shook my head. "Every time, Cavanaugh? Do you have to sing that every time we come out here?"

He nodded. "I do."

"So..." I started hesitantly.

"What is it?"

"Besides Willow and my parents, I've kind of been avoiding everyone for the last month."

Bo shrugged. "They all know, Em. It's not like we kept *that* a secret."

"I know, but my concern is that they're all going to be *looking* at me...at us. You know how I am, I don't like to have to prepare an emotional reaction." I leaned my head back and thought about how tense I'd felt at the DROP gala two weeks prior. The event was beautiful and no one treated me any differently, but I'd been a nervous wreck about what I'd say *if* someone asked.

"Well, remember what Dr. Bittman said at our last session. All you can do is thank people for their concern and be honest about your feelings if they ask. It's not up to you to determine if they're asking for you or themselves. Tell them how you're feeling." Bo gave me a soft kiss on my temple and went back to humming.

We'd seen Dr. Bittman once a week since Christmas, meaning we'd had another three sessions under our belt before taking this trip to California for our first PR buzz with Grounded Sound. Honestly, after Christmas Eve, there was a dramatic emotional shift in our relationship. Both of us felt it, but we wanted to keep up with therapy for a while to avoid any dark surprises hiding in our psyches.

That shift, though, was breathtaking. Palpable. Bo and I were calmer and gentler with each other than we'd ever been before. We were treating each other as human beings. Dr. Bittman had suggested we stop using the term "soul mate" with each other for a while. Just because it felt that way didn't mean we had to beat each other to death with the pressures of the tag. The assumption, she'd pointed out, was that each of us would be perfectly flawless. Infallible to the ends of time.

Turns out, we weren't. We needed to accept each other with all the flaws that made us who we were, and support each other along our path. Especially if we intended to walk that path together.

"Hello?" Bo raised his eyebrows as he leaned forward.

I shook my head to clear my daydream. "Huh?"

He grinned and put his hand on mine. "I asked if we were still staying with Willow."

I nodded. "My parents are out of town with The Six this weekend, remember? Even if they weren't, I'd still like some extra time with Willow. Are Regan and Georgia still picking us up from the airport?"

"Yeah. Have you talked to Georgia recently?"

It was so good to be having *normal* conversations with Bo, I felt like I wanted to stay on that flight forever.

"A few times. She's helping me out with something tonight after dinner."

Bo scrunched his eyebrows. "What's that?"

I shrugged and smiled. "Surprise. *Not* like the church surprise." I chuckled and flipped through my *Entertainment Weekly*.

"Yeah, we need to work on your surprises," Bo teased. He lifted my hand to his lips, giving me a quick kiss. "Seriously, though. I don't know how I'll ever be able to thank you for that."

"Just keep being the man you are," I whispered. My attention was quickly diverted to the page I was reading. "Holy shit!" I yelped, causing the person in front of me to jump.

"What?" Bo sounded startled as he leaned in.

"Look!" I pointed to a page of "Upcoming News" and splashed on the right hand side of the page were two studio shots. One of me and Bo, and the other of Celtic Summer, from our recording session in early December at the GS studios in New York.

Bo leaned in further, squinting slightly. "Keep your eyes and ears on the Grounded Sound Entertainment website. You're not going to want to miss out on the two albums they're set to release this spring."

The article spoke a little about the musical roots of each of the artists, discussed me, Bo, and Regan touring together for a year, and gave the name of the first singles we would be releasing. Which was news to us, but fine just the same. It appeared that Bo and I would be releasing "Crimson Minute" first.

"You need glasses," I teased as Bo relaxed his eyes and sat back in his seat. "This is crazy exciting! *Entertainment Weekly*!"

Bo's controlled smile was bursting at the seams with pride. "I've got chills," he admitted.

"Hey, look at this." I ran my finger along the bottom of the article. "Celtic Summer's debut album will be titled *Celtic Summer*."

Bo shrugged. "That's standard. And ours?"

I smiled as I continued the sentence. "Bo and Ember." My voice choked up just a little at the end. It was printed Bo & Ember, and no one would know just how much that ampersand represented. Intertwined. Never breaking.

"Sounds perfect to me." Bo grinned.

As I looked again to the page, my stomach sank just a little. I ran my thumb over the picture EW had printed of Bo and me. It was from our last recording session the day we ended up leaving New York. Bo was whispering in my ear, and I was blushing like a girl on her first date. That whisper, I remembered, was about "our little secret" as we'd called it.

The two people on that page had absolutely *no* idea what the next twenty-four hours would bring, let alone the following month.

Bo nudged me as I bit my lip. "What is it?"

I turned to look at him, and my heart swelled with gratitude that we'd made it through that dark time. We flirted with the edge of the cliff more than once, and we certainly weren't through all of it, but we were much stronger than the couple in that picture.

"Nothing," I whispered as I lay my head on his shoulder. "I'm just really proud of us."

Bo wrapped his arm around my shoulders and kissed the top of my head. "Me too."

S

Walking through the airport after retrieving our luggage, Bo and I were on the lookout for Regan and Georgia. About a second later, we heard a loud whistle at the same time that we saw Georgia's head pop up through the crowd.

Standing on a bench in the middle of the crowded space, Georgia waved her arms frantically.

"It's Bo and Ember!" she squealed like a rabid fan before jumping off the bench and running toward us.

"Oh my *God*," I teased back. "Are you *the* Georgia Hall? The one who owns *Sweet Forty-Two*? Did you see *Entertainment Weekly*?" I was speaking a thousand miles a minute, and it felt good.

We met each other in the middle of what felt like a thousand tired and travel-worn strangers as we danced and hugged. Two years ago you could have bet me that this scene would be happening on this day with me and Georgia and I'd have lost that bet three-fold.

It was *so* good to see her again. She texted me three days after my miscarriage. Saying she was shit with talking about hard stuff—which I'd observed firsthand. She'd said she hoped the text didn't come off as impersonal. Frankly, I was grateful for the casual communication. Each of us could talk when we were ready, and no one was waiting for an immediate response. The week following that, she'd sent an overnight package of her cupcakes. Four of them, to be exact. I ate two that night, and the other two were gone in the morning. I'd assumed Bo had eaten them, but we weren't exactly on smooth communication at that point.

"I missed you," I said as I squeezed the hell out of her.

Quickly, I exited that hug and dove into one with Regan. He held me tightly and whispered. "I'm so happy you're here. Thanks for not running off to Ireland on me."

I chuckled softly and hugged him harder. Regan and I had shared several texts over the last month, too. Ours started more somber in nature. After I'd ignored his first few texts in the two days following the miscarriage, he sent me another one and told me I better not take off for Ireland, the way he had when Rae died. That made me laugh and cry at the same time, earning him a three AM phone call. He confiscated my emotional passport, as he'd called it, and we'd talked and texted fairly regularly from that point on.

After all of the reunion hugging quieted down, we all stood across from each other for a few silent seconds. Georgia had a curious look on her face as she tilted her head.

"Whoa," she said inside of her exhale.

"What?" I looked around.

Georgia grabbed my suitcase and started walking toward the exit. "I don't know what the hell happened to you two, but someone better call Grounded Sound and tell them to change the name of your album from 'Bo and Ember' to 'Bo and Zenber.' Seriously, you're, like, floating across the floor."

Bo gripped my hand and winked at me as Georgia tossed my suitcase into the trunk of her car. Bo placed his in and shut the trunk. Georgia stood with her hands on her hips and smiled.

"Whatever it is you guys have been doing, keep doing it. You're all...glowy and shit. To go through what you've been through the last month and to look like *that?* You're doing something right." Georgia moved to the driver's seat, and the rest of us got in the car.

I, for one, was grateful to have the *baby ice* broken. They didn't need to know all we'd been through in what we'd later call 'the dark month." They just needed to see we were where we were. Bo and I committed to each other, in the confines of Dr. Bittman's office, that we wouldn't share all the negative pieces of our relationship with even well-meaning family and friends. While it was acceptable—and sometimes necessary—to vent, Dr. Bittman had reminded us, it was also our responsibility to make our relationship our own, and not one governed by outside opinions. The more people we let into our relationship, she'd said, the harder it would be to keep it *our* relationship.

"You guys are staying with Willow, right?" Regan drummed his thumbs on his legs as he spoke.

"Yeah, but she's going to bring us back there after our session today," Bo answered.

Despite just getting off a six-hour flight, we were all headed directly to Grounded Sound's West Coast offices for a meeting with Yardley. Willow would be there, as she'd been promoted to assistant sound engineer, and her first project was Celtic Summer's debut album.

"She's really good," Regan entered in the middle of my thoughts.

"Yeah, people can be surprising, huh?" Georgia said as she looked in the rearview mirror and winked at me.

Georgia had the day off, so she was going to be able to hang out with us at the studio. As soon as we arrived, the tanned and toned surfer receptionist—a far cry from Brielle in NYC—whisked us into the conference room, where Yardley and her assistant waited.

"You look well," Yardley said as we hugged.

I nodded and pulled a smile from deep within. "I'm feeling better all the time. Thank you for the lovely flowers. And for that mention in *Entertainment Weekly*!"

Yardley cracked a grin as we all took our seats. "We wanted to keep that a surprise. Looks like it worked, huh?"

"Yeah," Bo scoffed jokingly. "A huge surprise at thirty thousand feet."

Shortly after, Shaughn and Chris joined us, while Georgia ran out to grab lunch. Yardley updated us on what had been going on behind the scenes over the last several weeks. Celtic Summer had finished recording their album, and both of our albums were in post-production.

"We're ready to talk about publicity." Yardley nodded seriously as she handed out sheets of paper peppered with dates and events. "You'll see that our PR team has carefully crafted the build to your album release. Bo and Ember, your album will release at the end of April, and Celtic Summer's album will drop two weeks later. We want the anticipation at its peak by the time tickets go on sale for the tour, which will be the third week in May."

My heart raced with excitement. Several months ago this was all "in the future." Now, it was real, and the wheels were turning.

Yardley continued, sounding slightly excited herself, "The tour will start July first on the East Coast. I'd like you all to look at July fourth, please."

I scanned past the various Internet and radio interviews, dates where our in-studio recordings would be released, and finally landed on the Fourth of July.

Central Park.

"Are you serious?" Bo's tone was breathless as he looked up with as shocked a face as I'd ever seen.

"Jesus," Chris mumbled.

Regan and I eyed each other with gaping mouths.

"Get it out of your system, kids," Yardley said with a smile. "You need to be on your A-game."

"How..." Shaughn trailed off as she shook her head, a mischievous grin on her face as always.

Yardley took an assured breath. "Several artists are starting their tours in June. I was able to speak with a few labels, and we coordinated a one-day event where you'd all get to play. Not an official festival, just—"

"A one day bad-ass gig?" Regan blurted out excitedly.

Yardley smiled. "Precisely."

The room erupted into cheers and chatter.

"That's going to be a *huge* crowd." Chris's eyes bugged out as he stared at the sheet.

Yardley nodded. "It is, but it'll feel bigger because of the close quarters. You're scheduled at larger venues through the summer."

I zoned out while Yardley ran quickly through the rest of the dates and venues of the summer tour, which was going to end mid-October. I tried not to, but I started thinking about the baby. For a couple of weeks I had been so nervous about breaking the pregnancy news to Yardley. I worried how it would affect the tour and the other groups. There I was though, discussing the tour as planned, with the unplanned pregnancy no longer an *issue* for anyone in the room except for me.

I needed some air. I wasn't on the verge of a panic attack, but I was on the verge of being on the verge. I just needed a minute. Standing slowly, I tried to slink inconspicuously from the room, which was a challenge in a room of only seven people.

I heard the room go silent as I slipped through the door, but pretended like no one saw me. I made it to the main door before Bo snuck up behind me, gently placing his hand on my shoulder.

"Hey," he whispered. "What's going on?"

I turned around and took a deep breath. His eyes were concerned, urgent by way of empathy and not panic. The genuine pull of his eyes made me tear up more than my escape-inducing emotions did. It was the look I'd wanted to see in the days we'd returned home from the hospital. Regardless, it was there now.

"I just needed some air." I swallowed hard and tilted my head to the side.

"Talk," he commanded as he pushed the door open and ushered us outside, where we sat on a stone bench.

My lips twisted. "I was just looking at the tour dates and thinking about the baby." There was no reason for me to beat around it, even if I'd been quick enough to find a way.

Bo nodded and pulled my hand from my lap, interlacing our fingers. He looked like he was ready to say something, but I cut him off.

"I'm okay, though. There's...everything's fine. I just needed to take a minute to breathe about it, you know?" I gave his hand a reassuring squeeze.

"I know, but *I* need to talk about it for a minute."

"Oh." My voice dropped to a whisper as I watched his eyes fall to our hands.

Bo spoke softly. "You know that when we get home from this trip, we'll be able to pick up the ashes from the funeral home."

And, suddenly, there we were. Discussing the baby, the ashes, and all of the shit we'd avoided during a few dark and damaging weeks both of us would probably like to forget if it hadn't been for how much closer it made us in the end.

I bit my lip. "I know."

"I've been thinking about what we should do with them. We don't have to talk about it now, but I wanted you to know that I'm ready to talk about it, whenever you are." Bo leaned in halfway and arched his eyebrow, pulling me in the rest of the way.

We shared a tender, calming kiss in the middle of a busy complex filled with people carrying around their own brands of ashes.

"Wanna go back in?" Bo pulled away and ran his hand down my cheek.

"Does everyone think I'm cra—? Never mind, I don't care." I gave him a quick kiss on the nose and we headed back inside to discuss the details of the *Indie Tour*.

As I set my hand on the door to the conference room, I took one more cleansing breath, reminding myself that while sometimes we're granted all of our dreams, rarely are they granted all at once. I was ready to sing, ready to tour, and forced myself into a place of gratitude for the insane opportunity that lay before me.

CHAPTER

Roots and Wings

Bo

"DID GEORGIA SAY how long they'd be gone?" I asked Regan as we fumbled our way around Willow's kitchen.

He shook his head. "Nope. And, I was told not to ask. Girl stuff."

"Somehow, with the three of them, that makes me nervous." My eyes widened as I diced the chicken.

"We should probably start pouring the wine now." Regan laughed as he searched for the corkscrew.

Ember and I were staying at Willow's tiny beach house during our time in California, and we invited Regan and Georgia up for dinner. We knew we'd have plenty of time to hang with the other members of Celtic Summer, but Regan and Georgia were some of our closest friends with whom we hardly spent enough time.

We'd had a busy—but exciting—day at Grounded Sound's studio. After the briefing with Yardley regarding the summer tour, we were then given the opportunity to interview with reporters from various media outlets. We'd talked with just about everyone from the local newspaper's arts and entertainment section through representatives from different satellite radio stations.

The interviews hovered around our experiences recording our albums, excitement about the tour, and a bit into our histories with music. The last bit had made me feel like a bit of an outcast in the company I was keeping. Ember and Regan's deep roots in music were no surprise to me. I'd known Chris's parents weren't as supportive as mine were with his musical interests, but it was news to me that he'd made huge sacrifices in the name of art—including moving out of his parents' home and not speaking to them for almost a year. Finally, Shaughn's history was scattered between the UK and Chicago and encompassed everything from private lessons with several-hundred-dollar-an-hour instructors, to sneaking into after-hours nights at local pubs.

While I had a number of successes under my belt, and music had always come naturally to me, I found myself in awe at the raw, industrious talent around me. I was certainly looking forward to honing in my talents while I was given the chance to work with all of these wonderful artists.

"So," Regan started hesitantly, pulling me to the present, "how are things with you and Ember? Really."

Guys don't normally talk about stuff like *how things are going.* I know this, because I am one. But, I also know that I'm different. So is Regan. And, frankly, I needed another dude to process with. Even if he hadn't been through the same loss I had recently, we'd been through enough together to prove to me he had the guts to handle just *how* things were going.

"Better. But," I puffed out my cheeks as I exhaled, "it got fuckin' brutal there for a while."

Regan bit the inside of his cheek. "I thought so. Ember wouldn't say anything to me, but she seemed...just..." He shook his head and diced some peppers. "What are we making anyway?"

"Fajitas," I answered. "Don't use the same cutting board for the veggies as the chicken, though. The veg-heads will castrate you."

Regan switched cutting boards and seemed to pick up where he left off. "Like, I knew she was talking to me about how she was feeling about the miscarriage, but there was *nothing* about *you two* in there. And any time I talked to you it was the same. I wasn't there to see you, but—"

"No one was," I cut in. "It was kind of the perfect storm in the worst way. We had nothing going on and kind of wrapped ourselves in that house. I honestly have no idea how many days Ember spent without leaving the property."

"Ten," Regan mumbled.

I huffed. "That's about right, I guess. I went back to work right away. Which was kind of mistake number one."

Regan shrugged. "There's no playbook for this shit. I get wanting to escape."

I set the skillet on the stove and added the chicken. "Yeah. It's that damn fight or flight thing. I couldn't fight the grief, so I tried to run from it." I shrugged as Regan tossed in half the veggies. "I mean, it's not like I've never grieved before, but, I've never fled from it."

"Doesn't work." Regan's tone was dry, but his grin was sympathetically playful.

I clapped him on the shoulder and chuckled. "No, brother, it doesn't. Not even for a second."

"Yeah," he snickered, "sometimes it even makes it worse."

I rolled my eyes. "I think it *always* makes it worse. A hundred percent of the time in my case."

"So," Regan eyed the uncooked veggies curiously, "are they just...gonna...eat the veggies and...nothing else?"

"You basically lived with Ember on the road, dude. You know she'll add some soulless protein when she gets here. I'm just not allowed to cook it." I held up my hands in defeat. "I screw it up. Also a hundred percent of the time."

Regan shout-laughed. "Soulless?"

"Her word. Not mine."

He shook his head, eyeing the ceiling. "That girl and her one-liners, man."

"Things with you and Georgia...good?" I changed the subject.

"How are you feeling?" Regan changed it back. "Like, about the miscarriage itself. Not just you and Ember stuff."

I turned down the heat on the stove, plopped the lid on the skillet, and leaned against the counter with my beer in hand.

"Honestly? It's hard to say. In the span of a few days everything was changed a hundred and eighty degrees and then spun off in a whole other direction. I barely had time to get used to the idea of being a dad..." I trailed off, but started again as I watched Regan eye me suspiciously. "Who am I kidding?" I sighed. "I was so excited. I knew it was the wrong time professionally but, hell, it's not like we couldn't have still sold a record, you know?"

Regan nodded. "It really freaked Georgia out."

"Huh?" I lifted my chin, surprised.

"I mean, we're obviously not even engaged yet or anything, but we talk about that stuff. The wedding, house, kids... anyway, a few days after she heard about the miscarriage she didn't talk for like half a day. Out of nowhere. Then—and don't tell her I told you this—but she burst into tears when I asked her what was going on."

I took a swig from my beer, shocked at Georgia's emotion regarding our situation.

"Yeah," Regan continued. "I was weirded out, too. We've dealt with some serious shit, and cried a lot, but it was always about *us* stuff, you know? But she was freaked out about what would happen to us if we went through something like that, and she was *really* freaked out about you guys."

"Really?"

Regan opened his beer and leaned next to me, both of us staring at the stove. "That was after she'd texted with Ember for a couple days, remember. She said the same thing I'd noticed...that she was only talking about her and what she was feeling and how she was perceiving it. Even though she rips on you guys, it wigged her out to not see you two holding onto each other."

"We almost blew it," I agreed.

"What happened? How'd you get out of it?"

I set the beer bottle down. "She called me an asshole."

"Yeah, so?" Regan shrugged. "Georgia does that on the daily."

I laughed. "Let's just say that was the tip of the juicy "Behind the Music" segment, huh?"

"Nuff said." Regan held up his hands. "Have you talked about when you want to have kids now?"

I took a deep breath. We hadn't talked about it, but I hadn't stopped thinking about it. The first time Ember and I had slept together after the miscarriage was the night of the gala, a few days after Christmas. That was the first night we'd felt like a couple in weeks. Ember had been nervous, worried that it would bring up a whole host of shitty feelings. We kept reminding each other to be gentle. More for ourselves than the other person. It went smoothly and we both cried. We didn't talk about why we were each crying because, honestly, by that point we were exhausted from talking about our feelings.

The next morning, though, was different. Peaceful, beautiful. Like the third step after putting one foot in front of the other.

"Save your answer for another time, dude. Here come the girls." Regan pushed off the counter and pulled down three wine glasses.

I silently hated when he did considerate things before I could get to it. Didn't seem manly to get into a fight over who was pouring wine, though, so I let it go.

Willow did a quick scan of the room when she walked in. "Well, it's still standing, so you couldn't have screwed up dinner that bad." She winked as she set down a box of pastries from *Sweet Forty-Two*.

"Went to La Jolla, did ya?" I clapped and rubbed my hands together as I stared at the box.

"Yes," Georgia snickered. "I was a tool and went to my own bakery to bring things back here. Thank God it was just my mom there. I used to hate working at places where the boss would come in on their days off to get food, or whatever."

Georgia slapped my hand away and pushed the box to the back of the counter. "I still can't believe you live in *this* house, Willow. What a fuckin' dream."

"I've seen your place, Georgia. Neither of us are doing too shabby." Willow graciously accepted a glass of wine from Regan and stuck her head in the fridge, undoubtedly looking for non-animal protein.

"Well," Georgia added, "guess we can't hate our parents for making smart investments when we were younger, huh?"

Solstice and Michael owned Willow's tiny bungalow, but they'd rented it for years until Willow was old enough to live on her own.

"Amen to that," Willow said with her head still buried in the refrigerator.

Ember seemed quiet as she clutched her sweater around her. It was chilly by California standards, but a miracle based on the month we'd just had in New Hampshire. On a number of levels.

I mouthed, "You okay?" and Ember smiled as she nodded to the back door. I followed her through the sliding door, noting the hush that had fallen over our friends before Willow started to school Regan in the art of tempeh.

"What's up?" I asked as I sat next to Ember on a weathered and probably decades-old fallen tree trunk.

Her cheeks were rosy and absent of signs of distress, so any worry about her overly quiet demeanor faded.

"I had a great time with the girls today." She looked down at her knotted hands.

"Okay...I...don't...what'd you guys do?" I didn't even know if Ember wanted me to be asking the questions, but I knew asking was better than *not* asking.

"Don't be mad," she started. "But I had Georgia take me to her artist in La Jolla. Where she had all her work done. That's how we had time to get the cupcakes."

I scrunched my nose. "Arti—oh! You mean tattoo artist?"

Ember nodded and my eyes bugged out. Ever since I met her, she'd talked off and on about getting a tattoo, but I hadn't ever heard her discuss any concrete ideas. Still, any time she gave me a back rub she traced her fingers over the broad cross on my back, so I knew it was never far from her mind.

"What'd you get?" I smiled as my knees bobbed impatiently.

Ember lifted her left arm, and it was then I finally noticed the covering. She carefully peeled the tape off enough so she could move the dressing back to show me. Once her skin was exposed, her eyes shot to me.

"Like it?" she asked innocently.

My stomach dropped in the best way it had in months as I took her arm in my hand. "Oh, Ember..."

In the center of the inside of her wrist was a black pair of angel wings. Wings that looked remarkably like the ornament I'd given her for Christmas.

"Are these—?"

Ember cut me off. "They are. I snuck the ornament in my bag. I wanted them with me...always."

I was speechless for a few seconds. "They're beautiful on you. And, a wrist tattoo? Gutsy. I love it."

"Well," she blushed, "this is my chord hand. Now, whenever I play the guitar I'll see it, and be reminded of all of our angels above. Just like you said." Her eyes filled with tears, but the smile never left her face as she leaned her head on my shoulder.

I kissed the top of her head—something I took every opportunity to do because her hair always smelled like something different. Coconut, mint, fruit...it was always amazing. "I'm proud of you."

Ember's hand tightened in mine. "I'm proud of us," she whispered.

Just as the sun started its dance with the horizon, there was a knock on the sliding door. We turned our heads and found Willow holding plates of food, indicating dinner was ready.

"Well, my badass wife," I teased. "Let's go eat." I stood and held out my hand.

"I am badass, aren't I?" Ember grabbed my hand and stood up, walking hand in hand with me to the house.

I grinned and kissed her knuckles. "You have no idea, do you? You're amazing."

As we sat and ate with family and friends, each time Ember's wrapped arm caught my eye, I felt like it was a wink or smile from one of "our angels." We'd been given roots and wings, and it was our turn to soar.

Georgia and Regan stayed at Willow's until about 9:00, before finally yawning their way out the door. We knew we had a busy few days ahead with taped recording sessions and more interviews, so Ember and I headed to bed right after they left.

Just as our heads hit our pillows, Ember's phone buzzed with a text message.

She rolled to her side, and the room lit with a soft glow as she read it. After she was quiet for a few moments, I leaned in and kissed her shoulder.

"What is it?" I asked.

"Monica," Ember replied meekly. Her ears lifted as she smiled, though her sniff gave away tears. "They're having a girl."

Instinctively, my arm wrapped around Ember and I pulled her close. I didn't know what to say. I couldn't say anything even if I had words, because I realized it would have been around this time that Ember and I would have found out the sex of our own baby.

"It's good," she whispered while nodding, seeming to sense my hesitation. "I'm happy for them. I really am, you know."

"I know." I kissed her shoulder once more.

Ember set her phone on the bedside table and rolled back over to face me. "It's been a little weird with me and Mon lately, but we'll be okay."

"Weird how?"

"I think she's afraid I'll have a meltdown. She's reluctant to share things with me, or complain about the pregnancy on days when she's feeling like crap. I wouldn't tell her it was okay if it wasn't. I mean, God, I didn't speak to her for a couple of days after the miscarriage. That's all the time I needed from that situation, you know?" Ember spoke quickly, like she was talking to Monica and not me.

"Have you told her this?"

She nodded. "I guess all I can do is keep being there for her and she can keep being there for me. The fact is, now we're at two different stages in our lives. That's why we were both so excited to be pregnant at the same time. So nothing would have to change, you know? But, it'll change now. Not bad, just...different. She'll settle into mom mode, you and I will be on tour, and for the first time we're going to share less in our everyday lives and need to support each other more than before."

"I love the shit out of you, you know that?" I didn't need to talk with her about her friendship with Monica. She just needed to vent and verbally process.

That's something else we'd been working on with Dr. Bittman. Not trying to *fix* everything for each other. Just because one of us has a struggle, doesn't mean the other person can or *should* fix it. Sometimes support means being a set of ears and strong arms.

Ember brought her lips to mine, and I loved that I could feel her smile against my mouth. "I know. I love the shit out of you, too."

§

Halfway through the week, Ember and I and Celtic Summer were finally in the studio to do some live recording sessions. While we'd taped some back in early December while we were in New York, we were going to have a live feed streaming on the website today. Each group was going to choose pieces of three songs, and talk a bit about the process of writing and recording the number.

The plan was to release our first singles in a week or two, allowing us time to have two singles out before the album dropped. It was carefully crafted and expertly executed. And, I was thankful to be on the talent side of things for this round.

PR for a business is one thing. For entertainment it's a whole other animal.

Yardley entered the large recording room looking bright and relaxed in a flowing sundress that looked like something Ember would wear. It was much different than her New York attire. Her blonde hair hung free, instead of in the tight ponytail that looked downright painful most of the time. I grinned at her coastal costume change.

"Okay, guys," she chirped. "This room is big enough that whoever isn't playing can sit on those couches over there. That will help the cohesive image we're going for, too."

Ember chuckled. "It's hardly just an image, Yardley. Surely you know that, right?"

"I do. Honestly you're the easiest group of musicians I've ever worked with. Let's capture it on tape before the egos take over, huh?" She was so matter-of-fact that the five of us found ourselves looking at each other with wide eyes.

Which one of us would morph into Brutus with our power hungry greed? A Judas among us, perhaps? That's what we were each thinking, but we kept smiles on our faces to mask the sudden suspicion.

"Well, thanks for the pep talk, Yardley," Chris joked. "Let's get to work, shall we?"

Yardley's shoulders sank as she sighed. "Sorry, guys. Didn't mean to be a downer. Just being realistic. I've been involved with this world a long time."

"So have I," Ember said confidently. "We'll be okay. Let's get cracking."

Yardley studied Ember for a moment, noticing, perhaps, as I had, the shift in her demeanor over the last couple of months.

No longer was Ember downplaying her industry know-how, brushing off praise of her skill and history. She was ready to make something of this album, of our talent together, and didn't want to waste time worrying about potential personality conflicts. With a nod and a grin, Yardley turned on her heels and moved into the control room with Willow.

A second later, Beckett dashed into the control room from the exterior door. Ember gave a slight wave and a smile before turning for her guitar.

"Haven't heard from him in a while," I mumbled after checking to assure the microphones weren't on.

Ember shrugged. "Me either. Guess he's been busy producing our album." She winked and tuned her guitar, lifting her chin as her way of telling me to get my act together.

I watched as she tuned a few chords. The bandage from yesterday was off her wrist, and every few chord changes I caught Ember's eye as it flicked to the pair of wings on the inside of her wrist. The tattoo was more than just about the baby we'd lost, or my parents, or even Rae. It was Ember making an indelible statement that she wouldn't be held down by pain and grief. She would rise. Always.

We hadn't decided which group would play first, but as all of us were tuning, I saw Ember tilt her ear toward Shaughn.

"Viva La Vida?" Ember questioned as she took off her guitar and placed it in its stand.

Shaughn nodded and kept playing. As soon as I adjusted my ears, I picked out that Shaughn was playing the slow violin harmony. She played both guitar and violin, and was fluent in both languages.

Regan bobbed his head. "Right on." On cue, he began the sharp staccato part.

Ember whipped her head to me. "You know a piano melody for this, right?" Her eyes were provocatively enthusiastic. "I know you do. I've heard you play it."

"I do." I laughed.

"Let's play it!" She motioned to the recording room. "Ignore them. Let's have fun for a second. Together. We can do this, right?" Ember moved to the drum set and separated the base drum from the group, dragging it to the lead mic.

"Chris," she continued. "You keep the beat here and sing with me."

Chris grinned. "Abso-fuckin'-lutely."

I shifted the keyboard around as Ember directed Regan and Shaughn. "You both play those short notes at the beginning, then one of you take high and one low. You decide. Shaughn, you've played this a lot, right?"

Shaughn nodded. "It's a great warm up."

"Yay!" Ember clapped, and I realized I don't think I'd ever heard her say *yay* in her life.

I watched placidly as she moved mics and stands around the studio, talking to Chris about pitch and entrances. Finally, she turned to me. "You good, love?"

I gave her a thumbs-up, grinning like a fool at how at home she seemed. Today over most days in the last month.

From the control room, I saw Willow grin and Beckett mouthed, *what are you doing?* Ember flicked her fingers in a motion requesting they turn on our mics. "Getting along," Ember teased as she slid on her headphones.

Willow covered her mouth as her shoulders shook slightly against her laughter. Yardley sat back with a curious look on her face and Beckett looked enticed as he slid some controls and gave Ember the thumbs-up.

Ember situated herself next to Chris and looked over to Shaughn and Regan, whispering, "Five, six, seven, eight..."

Regan and Shaughn kept their eyes on each other as they settled into the rhythm of the song. Ember tapped the quick beat against her thigh. As she entered the song, Chris struck the pedal of the bass drum. Regan and Shaughn split into their different parts as I brought my fingers to the keys. It blended perfectly, like Ember had seemed to know it would. This song, in particular, always gave me chills, more so after my recent stumble inside the house of God.

Ember carried the second verse alone, as well, but Chris joined her as we all erupted into the chorus. I resisted the urge to turn on my mic, and pushed down the twinge of jealousy toward Chris that he got to sing with Ember in that moment.

No one knew how lucky they were to have the chance to sing with her until it was all over and they were left wanting more. I sure hoped he was enjoying it. The three people in the control room certainly were. Yardley's wide—but con-trolled—smile was laced with satisfaction as she watched her hand-picked musicians work together.

The song was over seven minutes long, and for that entire time, we blended perfectly. To a song that isn't your standard "jam" song, the five of us performed as a group, thanks to my wife. And those wings that gave her the courage to step out and own her true self.

At the close of the song, when the last note faded, Ember raised her hands in victory. She and Chris hugged as Shaughn and Regan high-fived. Yardley leaned into her mic on the other side of the glass and turned it on.

"Message received."

With an appeased smirk on her face, Yardley sat back in her chair and we all carried on with our session.

CHAPTER Twenty Three

Heaven when we're home

Ember

OUR WEEK IN California flew by. There were live streams, interviews, and a few small meet-and-greets. By the end of it, I think we'd finally convinced Yardley that this wasn't our first rodeo. Sure, we weren't seasoned by any means, but we all had class enough to interact with fans as if they were human…because they were. And, so were we. All that was left to do was sit around and wait for our April album release party, and prepare like hell for the tour. Which, basically, meant we had to sleep a lot.

The good news was the tour bus was about four times the size of one of The Six's RVs, so we likely wouldn't want to kill each other until three-quarters of the way through the tour. By Labor Day, if my calculations were correct.

The night before we were scheduled to fly back to New Hampshire, Bo and I were packing our suitcases, when I got a call from Tyler.

"Hello?"

"Hey, gorgeous."

I grinned. His greetings were different every time, but I favored "gorgeous" and "sweetness."

"Is Bo there?" he asked with a hint of urgency.

"He is, what's up?"

"Put me on speaker for a second."

I flagged Bo down, who was busy organizing his belongings perfectly inside his suitcase. "Tyler wants to talk to us," I whispered, tapping the speaker button. "K, Tyler, we're on."

Tyler took a deep breath. "All right. When you guys left, the addition was almost complete."

"Yeah..." Bo said, baiting Tyler for more information.

"It's done and I'll be painting it tonight. Well *I* won't be painting it..." he drifted off in soft laughter. "But what I want to ask is if you can give me artistic license for the first bedroom at the top of the stairs on the right. Rae's old room."

Bo and I shot our eyes to each other at the same time. We hadn't once discussed what we'd do with that room. For about a minute, I'd considered making it a nursery, before rationalizing that it wasn't wise logistically, being on the opposite end of the mile-long hallway.

"So...is that a no?" Tyler interrupted our long silence.

Bo swallowed hard, running his hand over his head, perching it on the back of his neck. "I don't know...I haven't really thought...what do you want to do?"

"I know this is asking a lot, Bo," Tyler replied. "But...I need you to trust me. I want it to be a surprise when you get home. It's nothing huge. Not a remodel, I mean, I'll have it done by the time you guys get home tomorrow night. But, since at the end of next week this phase of the remodel will be done, I wanted to give you guys a gift. On me."

I grinned at the humility in Tyler's voice, and my chest ached at the hopeful, but pained, look on Bo's face. Those two had been through a lot of crazy life together, and trust was being called out.

"Are you okay with it?" Bo asked me. "It's *our* house."

I smiled and responded as if there weren't a third party present by phone. "I know it'll feel weird but we have lots of Rae all over the house, and on my body." I winked as I lifted my tattooed wrist. "I think it might be nice to make some new memories there."

"I was hoping you'd say that," Tyler cut in, reminding us of his long-distance presence.

Bo sighed with a grin. "All right, Tyler. We trust you. We *will* be home tomorrow night, though, so…just…don't leave a mess," he teased.

Tyler laughed freely. "Okay, enough chatter with you two, I've gotta go work."

I pressed "End" and resumed packing. "You really okay with this?"

"You know?" Bo said as he zipped his suitcase. "I really am. I totally trust him. We've been through our shit, Tyler and me. And he's been great to you over the last couple of weeks. We can all move on, I guess, huh?"

I smiled, proud of the steps we were both taking to be emotionally healthy adults. Before I could respond, Willow knocked on the door.

"Hey Ember? Beckett's here and he wants to talk to you."

I shot a curious look at Bo, who shrugged.

"Okay," I called. "I'll be right down."

"I'll stay here," Bo said as he took off his pants and shirt and slid into bed. "I need a quiet minute after this week."

I kissed him on the cheek and walked down the stairs, where I found Willow alone in her kitchen.

"Uh..." I started.

Willow nodded to the beach. "Out there."

"Weird." I looked to Willow for a cue on what it was all about, but she had nothing to offer.

"Who knows? It's Beckett." She laughed and resumed combing through what looked like textbooks on sound engineering.

As I stepped onto the sand in the post-sunset dusk, Beckett was sitting on the large log to the left of the door.

"Hey you, what's up?" I wrapped a sweater around my body, having forgotten how chilly an evening ocean breeze could be—even in California.

Beckett patted the space next to him. His hair was tucked behind his ears and he wore one of those half-grin half-frowns that instantly had me concerned.

"Is everything okay?" I asked as I sat. "There's not something wrong with the album is there?"

Beckett shook his head and rested his arms on his knees. "No."

I looked around, waiting for him to continue. "Okay...so?"

"I'm sorry, Ember. About the baby." He looked to the sand as he spoke, and my stomach dropped.

Some days it felt like so long ago. Until someone handed me their condolences. Then, I was right back there.

I cleared my throat. "Beck, it's okay. I'm feeling better."

Beckett shrugged then finally looked at me. "I'm sorry I wasn't there for you, too. That was kind of a dick move."

"Beckett—"

"No, Ember. Let me finish. I was so psyched to be working with you and getting your first album off the ground, and it was great hanging out at your place in New Hampshire, then I fell off the grid. It was like...I knew you and Bo were married, but when I heard about the miscarriage it just made it all real. Like...your *life* was something...something more. Marriage, a family." He growled and ran his hand through his hair. "I don't know. I guess when I first saw you at that club before you were signed, I was kind of hoping—"

"Don't," I cut him off with a smile. "Don't say it."

"But..."

I shook my head. "I don't want you to say it because it'll ruin the friendship we've had for a long time. We've been friends since diapers, Beckett, and I don't want that to change. I forgive you, okay? For what you said and what you didn't say." I put my hand on his shoulder and he reached up, gripping it for a few seconds.

"You were always the peacemaker, you know. Of the three of us, remember? Willow and I would fight like cats and dogs and you'd make us friends again." Beckett's boyish smile lit up places in my childhood I'd long forgotten.

I nodded. "You two were ridiculous."

"Yardley's lucky to have you. That stunt you pulled with that Coldplay track the other day? Brilliant." Beckett stood, and I followed.

"It was hardly a stunt, Beck."

He laughed. "You owned it, sister. Bo's a lucky man, Ember. Don't let him forget it."

I flicked my eyes up to the window of the bedroom where Bo and I would spend one more night. "Well," I sighed, "I'm pretty damn lucky, too."

Beckett's eyes followed mine, settling on the glowing light from the room. "He's all right." He shrugged and I playfully smacked his shoulder.

"Beckett!" I teased.

"What! I thought he was going to eat me alive the first few times I was around him. His eyes never left me!"

"Can you honestly blame him? You stared at me nonstop." I rolled my eyes and opened the door.

"Well," Beckett said as we entered the kitchen. Willow was nowhere in sight. "Guess I'll see you back in New York for the release party in April?"

I smiled. "You better drive your ass to New Hampshire the second the album is done. We can have a secret listen."

Beckett leaned in and hugged me, planting a soft kiss on my cheek as he pulled away. "Right on."

Beckett left, and I hurried upstairs where I knew a warm bed awaited me. It was going to be a long day tomorrow, and I still had to run the details by Bo. Luckily, he was still awake when I got into the room.

"Everything okay?" he asked, setting down his book. He'd recently started reading in what little downtime he had, and damn it if he didn't look even sexier with a book in his hand.

I waved my hand. "Yeah. Beckett just apologized for not reaching out after the miscarriage." I shrugged. "He felt bad. We've been friends a long time."

Bo's eyebrows lifted. "That was...nice of him. Weird, but nice."

"Listen..." I sat cross-legged facing Bo. "I know the ashes are ready. They were ready on Wednesday, as promised by the funeral home."

Bo's face greyed slightly. He simply cleared his throat.

"They left a message on my phone," I continued. "I didn't keep it a secret, or anything like that. It was just...shocking, I guess. I mean, we knew they'd be ready—"

"Ember, it's okay," Bo cut in as he gently rubbed my leg.

I took a deep breath. "Anyway, I was thinking since we're landing in Logan that we should go to that funeral home on our drive home and...get them." I bit my lip and studied Bo's face.

His lips twisted, and his eyes misted over just slightly. "Makes sense. What do you want to do with them?"

I shrugged. "Let's not decide now. Let's not even talk about deciding. It's still kind of raw. The box is going to be tiny. We can figure out where to put it, and then decide on how to handle the ashes later. Like...summertime. Before we leave for tour."

Bo lay back on the bed and extended his arm. "Come here." He spoke softly, inviting me to curl up next to him. That was his way of saying he agreed with me and was ready to take a break from talking about it.

Just because one of us was ready to talk about something, didn't mean the other had to be forced into it. Likewise, just because one of us *didn't* want to talk didn't mean we could avoid it all day. It was a balancing act. I'd said what I'd wanted to say about the ashes and didn't need anything more from Bo until we landed in Massachusetts.

I felt like each day we were acing page after page of "Dr. Bittman 101." While we hadn't discussed how long we'd see her, Bo and I agreed we needed to meet with her regularly before the tour started, and keep her on standby while we were on the road.

I was happy to oblige Bo in his simple request, loving the feeling of his always-warm skin against mine. "Thank you for being mine," I whispered as I kissed his chest.

Bo kissed my forehead, taking the same deep breath he always did when his lips were against my skin. "Thank you for being mine."

§

I don't ever want to pick up ashes again.

The funeral home was extremely gracious and the whole process was smooth and uncomplicated, but it was still devastating. I know there were words exchanged and signatures scrawled, along with well-meaning smiles, but the details were a blur. All I knew when we left was I didn't want to go back any time soon.

As Bo drove us over the border into New Hampshire, I clutched the box in my hands.

"It's so small," I whispered, my lip trembling as I grazed the lid.

The size of a ring box, the silver cube was engraved with the date, as we'd requested when we were at the hospital.

"I feel like I've been shot in the chest," Bo admitted as he puffed out his cheeks in a sigh. He was preventing himself from crying.

"Hey," I cooed as I reached across the car, gripping his hand. "It's going to be okay. You know that, right?"

Bo nodded.

"Do you want me to drive for a while?" I continued. I was a mess inside, but was holding it together, and it looked like Bo needed to fall apart.

"No, I'll be fine." Bo refocused his eyes on the road.

I appreciated using driving as a distraction, so I let it go as I gazed out the window with the nearly weightless but oppressively heavy box in my right hand.

He was right. He would be fine. We both would be.

"It's just another process," I said as I leaned my head back. "Those processes you always talk about. We've got to keep moving forward and being *part* of the process so we don't get run over by it, right?"

Bo grinned. "Right again, Mrs. Cavanaugh. I really should watch my words around you. They don't taste as sweet when you serve them back to me."

We shared a light laugh in the midst of our storm as we headed for home.

We finally reached the house around 7:00 PM. It was pitch black and frozen. The driveway shined with a smooth coating of ice.

"This is bullshit," Bo grumbled as he shivered at the sight of the frozen wonderland.

I laughed. "Don't sound so old. It's January. This is how it's *supposed* to be."

"I am old," he insisted as he turned off the car. "I'm over thirty, run a successful nonprofit, I'm married, and I own a house. How the hell did I get so old?"

I rolled my eyes. "Hey, Tyler's not here," I said as I surveyed the driveway.

"So." Bo shrugged.

"He had that top secret project thing..." I unbuckled my seatbelt and reached for the door, but Bo snapped his fingers, stopping me.

I sat back with a grin, and waited for him to carefully skate around the front of the car and open my door.

"Thanks," he said as he helped me out onto the slick driveway. He always had a lighthearted grin when he opened the door. Frankly it looked like the grin I'd seen his father wear in the pictures around our house.

I'd take it any day of the week.

As we entered the house, I called out for Tyler in futility. "Hello?"

"Holy shit!" Bo exclaimed inside a whisper. "Look at this place!"

My jaw dropped as I followed Bo into the dining room. The paint was crisp, the new furniture perfectly situated, and the addition was perfection. Although it was only a couple hundred square feet, the sunroom that had access from both the dining room and the kitchen looked like it doubled the space on the first floor.

Painted a pale sunny yellow, the room held a small wood stove, an oversized coffee table, and comfortable looking seating. My mind flew forward ten years and I could see me and

Bo and our children around that table playing board games after dinner.

"You did good," Bo said as he put his arm around my shoulders.

"Me? Tyler. I just picked out some furniture."

"Still," Bo replied. "This is amazing. I had no idea it could look so bright in here."

He pulled me closer, and I was left wondering if he was still talking about the house at all.

As excited as I was to see everything with the downstairs renovation buttoned up, I couldn't help the telltale heart beating upstairs in Rae's old bedroom.

"Is it bad I want to ditch this scene and run upstairs?" I asked.

"Hell no, this is like Christmas." Bo leapt in front of me and bounded up the stairs.

I took my time, breathing every other step, still clutching the box in my right hand. I hadn't found the perfect place to set it down, since there was no such place in existence.

Bo paused in front of the door, squinting at something. "He left a note."

"Again," I teased. "You need glasses." I shouldered up next to him and unpeeled the note from its taped position on the door.

Tyler's handwriting was disturbingly neat, though I don't know why that surprised me. I took a deep breath before reading the note aloud.

Hey you two,

Thank you for giving me the opportunity to do this for you. For trusting me. I'll see you tomorrow, I'm sure, but I wanted to give you guys some space to take in what I've done here. If you hate it, I can put everything back the way it was. I moved what furniture I didn't use to the garage.

It's a shared space, with elements from each of you represented. I know the last couple months have been tough, but the way you're pulling through is awe-inspiring. Keep holding onto that and do it every day. Whatever it is you're doing.

I think I have some idea...

Xo
Ty.

"Ty?" I questioned, my heart beating a bit faster in anticipation.

Bo grinned. "All our high school friends call him that. He must *really* like you." He winked and placed his hand on the doorknob. "Ready?"

I nodded. Bo turned the knob and let the door swing open as he flicked on the light.

"Oh my god," I whispered as I brought my hand to my mouth.

"Jesus..." Bo trailed off as he walked deeper into the large space.

The walls were still the same crisp white they'd always been, but there was gorgeous fabric hanging on the walls. Tapestries of blues and greens and purples surrounded us as small lamps around the room gave a glowing light, rather than a bright overhead light.

The room was in the upstairs front corner of the house, and had the luxury of two sets of windows on two different walls. Where those two walls met sat a small narrow table with an incense holder on it and a mason jar filled with incense next to it. On the floor in front of it was my yoga mat; its accessories were stacked neatly under the table.

"Look at this!" I squealed, heading for what would surely be the best spot indoors to do morning yoga.

Bo was quiet as he turned for the wall opposite the yoga center. There stood a bookshelf that came to his shoulders, and pillows were scattered at his feet.

"Come here," he said quietly as he reached for something on the top of the shelf. "He left another note." Bo read it silently and handed it to me as he crouched in front of the shelves.

Hey again,

I hope you like what you see so far.

Ember, you need to have a place to do yoga where you can leave your mat all the time. You never know when the need will strike.

I want this room to be a spiritual retreat for the both of you. Prayer. Meditation. Whatever. Leave all anxieties at the door and come restore yourselves in here.

Bo, I've set up this bookshelf so both you and Ember can explore your questions, and discuss answers together. The pillows are for your knees. Thank you for teaching me how to pray.

"You taught him how to pray?" I asked, setting the note back on the top shelf.

Bo shrugged and gave a sly grin. "That's a whole other long story."

"Great," I mumbled, kneeling next to him.

The top shelf had my name scrolled in blue letters against the pale wood. Beneath it were yoga books, Christian prayer books, Buddhist meditation books, and the list went on. There was at least one book for each major religion or practice.

Suddenly, Bo let out a huge laugh.

"What?" I drew my attention down to the next shelf and let out a laugh to match.

On the shelf labeled "Bo" there sat a single book. *The* book, as far as Bo was concerned. A thick hardbound black Bible with an embossed gold cross on the front sat front and center on the shelf.

Bo plucked it from its spot and thumbed through it until he reached a place where a bookmark was sticking out. I guessed it was somewhere in the Old Testament by how close to the beginning he was. His hand went to his mouth and he closed his eyes tightly as his knees anchored on two of the plush pillows.

I moved my clenched hand to the shelf, gently setting the box of ashes next to the place Bo's Bible would sit. There was a good place for the box, it turned out. I just hadn't known till that moment that it existed.

Kneeling on a pillow next to Bo, I looped my arm though his and leaned my head against his arm. Bo put the Bible open side down and sat back on his heels. His eyes were wet with tears, but he smiled.

"This is amazing," he finally said, wiping under his eyes.

"Stand up for a second," I said as I rose to my feet.

Bo followed and grabbed both my hands. "What?"

The lip tremble I'd battled through the afternoon gave way to soft flowing tears.

"Whatever we go through, I want us to always come back right here," I started.

Bo looked around for a moment before settling back on my eyes, silently begging me for more.

"Not just this room," I continued. "I mean *us* on our knees, comforting each other. Praying for help. Wherever it comes from. That's how it should be, and I promise you, Bo Cavanaugh, that I will spend every day that I have left on this earth fighting for us."

Bo's face cracked into a broad smile as his hopelessly blue eyes flooded with tears. "I'm fighting right next to you. Never against you. I promise."

"We have so much ahead of us. Our album, the tour, Monica and Josh's baby. There are so many opportunities for us to fuck it up." I laughed through my tears. "But under each of those things is unpolished grace. If we dig in and buff it out, we'll get to that next level with each other."

Bo's thumbs wiped my cheeks. "I want the world with you, Ember. I don't want a damn thing if you're not next to me. I promise I'm never leaving your side again. It's ugly out there."

"It is," I agreed, my tears starting to dry. "Everyone's crazy."

Bo laughed and pulled me close, holding my head to his chest. "You know," he spoke softly, "I never thought you could look more beautiful than you did that first night I spotted you through the crowd at Finnegan's. I've been wrong every single day since."

"I love you, Bo." I leaned my head back and kissed his chin.

"I love you, too, Ember."

We'd been there many times before, and in that moment I knew that's where we'd always be, even if we were out on the road, on a stage, or sitting at home. Just the two of us, under the soft glow of lights somewhere, swaying back and forth.

That was us, and that's how it would always be.

EPILOGUE

Bo
Two years later...

ALL OF THE highs and lows over the previous two years suddenly seemed inconsequential as I watched a perfectly serene Ember breathe through another contraction.

It was nearing dawn, and we'd arrived at the birthing center an hour earlier, after spending the night in our home trying to relax and get as far along in the process as we could. I say "we," but it was all her. She was magnificent. The baby had been hanging out, growing beautifully inside Ember for forty weeks and one day, and it was finally time to meet him.

The contractions had started late afternoon the day before. Ember had called it "cramping," but her mother and Willow kept a close eye. She was past due, after all. Sure enough, we tried to go to bed that night and Ember couldn't get comfortable. We encouraged her to rest, knowing it was about to happen.

I couldn't rest, either, but none of that mattered as I watched her take her masterfully trained yoga breaths as she labored with our baby.

"You're doing amazing, love," I coached in a whisper as she rocked side to side on a huge medicine ball, resting her head on my chest as I sat in front of her.

When the contraction was over, Ember looked up and grinned, her cheeks rosy with exertion. "That one was a bitch."

"Ember," Raven playfully disciplined as she quickly worked Ember's long hair into a braid.

Ember rolled her eyes. "Now is not the time, Mother. Not the time."

Monica's eyes widened as she sat in the chair by the window. "Shit's gettin' real now. She's losing her sense of humor. When I stopped laughing at Josh's jokes, April was born an hour later."

"I remember," Ember nodded, allowing a brief smile to cross her lips before chewing on some ice.

Two years ago, somewhere in the insane time between *Bo & Ember* being released and our tour starting, April Rose Dixon had come into this world, with Josh and Ember by her mother's side.

Ember and I had been in New York for a slew of pre-tour interviews when she got the call that Monica was close to delivery. Like the best friend she'd always prided herself on being, Ember dropped everything and left New York within twenty minutes, arriving at the hospital in time to see April be born.

I'd stayed back to field more interview questions, knowing that this was something Ember and Monica needed to go through together, even though it was *also* a Josh and Monica thing. Monica had been hesitant with Ember through her entire pregnancy, and finally, when her daughter was born, Monica burst into tears and said while she couldn't, in good conscience—no offense, she'd said—name her daughter November, she wanted to honor her best friend in some way. So, April it was.

While Ember couldn't stay at Monica's bedside for long, given our professional responsibilities, Monica, Josh, and their infant daughter were in attendance for our Fourth of July show that year in Central Park. Baby April was swaddled against Monica's chest as Monica danced and swayed along to the music she'd been such a part of. Our history.

The entire tour was an epic success. Our album flew to places on the chart I'd never thought we'd be, and *Celtic Summer* was always near us numbers-wise. That we'd made the chart at all was head-spinning enough. Ember got pregnant while we were writing and recording our second album the previous summer. We weren't exactly shocked, since we'd decided to start trying once the tour was over, but that hadn't stopped the nerves.

The day Ember found out she was pregnant I'd found her in our "prayer room" crying. She was scared, she'd said. So, we knelt. We prayed and smiled and cried until we both felt better.

During the pregnancy, Ember had decided that she'd save the placenta and plant it with a tree—or something. I was still fuzzy on the details, but the point was, Ember had asked if we could sprinkle the ashes of our angel baby into the ground when we planted the tree.

There was nothing to decide on. It was a "yes" immediately from me. Ember's careful thought and planning on the matter was so sincere, I knew it meant a lot to her, and it seemed like the most beautiful way to honor both of our children at once. The one we never got to meet, and the one we'd soon bring home.

"Shit," Ember hissed under her breath as her hand gripped around mine. "Another one already."

"Just breathe. You've got this." I took a deep breath of my own, anxiety and anticipation bursting at the seams.

Willow, who'd flown out with Raven two weeks earlier rose to her feet and took Raven's place behind Ember, pressing her hands low on Ember's back.

Ember groaned in apparent relief. "How could that possibly feel so good?"

Willow grinned. "Because I know what I'm doing."

After assisting in the production of Celtic Summer's debut album, Willow had decided the music industry wasn't for her. During her time spent with us after the miscarriage, Willow had developed a deep passion for maternal care. She'd spent the previous year becoming certified as a doula. I barely understood the definition, but I didn't care, because whatever Willow was doing was helping Ember through this intense experience.

"I'm going to get some tea," Raven said as she stretched her arms overhead.

"I'll go with you," Monica answered, standing from her chair and revealing a barely swollen stomach.

Halfway through Ember's pregnancy, Josh and Monica announced they were pregnant with their second child. Ember and Monica got to go through pregnancy together after all, even if it wasn't the way either of them had thought it would be. Once they exited the room, the midwife came in.

"How are you feeling?" she asked hopefully.

"Like I have a human barreling through my body trying to escape," Ember replied dryly. "There is *so* much damn pressure."

Willow suppressed a laughed as she continued massaging Ember's back.

"She's doing great," Willow encouraged. "The contractions have been really close for the last half hour."

And, she really *was* doing great. It seemed like forever ago that we'd sung on stage together for the first time, seconds after we'd met. That girl was still there, inside the forest green eyes of my wife, but she had morphed into a stronger, more confident, soulful woman. Pride didn't begin to describe how I felt about her.

The midwife nodded and asked Ember to shift onto the bed for a moment so she could do a "check." That in itself made me queasy, and Ember didn't seem to take too kindly to it, as evidenced by her death grip on my hand.

"Perfect." The midwife smiled as she took off her glove and Raven and Monica walked back in. "Whenever you feel the urge, you can push."

Ember's eyes shot immediately to Monica as she said, *"Now* shit just got real."

§

A half-hour later, Ember had moved positions several times. From squatting, to being on her hands and knees, she pushed with everything she had.

She'd told me throughout her pregnancy that she didn't expect much in the way of coaching from me, and that's why she'd asked Willow to come as her doula. That was a blessing, because I was speechless from being in awe, and a little terrified about what was going on. All she'd asked was that I be there for emotional support, and I was doing the best I could.

"Okay," Willow said calmly. "The head is *right there*, Ember. Just a couple more pushes and he'll be out. You're doing amazing." There were tears in Willow's eyes and a slight tremble in her voice, but she kept her composure.

Ember took a deep breath and turned her head to look at me as I stood next to her bed, my hand on her shoulder. "Okay, I want to turn over and sit up. Bo, can you sit behind me? To, like, support my back?"

It was the first direct request she'd had of me through the whole process, and I was overjoyed that it seemed to be something I'd be able to handle. As Willow and the midwife helped guide Ember to her desired position, I slid off my shoes and got in the bed, helping to ease Ember into a comfortable position.

"Ugh," she groaned as she threw her head back. "I have to push."

Willow eyed me intensely. "Sit forward to help keep her upright. He's really close, okay?"

Ember looked over her shoulder. "Bo, I'm scared." There was a vulnerability in her eyes I couldn't ignore.

I kissed her temple and swallowed my own fear. "This is the end, Em, okay? You've got this. I'm *right* here."

Ember nodded, fresh determination settling across her face. My heart raced as I watched sweat trickle from Ember's neck down the center of her back. Her ribcage expanded as she drew in a huge breath, and her hands tightened around my knees as she leaned forward and pushed.

"Oh, God..." she moaned quietly, never reaching the volume of a yell.

"Excellent, Ember," the midwife said as she watched carefully. "Okay, blow, blow..."

Raven and Monica moved to the end of the bed and started tearing up. Initially I felt at a disadvantage, out of the loop as to what was going on. That was until I heard Ember's final cry and I looked down to see her reaching forward and pulling our son the rest of the way out of her body.

"Oh my *God*," I blurted out as Ember collapsed back into my body, our screaming newborn son on her chest.

"Bo..." Ember craned her neck to look me in the eyes. Her smile was now *exactly* like her mother's as her eyes filled with tears. I'd never been more in love with her than that exact moment. Except the second after. And the one after that. Somewhere in my soul, I knew that feeling would continue forever. Each second, as they all had, would be better than the last.

I felt like my chest was going to explode. Never in the history of my life had I seen anything more beautiful than the sight of my perfect wife holding our newborn baby. Our son. All I could do was cry. I knew there were all kinds of things in the birth plan I probably should have been paying attention to. Something about delayed cord cutting and how to save the placenta, but nothing else mattered at all as I listened to the blissful cries of Jackson Spencer Cavanaugh.

"Hey, buddy," I finally managed through intense tears, reaching my hand over Ember's and rubbing my thumb across his cheek. "I love you so much. Your mom's amazing, you know that?"

His strong cries drowned out every other sound in the room. I wanted to wrap him up, take him home, and never let him out of my sight. I had this primal urge race through me that made the hair on the back of my neck stand on end. As I watched the way Ember smiled at him, I saw every dream I'd ever dreamt fulfilled.

Ember chuckled through a soft cry. "You're amazing." She lifted her chin, kissing me on the lips before kissing our son's head. "Hey, Jax, don't let him fool you. Your dad is pretty incredible, too."

Surrounded by family, old and new, I held Ember as she held our son, and we prepared to embark on our most incredible journey yet.

The End